Within
Paravent Walls

Within Paravent Walls

Laura Gentile

E. L. Marker
Salt Lake City

Published by E.L. Marker, an imprint of WiDo Publishing

WiDō Publishing
Salt Lake City, Utah
widopublishing.com

Cover painting is "Mirror Portrait" by Oskar Zwintscher (1870–1916)
Cover design by Steven Novak
Book design by Marny K. Parkin

ISBN 978-1-947966-14-7

Printed in the United States of America

To my Mother, my Heroine,
&
To Vlad, my Beloved

Within Paravent Walls
A Widow's Portrait

L ADIES AND GENTLEMEN, YOU ARE NOW LOOKING AT THE
last portrait of Estefania von Zweighaupt, born Viennese, the
fifty-five-year-old moribund widow of the renowned artist Severin von Zweighaupt, completed three months prior to her death.

"The insular painter, Goyème Cameliano, requested by Estefania herself, agreed to eternalize the woman struck by a lifelong
malaise on canvas under the sole condition that he would not be
forced to look her in the eyes. The accomplishment of the portrait
was the greatest testament to his faith, he claimed. By the time
he painted Estefania's features, her appearance had already been
hag-ridden and struck by sheer madness and delusion. But he still
did what so many other male painters did before him; he created
an idol.

"Nobody was better fitted to enjoy idolization than Estefania,
and she revered every instant of Cameliano's gilding gaze scavenging her face and body, ignoring her deflecting eyes. The triumph
for Cameliano was that he found his truth of Estefania by disre-
garding hers, which had always been an established fact. But she
deliberately embraced his intentions to cover it up.

"This museum compels you to look at the end of human life, the
beauty and ugliness orbiting it, and the truth of all the individuals
who have lived in this mansion. Museum and mansion became
one under Estefania's and Severin's ill-fated marriage, and I caution you, every piece of art that you will encounter bears its own

story and perspective. It is easy to get absorbed, to get drawn into them and their inner mechanisms, because nothing bears more life than the human imagination coming into contact with a work of art.

"For Cameliano, the hunchbacked maestro who painted bowing to the portrait, the intensity of avoiding direct eye contact with Estefania ignited his imagination and energy to such a degree that his creativity reached a transcendental state. He made her soul transparent with the strokes of his brushes. Once completed, Cameliano turned his back on the pre-mortem painting, on Estefania, on the countless hours, and lived with its mental duplicate until he too, was no more.

"On the oval-framed painting, Estefania has a glacial peppercorn-colored stare underneath a pair of perfectly arched eyebrows. In truth, her eyes had already faded into a smothered ocher color, and her eyebrows looked like a disarranged puzzle of mummified hair. The idealized widow has well-spread facial freckles the color of dark-roasted coffee, and two mischievous wrinkles next to the crevice in between her beetroot-colored lips. Again, in reality her complexion had already degenerated into such a translucency that one could see the blue veins through her sick skin; Cameliano painted what once was, and the vivacity of the widow's lips resembled two leaking snails.

"The yolk-yellow gown that the Widow von Zweighaupt is wearing here gives her a heavier and healthier posture. The entire sleeves, the décolletage, and the hips had been upholstered to hint at fertility, represent femininity, and project virility. Underneath the gray layers of cotton and silk, her deteriorating yellowish skin enveloped the material with a viscid smell. The nurse in attendance spilled the secret that because the painting process was done in close quarters, the widow suffocated her lower body with voluptuous cloth so the thigh-warming odor did not transcend to her nostrils or Cameliano's, because it was quite nauseating.

"As you can see, a pair of daffodil yellow gloves and an amber crystal egg are lying on the desk she is leaning on. And if you look at Estefania's hands, you can behold something quite remarkable. Her hands are the only body part that Cameliano painted as they were; in a thick and lifeless tone of yellow, like the filter of a cigarette that has been subjected to a dirty tongue and teeth. The gloves stand in direct opposition to her hands and expose the painting's truth.

"The haggard widow wished to be preserved on canvas, as she could not allow the world to forget that she had existed.

"The more you observe the movements within the portrait and release your imagination, the more you will detect how the thick fabric engulfing her silhouette resembles waves of loose skin trying to fluff up her shrinking muscles and shredding bones.

"Poor Estefania spent her days and nights softening within her antique bed, complying with uncontrollable muscle spasms in her limbs and awaiting frequent shivers from deep down to crawl their immaculate way to the surface. She would push her body into the sheets, pressing it on the mattress, stiffening her corpus as her tongue lurked embedded in her mouth like a stranded and undercooked piece of meat, immoveable and floppy. Her teeth would clatter in an uproar against the fleshy hindrance, and she would force her hands under her buttocks.

"'I will not think of it. I must feel it. I must live it. I must die with it, but what I can control are my thoughts,' the widow used to claim. Untimely entombed in her own body, she was doomed to disintegrate amongst her stained blankets like a nineteenth-century invalid and wait for the disease to swallow her whole.

"The vain widow attributed her derelict physicality to a curse, pledging she had done nothing to deserve this insufferable state. Never did she consider that she had been a woman more concerned with death than with life. If a taste could be assigned to that exuberant *femme d'artiste*, it would be the mournful and traumatic taste of excessive salt.

"In contrast to her husband, who was buried in the Zweighaupt family mausoleum in a secluded part of the public cemetery that marks the tripoint between our country and two others, Estefania was buried in the rapturous heart of the front garden of this very mansion, as her remains had been denied access to the mausoleum decades earlier by none other than her mother-in-law, who never stopped holding a grudge against her. If one can trust Estefania's nurse, this burial arrangement might have been for the better, as the widow is believed to have said that after sleeping for years next to someone who fears you, abhors you, and whose love and devotion is to want you dead, she didn't want that destabilizing force extending into her afterlife.

"As you can see here in the portrait, she is holding a portable blackboard in her right hand and three pieces of chalk in her left hand, next to the crystal egg. If you look closely, a mirror-inverted word can be detected on the blackboard: "Aleirbag." It's in reference to her daughter, Gabriela, the nerve-wrecker, as she called her toward the end of her life.

"Ladies and Gentlemen, your history starts with your mothers and fathers, grandmothers and grandfathers. You may be swimming against the stream, or you may be holding on to those very roots, but whatever you are doing, you are never without them. Your lives are a reaction to them, good or bad; every love story contains six people from the very beginning, in one form or another. Replicate them, get rid of them, but they existed, and cutting off their influence is a lifelong struggle that not all of us survive wholeheartedly."

The Zweighaupt Powerhouse:
A Murder-Suicide

MANUKA VON ZWEIGHAUPT, BORN NUSSKLUFT, AND Balduin von Zweighaupt, also known as the "Zweighaupt Powerhouse," sprang from the most influential, oldest, and renowned artistic family of the local bourgeoisie. The fearless couple were themselves an institution, relentless and absolutely reckless where their art and space were concerned. Always in conflict, they dismantled each other on canvas. It was the only way their muses could flourish, by contradicting and fighting one another off with oil colors, dust, shards, and the smell of their own blood. They were also famous for their post-creative orgies; every time they survived a collaboration, their libidos were buzzing, as was reflected in their pandemoniac masterpieces.

Instigated by the Zweighaupt Powerhouse, the cultural boom on this side of the tripoint caused a sudden and ever-increasing migration of *connaisseurs d'art* to the town of Arracheusebourg. In contrast to its neglected neighboring cities, it was a stronghold of sponsored prosperity and functional multiculturalism in the forum of art and eventually made a name for itself in the whole world.

The Zweighaupts always selected their intimate circles opportunistically, and every celebration soirée rotated a different circle of their pseudo-amorous conquests as taste and mood varied. They were as skilled in creating as in selling their art, and in no time they were the town's richest couple. They supported local

businesses, gaining a respected reputation and a most welcome
control, despite their sexual appetites and frivolous indiscretions.
In homage to their predecessors, the egocentric couple revived
the *Zweighaupt Casa Padronale Dell'Arte* on the edge of the town
near the black lake.

Both abominably eccentric, inconsiderate, careless, and megalomaniacal, they engaged in overt, violently volatile behavior in
the middle of a crowded street, abusing each other verbally like
untamed children in the bodies of adults, spitting and kissing,
hissing and throwing whatever lay in their fight's way because
they could allow themselves this treat of bad behavior in exchange
for money.

Their unhinged and open quarrels always ended with an unexpected yet always appreciated applause from the blindsided and
engaged onlookers, as they thought it was part of their performance art, a kind of *amuse-bouche* to show what their next sala-
cious piece would be about. They both despised that they were
born and copulating stereotypes and thus tried to make the best
out of it by making their lives public property and a crafty spectacle and letting their audience be a vital part of them.

They were more than tolerated—they were the sole source of
entertainment for a society of gourmands, spreading their success
and guaranteeing the financial security in the town. They took
everything they touched too far, including their family name—
that was their unique signature. It was what the Zweighaupt family was all about; their legacy even took death too far.

When their son Severin was in his thirties, they had had enough
of the bazaar of life. All their artistic possibilities exhausted, they
longed to go out in a big bang, one last masterpiece, one final
performative outcry. As they were the *Übermenschen* in this town,
with all the money in the world and a smooth hand for corruption,
they acquired all the shady legal rights to commit their final piece
of showmanship.

A lot of signed paperwork was required, covering all the gray areas; oral and visual statements were conducted on tape, and interviews were recorded so that no one could be blamed or prosecuted for what was planned. They made sure Severin had everything he needed, was mentally stable and understanding of what they had set out for themselves, and of course they both assured him that he would be the sole heir of their empire.

By then, Severin was married to Estefania, much to the discontent of his mother, who considered her a disgrace to their family name. Estefania came from a low-key artistic family that erupted nowhere near the bourgeoisie. Their roots in naturalism and realism, Manuka often referred to them as a *"dilettante-clan."* Around that time, Estefania was denied a reserved place in the Zweighaupt family mausoleum. Lady Manuka treated it like an eternal resting oasis for snobs whose investment habits did not stop at their deaths. As a consolation prize, Estefania and Severin would both inherit the infamous mansion.

The Zweighaupt Powerhouse, after handing in all the preposterous paperwork and feeding the gorge of bureaucracy, were glad the day had come. They invited a sculptor of their choosing (mentally insane, of course), the town drunkard (better referred to as the key-witness photographer for the council) to document and enforce protocol, three sketch artists (previously tested to actually have the stomach for the project, but they were, in fact, apathetic sociopaths), and the most celebrated obituary writer, poet, and art critic the Zweighaupts could find. (The latter was a wanted necrophiliac who always wrote under a pseudonym.)

Before a life-size piece of blank canvas, the Zweighaupts positioned themselves opposite each other as the centerpiece, with their invitees as their active spectatorship. The couple chose their body postures carefully and with a sharp visual skill set. Balduin pointed a gun to her head from two meters away. Both stood proud and straight. Manuka, with a malicious yet caring smile, held her hand out to him filled with sleeping pills, like wedding almond *dragées*.

The impeccable execution of their initial plan did not work out as anticipated. It should have begun in slow motion, changing certain facets of expression or movement for the artists to capture in sketches, and later handed over to Severin for completion of the full painting. Their bodies would have been measured, touched, and preferably sexually exhausted before the time of demise in order to release all kinds of death-related anxieties and tensions. The knowledgeable hands and phallus of the sculptor were indispensable, as he was paid to know them inside out and carve their likelihoods out of stone for the envisioned double pre-mortem statue. Photos of the entire procedure, wasting one film after another, would have been taken. The poet would have used them as his source of inspiration and would have composed under influence.

What would have happened next would have been uniquely for the sketch artists, as their work would have continued and they would have needed to capture the essence of the event for Severin, who was not looking forward to this corporeal maelstrom caused by his parents, or parent, as it was never really clear whether Balduin was his real father (it had been a savage and disoriented night). Balduin would have shot Manuka's brains out, he would have lied next to her in her mess, and he would have swallowed all the pills she held clutched in her fist. He would have died rather quickly to not lose track of his wife in the afterlife. A physician would have been called, would have checked whether they had accomplished their deaths, and both would have been ceremoniously escorted, in more or less one piece, in two coroner *caroches*. And voilà, a perfectly executed and legally bound murder-suicide.

The Zweighaupt Powerhouse's vision faltered, and their deaths entered history in an unforeseen manner. Balduin had, in general, a rather hard time keeping up with Manuka's manias, impulses, and appetites, especially her erratic and perfectionist behavior

before their death-procedure. He had taken an overdose of Silde-
nafil to manage their *carpe diem* sex escapades shortly before their
carnal demise. Exactly one hour before the notorious rendezvous,
they granted themselves some privacy and solitude to gather their
thoughts, say goodbye to their own flesh and bones, and conclude
a self-destructive peace with their skeptical faces in the mirror as
they superimposed futuristic decay upon them.

While Manuka was monumentalizing herself with ferret fur,
surrealist makeup, a baroque hairdo, and synthetic discords of
essential oils and perfumes, Balduin suffered from a resilient erection that tried to lure him back into a willingness to grow old. In
agony, he prepared himself some Absinthe and let the green fairy
give him the vitality that matched the size of his artificial phallus,
hoping to develop an extensive death wish to match his wife's,
who was oozing with alienating ease. He needed drugs to attend
her spheres of calm lunacy. He insisted that he belonged there as
well, in the Olympus of art martyrdom.

By the time the Zweighaupts were both scheduled to obliterate
themselves, Balduin was so drunk he saw his better half thrice. His
persevering erection was undeniably the elephant in the room, yet
everyone ignored it as they were running late; these were professionals, after all. Balduin would see this through with an acquired
sense of humor. They assumed their artful positions, Manuka in
all her madwoman glory and Balduin cocking the gun. Manuka
blew a last soul-abandoning kiss at her husband, and Balduin, in
a sudden rush and folly, fired his shot.

A shot that went right through the window behind her. "For
Pete's sake," she screeched. Rearranging her hair and removing the
sweat from her upper lip, she ordered him to get the job done. If
there was one thing she couldn't stand, apart from her son's wife, it
was somebody else taking the liberty to make her look like a fool.

Balduin licked his lip, tried to focus, closed one eye, the lazy
one, and pointed the gun at his open-mouthed wife once more.

The shot blew off Manuka's left ear. As she hollered in pain, she started to curse him.

"Are you kidding me? You useless son of a—"

Balduin's next shot accomplished the deed, energized by an urge to shut her up. The bullet peeled her face, squint-eyed, mouth open, her brain dropping out the broken window like cauliflower and cottage cheese.

Balduin first succumbed to an embarrassed laughing fit, then quickly deteriorated into a state of sheer depression and absurd sense of loss. He came back to his bilious senses and remembered the pills now hidden in her twitching fist. The widower glanced at her wedding ring and contemplated a solitary life with his son, but then the mayhem of his marital allegiance resurfaced, and he decided not to betray her. As he approached her stupefied corpse, gazing at her detached ear and her scattered head and the stupid emasculating look of surprise on her blasted face, he inhaled the smell of her boiling blood and vomited all over her blood-coated fur.

Balduin took the pills from his deceased wife. As he could not stand the grotesque aspect of her, still howling in the hindsight of his short memory, he lay down a few steps away from her, as authorized, and there he swallowed them. It took a while until he lost consciousness, the pills having a petty and passive-aggressive lack of quality; as usual, Manuka bought the cheapest rubbish, he thought. Well, to be fair, he took a few shots at killing her, so he considered them equal and accepted the stomach cramps, hallucinations, and flatulence that guided him into his gagging and salivating death.

The photographer fainted twice, but the sympathy he felt toward Balduin revitalized him every time. He never stopped asking himself in therapy if the money was really worth it. It paid for the therapy, anyhow. The sculptor was far more fascinated and intrigued by the physicality and posture of the couple's corpses, imprinting the sight in his brain to later help him recreate a miniature sculpture for his private nocturnal amusement, but he completed the job as requested, naturally. (Now their pre-mortem sculptures are found in the marketplace in the middle of Arracheusebourg as a touristic highlight that remembers the village's patrons.)

The three sketch artists excelled and filled pages after pages, high on adrenaline, deriving a flaccid happiness from the gut-wrenching scene. They kept the copies and gave the originals to Severin as planned, the copies later serving as their career debuts and gaining them world notoriety. As for the poet, he had the best and quietest orgasm in his life and could replay his sexualized memory over and over and never get bored or ascetic. His poems, studies, and essays of the incident, including the magnificent obituary that did the couple absolute justice, were picked up by a publisher. To this very date, they continue to be bestsellers in the world of art fanatics. People from all over the globe come to see the cultural sights and landmarks accompanied by the literature.

Severin and his wife locked up his dead parents in the family vault, which became a tourist attraction and a mecca for tasteless art students on their lunch break in no time.

An Inheritance,
a Muse,
and a Monologue

S EVERIN AND ESTEFANIA INHERITED THE SCANDAL-RIDDEN
estate, pregnant with the shortcomings and malignancies of
Severin's ancestry. Estefania initiated the mansion into her property by choosing the room where the Zweighaupt Powerhouse
killed themselves as the master bedroom in defiance of and repug-
nance against Manuka. This would be the room of new beginnings,
the room of madness, of death, where everything needed to be
cleaned and fixed for the next couple to flourish.

Severin had respected his parents as artists but had no idea who
they were in relation to him, except for his mother's temporary
obsession with her pregnancy and motherhood, forcing Balduin
to paint her naked in obscene poses holding her big belly, and after
Severin's birth, showcasing her breast pressed onto her infant's
face, flirting with her painting husband who felt like the cock
of the walk. Without their creativity and the expression thereof,
Severin's parents would have been nothing. He was always terrified to discover the consequences of that fact, and that was why
their deaths felt like a blessing. He would never have to find out.

Severin's childhood had been invaded by strangers walking
off with his mother, then with his father, hibernating within the
severed anatomy of the house while he was both paraded and
rejected, subjected to his parents' unreliable whims. As he was

carried and dragged across the art-flooded mansion, holding on to sinister corners, he fantasized about the inner life the paintings and portraits offered him, and he dozed off in the materiality of the household he was born into.

Sometimes, when his mother would exit a room, she would not be the same woman that had entered it. As soon as he got used to her façade, she would change again. The only consistency and coherence Severin's parents exerted was to be found in their work; otherwise they made no sense.

The mood that slithered through the mansion when it was only the three of them was unbearable. It arose from the nothingness inside of them, their parenthood. They refused to be put into a box. To be trapped. Judged. Exposed. Seen as a sole identity. Their vanity was more compelling than the love for their son.

Severin grew up staring at paintings for hours cross-legged, the sexual sounds around him erased from his mind and the welcome muteness settling in, the colors of his imagination stirring within, a rambunctious swamp. Everything his parents repressed, Severin contracted and kept, collected almost, with the ambition to revive it when needed.

When his parents were working in their separate ateliers, the *cavatina* bellowing out of his father's record player and the *cabaletta* of that same aria bursting from his mother's, Severin sat quietly locked in his room, imagining and composing artworks in his head interwoven with the contradictions of his parents' energy that resulted in a strange, occasional harmony.

When Severin started to paint as a young boy, his parents felt disturbed by his artworks that favored depictions of disembodiment. Tense hands, a lonely foot, a cheek holding a tear, shut knees, nails and hair lying on a tile, eyes that had no life inside of them, hair locked around a pulsating finger. They thought his worldview was broken and felt a hint of pride to have given life to an artist. When Severin fell in love with Estefania, it was the first time he acknowledged a human being in all her entirety, as a functional whole, as a woman. While his parents never stopped being enigmas to him, Estefania's physicality felt graspable to him, a promise that would not withdraw itself. In Estefania, he saw a world to be painted.

The Zweighaupt Powerhouse's voices never resigned from their son's mind. They were all he had, and he held on to phantoms. Their oval-framed murder-suicide paintings decorated a long corridor in the mansion, peeking out of the tenebrosity.

The mansion became a gallery and a museum that exposed all his works, and people traveled and paid to see it. It was a flourishing business. Severin's art was defined as "Emotive Escapism." Certainly, Estefania had an influence on him, creating a safe space away from the rabid psychosis of his parents.

Estefania's mother was named Rosemarie Viennese, born Stutenzucker, a manufacturer of healing and sanctuary dolls that were stuffed with herbs and spices; her father Amond Viennese was a craftsman who specialized in collages of photographs, objects, paint, and mirrors.

In the Vienneses' opinion, art was meant to exorcize, enchant, heal, or curse people, the dead as much as the living. Once the inner art reached materialization, it could be injected with many kinds of energies. For example, the gaze of a painted woman's face following the viewer around the room would be an appreciated accomplishment for the Zweighaupt Powerhouse, but for the Vienneses there would be something wrong with it, and the attention should not be returned.

Most of Amond's clients were families who mourned the loss of young children. Other families would turn their grief into resentment, badmouth a deceased family member and thereby ignite an ill-intentioned presence that would not stop vandalizing their household. The dead outcast would only be made aware of the family's true feelings after it was too late, which could be quite infuriating.

Families who lost a child would not accept its untimely death and refused to let it go. The child's energy would remain, but it would suffer disorientation in the transitional sphere as two opposite forces claimed it.

The family would leave the room of the deceased child unaltered, frozen in time. They would sniff the clothes in the wardrobe, sleep in the deserted bed, suffer horrifying dreams, and smell the lingering odor of their offspring on the pillows. The parents would engage in a fantasy that led nowhere; it made them believe in signs and hear weird sounds, or they would suddenly hear the voice of the child, hear it breathing, brushing its teeth in the bathroom. They would chase the image rising from death, expect it, but then enter an empty room with a shrine of deadened memorabilia that made them lose their minds.

One mother's longing for her child went so far that she would sleep sitting cross-legged and covered by the insulating blanket on her daughter's urine-drenched sheets where she had simply stopped breathing, inhaling every trace of her beloved's life.

Before the bereft parents dedicated themselves completely to the phantasmagoria they created for themselves, they would seek Amond Viennese's help. He would come to their houses, spend an hour in the child's room alone, pick up the energy that resided in it, and decide which methods needed to be applied. In most of the cases, the child was torn between two worlds. The vulnerable somnambulist energy of the child wandered around completely paranoid, having lost all its senses and living through stages of feeling the parents' mourning, which shattered its awareness and metaphysical body.

The child perceived the earthy emptiness death had caused, the resilient trauma and residing loss that remained where the trade occurred. Simultaneously, the child's life-mongering energy felt a metamorphosis within itself, having lost all matter and yet still being summoned by intoxicating ideas, an aching fluency of desires, a liberating rearranging buoyancy. Contrasting forces tried to claw what they deemed theirs.

The *netherwaves* tried to engulf the unquiet child, to embalm the whirlwind energy and finally absorb it in their hegemonic cloudiness so it could become a form again. Amond would take the child's favorite plaything, a piece of worn cloth, a toothbrush, or milk teeth, a list of the child's fears, a photograph, or nail clippings from the father and a strand of hair from the mother.

The collage he would create would harmonize all the elements at hand: life, death, the child, the memory, the grief, the parents, the body, and the final separation. The process of reconfiguration calmed the parents' minds. They possessed a peaceful relic to set their child free, and the simulacrum they had fed would fade away.

Families who were plagued by a tenacious presence, however, required both Amond's and his wife's help, as Rosemarie was more familiar with unwholesome and unapologetic characters.

Based on a photograph, taken as close to the death of the individual as possible, Rosemarie would manufacture a doll to the likeness of the deceased person. Then, all the affected family members gathered objects that they associate with the deceased in the worst and best way, based on experiences that linked them to the individual.

Amond and Rosemarie would crush myrrh and salt and shred the items to pieces so that they could mix them. Depending on the intensity of the deceased's drive, Amond would supply either a small, medium, or big mirror, serving as a receptive canvas. He would benedict it, then moisten it with red paint (for the worst cases), then glue, sprinkle, and press the shredded objects on it until every reflection disappeared.

Once, as Rosemarie covered the last crevice of a twenty-seven-year-old deceased man's mirror, a shrill and flamboyant reflection originated from the doll's glass eye onto the mirror and catapulted itself into her pupil, which caused her to have weakened eyesight and an incessant eye twitch that never went away.

The doll would be roped tightly on the mirror face down, for eternal and inescapable introspection, bound to the object, forever staring into its own dark space, a never-ending confessional box. Thus the gateway would be shut, the energy captivated and forced to confront its self-erasing state. It was barred from the world of the living as it was unwanted, and it ended. It had no insight into this dimension anymore, as its vision was turned to blindness and vulnerability behind the glass of the mirror. Cases varied. This state was deemed worse than death itself.

Manuka distanced herself as much as she could from Estefania's family. She would never admit it, but they scared her to death. She badmouthed them, calling them pseudo-shamanic impostors who shouldn't call themselves artists—though others would, they never did.

Severin, who acknowledged the Vienneses as individuals but not parents, separate from his wife, admired Amond's work and the philanthropic aspect it entailed. After his parents' murder-suicide stunt, he dedicated an entire room to Amond's collages, as there was something about them that appealed to his soul and kept his subconsciousness busy in inexplicable ways. Estefania followed his example and put every single doll made from her mother's hands in separate display cabinets—her mother always claimed every doll needed her own space, otherwise they would scratch each other's eyes out, they were just that vain and self-indulgent. In contrast to Severin, Estefania did it less because of admiration for her mother but more to keep her close, where she felt she could control her, having the antidote to the poison ready.

Estefania had been well-trained as a model and sitter for paintings and sculptures. She had an extraordinary physical endurance and understood how to deform and twist her own body. She never complained of being too cold, or too hot, or uncomfortable; if anything, she sought out discomfort and thrived in it. She portrayed tormented bodies, aching chests, desirous throats, and caring hands. Estefania knew how to read an artist and their visions; her body would guide them through the melancholia and loneliness of a female body. Its unclaimed ecstasy.

The majority of artists that worked with Estefania admired her naturalism—she would sit completely unmade. They all claimed that it fascinated them how disinterested she was in beauty ideals and unaffected she was by the times she lived in. Estefania had been recommended to Severin, and that was how they met.

In contrast to the other artists, Severin didn't dive into erotic scenarios with her in his mind to fuel the platonic intensity of the artworks, and Estefania could see that from the beginning. It both stunned and intrigued her. She didn't know how to react to his non-sexualization of her, and as she stared at his silent face, she recognized a familiar pain, a sense of not being there. She felt connected to him.

Estefania wanted to divulge his mental image of her, what he saw in her, what her voice sounded like to him, how he felt about her. Severin had coveted something wholeheartedly that Estefania had lost over the years and had been overseen by the other artists. Even though she did not have access to Severin's imagination, she felt safe with him, and he realized that she had no idea who she was. To him, all of these other portraits of her were lies. She had performed as a shape-shifter with no sense of identity.

In contrast to those who fetishized her eyes, Severin told her to close her eyes and let her body move according to the loss of her sight. Listen to the music. The sound of her mind. The images that arose with every heartbeat. What every breath carved out of her stomach. Severin would hover, casting shadows over her naked body, pirouetting slowly around her to destabilize her. Evoking the stories her body produced. Her warm scent engulfed the room. She rediscovered herself. She gained access to key memories of her childhood.

Severin recognized every single change of breath, every alteration of her body, the peachy hair on her skin fluttering like blades of grass in the wind. Something was coming. A door was opened, then another. Estefania moved through them, and he was right behind her, recording her sensations with his brushes.

Severin let her go completely. Estefania faced the little girl in herself and was reminded of what had happened to her. How helpless she was and abandoned, how she screamed for completion and protection. At times Estefania couldn't take it; sometimes she hyperventilated, staring at her soaring inner scars and dysfunctional self-esteem. How she tortured herself, settling for less than she deserved, suppressing her needs and emotions. How she would push her identity further down into a cacophony of fiend-infested darkness where she couldn't hear her proper voice anymore, just pleasing those who demanded a distorted version of her.

It was through Severin's unparalleled methodology that she unveiled a deeply rooted secret, a trauma that had been hushed down so that it could be forgotten.

Severin knew what one could find in the depths of one's soul if one dared to seek it. One night, Estefania remembered an incident that was so deeply repressed it made her teeth clatter, but now she was able to carve it out of her system and confront it with Severin by her side.

After over a hundred sketches, paintings, and bodily introspection sessions that all uncovered her childhood persona and who she really was beneath her own skin, not who she thought she was but her actual untouched psyche blowing through her blood vessels, she returned to that one fatal moment. She must have been around five years old. She was already sleeping in her bed. Everything seemed to be fine. In the middle of the night she woke up because she heard someone sitting right outside, against her bedroom door, scratching the walnut wood.

Terrified, breathing rapidly, she sat up in her bed. The house was so quiet she didn't think it was a stranger sitting there, yet she couldn't muster up the courage to ask who it was. She felt paralyzed by her fear, maybe because deep down she knew who it was. She heard a consistent murmur, grunting, a bit whimsical yet threatening, and once she leaned in, still in her bed, she could hear those desecrating words.

"Get out of here . . . I just want you dead . . . Get out of my life . . . You are nothing, a pestilence . . . I abhor you . . . You don't belong to me. You need to be undone."

She knew those horrid words were addressed to her. They felt like the icy tip of an arrow meant to conjure up destruction, coming from the most venomous abyss imaginable, rammed right into her chest with the utmost authority, entitlement, and pleasure. Estefania recognized the voice. How could she not? Tears rolled down her cheeks. What could she have done to upset her own mother so?

She started hitting her legs with her fists to hurt herself, to numb the words still being uttered like a despairing chant. She was so scared, sitting on her bed listening to her mother's cursing. Did she know she was awake? Was this the first time? Would she enter the room? Was Estefania in danger? Did her mother mean her harm? She cried viciously and yet barely made any sound.

Suddenly, she heard the heavy body of her mother as she leaned all her weight against the door, pressing her face against the wood and dragging it to the little slit where air would circulate, and sniffed. The silence was horrendous, the breathing like daggers. Estefania heard her whining, breathing through her mouth, leaning even heavier against the door until the doorknob was grasped. As soon as she heard the turning of the knob, Estefania crawled back under the blanket, not knowing what to do. She pretended to sleep. Maybe her mother would disappear. Estefania's heart beat to the rhythm of terror, her body in a tremor, her breathing so quick she couldn't be asleep, not with this overdose of adrenaline.

Rosemarie entered the room. She left the door open, the light penetrating the room. She stood there in her white nightgown, see-through, naked underneath. Her nails were long and sharp, and her bony fingers looked like hooks or branches. She was biting her tongue, shivering, drooling, her hair a mess. Rosemarie clenched her fists. Then she collapsed on the floor, kneeling, her ear facing the ground, grunting like a conjurer, listening for voices and death, her shivering hands hovering. The whispering exchange of malevolence continued until she stood up again with a readiness that made the earth stand still.

Estefania heard her steps on the wooden floor, creaking as her mother approached. She should feel safe; this was her mother. But she felt like she would die. Estefania kept her eyes tightly shut, wishing the evil to go away, praying for her safety. She wanted her mother dead. Rosemarie was so close, Estefania could smell her, but she didn't dare open her eyes. Her mother leaned in. Estefania felt her breath on her face. Rosemarie's deranged gaze pierced right through her. Estefania felt the static between them.

Rosemarie knew how to read her daughter's fear-infested body. Still Estefania wouldn't open her eyes, she didn't want to see. Her mother dragged her lips across Estefania's cheeks to her left ear and started whispering.

"I know you're awake. You can keep your eyes closed, it's not a hindrance to me. I prefer them closed. Remember the night you were sleepwalking?"

Rosemarie didn't wait for an answer; this was intended as a monologue.

"You climbed right up into the attic and only I heard your tiny steps walking around up there as you were distracting me, disturbing my sleep, as usual. And of course your father snored his way right through the noise you always make.

"I thought this was perfect, your nightly crusades. Accidents happen, and you were already up there, you'd made it that far all by yourself. It was as if you had invited me. I came to rescue us from this terrible bond we have, remember? There I stood, right behind you, and you couldn't see me. You stood right in front of the open window—all you needed was a little push, and you would have fallen right through. The idea made me rejoice.

"I got closer and placed my hands on your back. I could feel and hear that you were in a deep sleep. The glory my fingers perceived. All the voices in my head hollered, 'Do it, end her, nobody will ever know!' I was so happy. Pure euphoria. I extended the moment, the suspense; I envisioned my future without you. Your little coffin, your grave, your body out there subjected to all the restless elements. Your blue corpse, how ugly you would become, your young skin disintegrating, your girlish scent rotting into a pungent stench, losing all your appeal. I was ecstatic to the bone.

"As I applied more pressure to your back, your father started calling my name. I heard him moving around. Of course he found us. Once again I was cheated by you, by your very presence in my life, and so I turned you around and slapped your face, to wake you up. What a nightmare. I told your father I sensed you were in danger, so I got out of bed to look after you and found you right in time to save you. He was eternally grateful. You were crying, believed me as well, and I became your heroine.

"It is rather peculiar, all the evil spirits your father senses, combats and conquers, and yet he is so blind when it comes to his own kin. I just wanted to tell you that you are the greatest regret in my life. I regret to my very marrow that I didn't throw your worthless body out the window when I had the chance. I could have tricked them all. You should have died then and there. Now I have to live with this remorse, and endure you and your meaningless existence."

Estefania almost choked on her own breathlessness. She felt her mother's cold face distancing itself again. Her mother staggered out of the room and closed the door.

There was not enough blanket in the world to cover and warm up what Estefania had felt in that very moment, in the aftermath of those words.

The next thing she recollected was that, shortly after that night, her mother disappeared for a year or so and came back a presumably changed woman, and that had been the fresh start which buried the past alive.

The Zweighaupt Triplets

A FEW YEARS AFTER THE DEATH OF SEVERIN'S PARENTS, Estefania gave birth to triplets: Jacqueline, Gabriela, and Gunnar.

Estefania's pregnancy had been extremely testing and strenuous. Her mood swings stemmed more from an innate frustration with life and the idea of a family brought into this world than from hormonal fluctuations. The notion of her being the guidepost for her kin infected her with a compulsion to blame what she had created. While she meandered through the house, her arms in a less holding and more of a pushing downward position on her belly, speaking to nobody, shaking her head, humming, she coerced her body into a state of apathy and indignation.

Hallucinations irritated Estefania's eyesight, her vision blurred. Light-sensitive headaches caused her to confuse real sounds with non-existent ones. She claimed that something inside of her made her thoughts stutter, that she could feel a gargantuan tension between the three of them in her belly, that something wasn't quite right. She resigned into secluded rooms in the mansion, away from the visiting tourists. She could taste her children on her tongue, the colors they wore. Jacqueline was yellow. Gunnar was blue. Gabriela had always been red. All their weight. Their history inside of her. And she remembered her mother's synesthesia and was startled as guilt crept up her throat.

The mother-to-be felt infiltrated, watched, disarmed, and prohibited to make peace with herself. Three infants were now taking up her space and body. She had become a hostage. She became estranged from her body and herself. She contemplated that these children were compromising that bond, that they were more exigent than expected, had more needs and attributed more importance to themselves than she had ever anticipated. She was convinced that this was it, the end of her existence.

When she reached out to the little girl in her, nothing erupted but the dense muteness of her own children in her belly. She felt helpless, alienated from her mirror-image, perceiving her body as a shallow vessel, possessed by human beings that she never met, draining her energy and suppressing her proper self, which she considered absent again. They killed her, she thought. Chased her away, their own mother, there was no love there. Oh, the deep turmoil. She made the unborn responsible for that loss, and yet never uttered that statement of guilt and blame out loud. She didn't have to.

Overwhelmed, she surrendered to impending motherhood, terrorized by fears and doubts, reflecting about her own mother whom she saw as an agent of trauma transferal and as the ever-expanding root in a vicious female circle. Estefania suddenly suspected no difference between herself and her mother. They were one and the same, both terrible and detrimental. Severin's worries increased as the communication with his wife deteriorated. Their bond had been failing slowly, and his ability to decipher her was led astray. He felt exiled by his wife.

Estefania tried to deracinate the hostile voices that pottered around her mind, yet she felt threatened and paranoid, lamenting the state she had put herself in. She wanted them out, then everything would be normal again.

Jacqueline arrived first, followed by Gabriela and Gunnar. The doctors gave Jacqueline a few days to live. They said it was a miracle she was not a stillborn, given the irreparable heart abnormalities and acute malfunctions. She had been severely underdeveloped, they said, and she suffered from the lack of space in Estefania's womb.

Gabriela and Gunnar were silent and sleepy infants, but Jacqueline always had her eyes wide open, absorbing her environment, sucking up the atmosphere, clinging to the surrounding images. She even slept with her eyes half-open. She made engaged and jolly sounds, always in the moment, and seemed to already have a sharp awareness and presence as her glance uplifted the atmosphere of a room. Jacqueline did not seem to feel that she was not going to make it, that any day could be her last—or maybe she knew, and therefore she would not let life escape. She always grasped for fingers, hands, her parents' faces. Whatever she found within her body's radius, she tried to hold on to with all her might, stretching out her limbs as much as she could.

Severin and Estefania reacted very differently to the physicians' news. If Jacqueline would have been less energetic, it would have been easier, they thought. If she would just sleep, be quiet, disappear slowly into a different world, it would be easier. It was cruel. They bonded so fast and intensively with her that the other siblings were ignored during Jacqueline's short life. The anxious parents needed to freeze and collect every single moment with Jacqueline, their little doomed daughter. They treated her as a passing blessing that would unjustly slip away against their will, never to return into their convivial arms.

During the nine days that Jacqueline was alive, Gabriela and Gunnar were taken care of by three empathetic nurses. Severin would not capitulate to the facts as long as she was alive. He did not cry as he tried to remain hopeful. He would not live the life of his daughter by falling apart and not giving her anything but anticipated grief and collateral heartache. He wanted to imprint paternal love on her body. Maybe she would be strong and regenerated enough to stay, and maybe his intense affection would work its magic.

Estefania was silent yet very physical with her; she would not let her go, caressing her soft cheeks, breathing her in, diving her nose right into the warmest spots of Jacqueline's skin. The yellow scent. The white taste. She absorbed her baby, never letting go of her infant's lively scent. She recognized it anywhere and conjured it up like a spell. It filled up her head, and she made this scent hers. It was in her and remained locked up in there forever.

Severin decided his dying baby girl must not be forgotten, he could not allow that. Her life must be documented, her body and her character captured. He returned to his art for help. He forced himself to commit to the task that would forever keep his daughter alive in the material and transcendent universe, in his own aging memory.

Severin's introduction to fatherhood was botched and butchered by loss. As he worked, he couldn't hold back his tears. He tried to compose himself, but his tears mingled with powdery pastels, making the paper salty and bitter. He drew Jacqueline in so many ways: the whole body, her face, hands, sometimes in Estefania's arms. In the latter, of which there were quite a few paintings, one could see what Estefania would resort to in order to deal with the horrendous situation. His hands would draw what his eyes saw but had not yet realized.

Jacqueline would be lying in her mother's arms, looking up to see her and connect with her, but Estefania would not look back. She would turn her gaze away and stare out the window, looking at the tree crowns blowing in the wind. Holding Jacqueline's hand to her face, she would fantasize an inner image of her daughter, forcing her mind to blend the memory of Jacqueline's scent with the imaginative reproduction.

While Jacqueline was alive, Estefania grew accustomed to her death. She used Jacqueline's body to make an imprint of her on her memory, without looking at her. She distanced herself from the real body of her daughter as long as she had the possibility. She toughened up during her infant's life so that she could survive the fact that she would outlive her very first offspring in such a brutal manner. Severin would not interfere; everybody mourned in their own way and that needed to be respected, he thought.

Severin and Estefania barely spoke during those days. They clung to Jacqueline, existing in this stuffy microcosm of impending tragedy and death, torn between impatience and denial. Jacqueline became fiction while she was a fact; her body became object and source while she was breathing. Twenty-four little pieces of art had been accomplished, and on the morning of the ninth day of her life, she didn't wake up.

The nurses were exhausted as they had doubled their workload, but they could not refuse the grieving parents who paid them double their salary during those days to take care of their other children. Gabriela and Gunnar behaved like functional healthy newborns, as if their sister had never existed, which infuriated Estefania. They slowly resurfaced in their creators' minds in the form of consolation and hope.

Now that Jacqueline was dead, Estefania would not keep her eyes off her, rocking her body back and forth, gazing at her daughter's glacial eyes.

"Close her eyes, Estefania."

There was an earthquake on Severin's lips that he tried to suppress.

"She was the good one."

That was the first time Severin had preferred his wife's silence to the expression of her thoughts. He refused to be contaminated by her toxicity.

"We had our time. There is nothing we can do. Would you please close her eyes? I can't stand it, Estefania."

Severin's hand compressed his jaw, the skin around his eyes red, his face overrun by grief.

"My body killed her. I made her sick. I carried a dying child for nine months. I had her in me, Severin. I carried her. And now she's dead. I don't understand. I don't understand. I never touched her. She knew me and stayed. I lost my child. There must be life in her eyes. Eyes are the portal to the soul. It must be. She must be in there somewhere."

"We have two other children to take care of, Estefania. Please, listen to me. We have to be there for them. We'll get help. We cannot abandon them. They need to take Jacqueline's body away now. Please stop staring at her like that. Let go. You're upsetting everybody."

Estefania shook her head, pressing Jacqueline's face against hers as if to evoke an awakening of her daughter's soul.

"I couldn't return her gaze beforehand because it terrified me. She didn't know, she didn't know it would end, so soon, but I did, I am the one who kept her alive all these months, I gave birth to her and I brought her little body in this barbaric world. And she scrutinized me with those eyes, those longing eyes, and I couldn't even peek. I couldn't look into a face that was expecting death yet experiencing the start of life so avidly.

"I can explore her now, Severin. Now that it has indeed happened, now that I will not see her crushed, her first expression of pain or comprehension of what her death is. Now that she has overcome her demise, now that she is over the hill, I can stare and see how magnificent she is without being afraid and outraged by her fate. She is calm now as nothingness has taken over. I still feel her. No sign of life on her face. She had no negativity in her life, just a fact that we all share yet came tastelessly early for her. Nothing bad has happened yet to her, right, Severin?"

She suddenly started to hyperventilate as she held her daughter against her chest. Then she began, the tears incessant, her breath ragged. Never again would Estefania cry. From this day, this moment, until the very end of her own life.

She unbuttoned her shirt and took her left breast out and pushed it into her daughter's lifeless face.

"Maybe if I—maybe if I give her my—she will—maybe there is something in—I mean, I am the mother, after all. I am her mother, Severin. Maybe if she drinks a—"

"No, this is not happening. Look at me. I'm here, all right? This will not work, I wish it could, please. You have to let her go. You are killing yourself here. Our daughter is gone. Our child is not here anymore."

Severin was sobbing, enduring the sight of Estefania's breast clinging to his daughter's uninvolved and disconnected face and how the last tears of her life rolled down her face, throat, and onto the infant's loose face.

"I can't watch this. Give her to me. You need to stop this lunacy."

As he approached her, Estefania started to laugh. Her uncontrollable fit of laughter was so loud that the baby wobbled in her arms. Perplexed, Severin dragged the infant away from her. The nurses reassured him that this was normal; she was hurting and traumatized, they said, her hormones still all over the place. She was confused and reluctant to believe the truth and needed sleep; everybody handles it differently. As Severin said goodbye to his child and handed her over to a nurse, Estefania jumped out of her bed, stumbled toward her dead girl, and whispered into her ear, "Come back to me, Jacqueline. Find me. Don't leave me. I'll wait for you to come back."

After the nurse had walked out, Severin turned around. Estefania was looking out of the window again as if nothing ever happened.

"I want her heart."

"What?"

"I want her heart."

"Estefania, listen, you are not well."

"I won't leave without it, Severin," she screamed and then directed her gaze at the nurses outside of her room and howled.

"I am her mother. I have a right to my daughter. I made her, every single particle of that body belongs to me. She is an extension of my body and she is dead, dead like a clipped nail, like dead skin, like hair, like everything that comes out of my body. So I want her heart."

"Mrs. Zweighaupt, there is no need for self-harming gestures. What you insinuate would entail an insane amount of paperwork, and I don't know if it's even possible or ethically justifiable."

"You will give me her heart before we cremate her. Whatever the cost, I will have it. Put it in some chemical liquid, some mummifying stuff, formaldehyde, whatever. I want it in a glass jar, with clear liquid so I can see it. Go, go, cut her open, I will sign all the paperwork, but do it now. I want to go home. I go home with my little Jackie. I am her mother. It's my right. She belongs to me."

Severin was speechless. As the nurses nodded in contemptuous agreement, they tried to catch his glance to obtain his confirmation. Severin blinked and left the room as his daughter was taken to the morgue.

A Couple's Shadow

E STEFANIA AND SEVERIN WALKED UP THE STEPS OF THEIR mansion, Gunnar in her arms and Gabriela in his. Estefania dragged death along with her as she heaved her empty body over each step, clinging hollowly to her attention-seeking infant. As soon as the twins were put down safely, she rushed out to the car again, and like an addict she grabbed the glass jar that contained Jacqueline's heart. She carried it close to her inconsolable chest, then caressed it and put it on the all-overseeing chimney piece.

"The heart that broke my heart," she whispered as she watched her daughter's dysfunctional organ float in chemical liquid like someone who was staring into a snow globe, shaking it in desperation and need for a better world where time stood still and pain ceased to exist.

"What's next? Her hair in a scented sachet?"

"Don't ridicule me, Severin. What kind of a woman would I be if I could let her go so easily, so quickly? You only knew her for nine days. How do you think I feel? It's nature's will. I want her in this house, in our home, in some form or another. I don't want a tombstone to be all that is left of her on this earth. Can you understand that? Where did you put your paintings of her? I want to see them, Severin."

"That's why I didn't want her to be cremated. It would be too abrupt. We both were her parents. Her loss is mine too. They are in the little room next to the chamber with your mother's work."

As Estefania slowly walked away from her husband, she mumbled that she wanted Jacqueline's body to be buried where nobody would find her, that her death had been a sign of her physical weakness, that her body had been unfit for motherhood, that Jacqueline's body would be her secret, buried in sheer solitude and far away from all the madness.

Holding her loose-skinned belly that now felt like non-discarded snakeskin, Estefania paced insecurely toward the room, feeling a faint sensation of fear that her request had been met. She stumbled alongside her mother's stale dolls, avoiding their narrowing eyes of glass. She dragged herself across the room. As she reached the edge of the chamber with the unseen paintings of her daughter, she halted in agony. It was an almond-white room. Severin must have worked for hours, even though she could have sworn he almost never left her side during those nine days. It smelled freshly painted and it was not intended to house a life. Severin's memory of Jacqueline moved over the walls within oval frames. Twenty-four reminders of her daughter.

"Deceased," it read in the deadbeat papers. "Little Jackie, nine days old, has left us all (her burial site unknown), and alongside our condolences, we congratulate the births of Gabriela and Gunnar, the new generation of the Zweighaupt family."

Suddenly Estefania could smell her again. There she was. Estefania took her shoes off and entered the room like a sacred space. She felt Severin's heaving pain as she stood in the middle of it, next to a walnut wood bench, eyes closed, sensing his tears and hardship. The unconquerable heartache of the room mirrored the father's dedication to erect a forget-me-not monument for his disintegrating daughter, a silent room for contemplation, lethargy, and remembrance.

The windows had always been barred, and now the small appendix seemed like a chamber that had inherited a sad secret and felt like a cell that kept Jacqueline's soul prisoner in the opposing mirrors on the doorframes. Their multitudes would not let her go, a coffin with only fleetingly evoked memorabilia as its content. It was a shackling shrine that alienated Estefania from her own sorrow and incapacitated her health. She felt excluded as this room manifested her husband's overarching pain that polluted the stiff air.

Severin's materialized anguish made her feel like she found herself in a competition of grief. Something had died in him. She could sense this threat amongst these four stonehearted walls. She could not accept his resignation.

Estefania could not stomach the paintings, and yet one caught her eye immediately. The one where her head was turned away from her daughter as she tried to reach her mother's face with her hands, which was shortly before she took her hand to smell it, but this painting seemed violent to her. This representation of events demonstrated rejection. Was this how it came across? Was this what it looked like from his perspective? She sensed some irritating truth in this miserable painting, a truth that she declined to accept. She suppressed this creeping feeling hollowing her stomach. She did not want to justify her actions again.

The painting conveyed something to her, acting as a mirror that pierced right through her conscience. Furiously, she branded it a vile misrepresentation of her stolen motherhood. The villainous pregnancy voices gnawed at her sides. *It's not what it looks like.* It's not what it looks like, she repeated in her head. *I am a good mother. I gave her everything. I couldn't see her like that.* Estefania felt faint again, looking at the beige marble floor in disorientation, and realized she was bleeding. She put her porcelain-blue dress between her legs, soaking it in her blood to stop it from running down her legs. She lost consciousness and fell on the floor. The conquering voices stampeded over her immoveable chest.

After Severin put Gabriela and Gunnar to sleep, he went to Jacqueline's memorial room. As soon as he caught a glimpse of his wife lying on the floor, he ran toward her. After he put her legs on the bench, he held her head in his lap and focused on the blood she had lost. He wept in exasperation.

"Why won't you confide in me? Tell me what's going through your mind. Why won't you let me be a part of you? I'm here. You must know that. Please don't go. Please don't go back. Stay with me. We're strong enough. I'm calling you. Hold on."

Severin hollered the housemaid's name, Rhubarba Lightfoot, through the halls, and told her that medical help was needed immediately. He cradled his wife's pasty body that seemed to come asunder beneath his touch. Her matter and her thoughts became fugitives, slipping away from him. It was like she was drowning somewhere in a dark lake and she would not swim, refusing to signal for help. She would feel comfortable in the wet bed of her impending death and just succumb to her corporeal heaviness that made her the lifeless anchor of her own memory above the water level. He rocked her body back and forth like the dependent corpus of a child. He hummed, transferring the soft waves of peacefulness and much-needed tranquility to her body. Her eyelashes twitched like severed tangerine feathers, and she slowly opened her eyes.

"I am a good mother," she whispered sharply.

Two sturdy medical assistants and a doctor arrived, and she got carried up to the master bedroom. She was prescribed prolonged bed rest and therapy. The latter she declined on the spot.

Severin was flabbergasted by his wife's newfound introverted invalidism. Although they both made it through her arduous pregnancy and the death of one of their children, he realized the aftermath of these life-altering occurrences would not bring them closer together as he had hoped.

Estefania's despondent face stared at him with fiendish ambivalence. He endured her behavioral abnormalities, rapid and volatile changes in temper that escalated into violence and wrath, and even though he always made it known to her that he was there for her and he would stay by her side, she turned away from him in irritation and contempt. Beneath the nebulous winds of the dismal voices, her bad conscience lit up inside of her, tormented by the sight of her withering husband. Yet she was unable to grasp him and silence the internal struggle that tore her apart.

As Severin smothered his grief to take care of his two infants, the image of an egg kept creeping into his mind when thinking of his wife. He would be haunted by it even in his dreams. The egg always kept its hard shell. You could knock it against a bowl and it would pull itself together with all its force to defy its shattering. It would rebel against transformation. It would never disclose what it contained and what secrets it incorporated. After a while of persistent aggressions, outer influence and ill will, the egg's sheltered and strong-minded shell would eventually crack, and suddenly it would desperately identify itself with the numerable splits, feel the rise of a new personality, and change its viewpoint.

There were only a few cracks at the beginning, to ease the transition and get comfortable with imperfection and vulnerability. There was a very thin skin that was the ultimate binding and separating matter between the inner life and the outer universe. Both perspectives had a blurred vision, and yet they became intimate, gaining a sense of each other and developed a haptic relationship. The egg would slowly bow to the dominant perseverance of the ambiguous outer penetration.

Seeing its cracks as an artful and static mosaic instead of traumas and failures, the egg embalmed itself in the fantasy of a better consciousness. But the egg was never meant to exist on its own. It was emotionally bound to other eggs sharing its fate as this egg led the way forward. After it had grown accustomed to its ideal state, an outer influence applied the final aggression to the egg's corpus so that it started to leak. Its lively fluid expelled, the energy shattered and scarce, the matter of its identity became hopelessly irrevocable. No longer could the egg maintain itself. Everything lay out in the open.

The egg felt cheated, the mosaic was gone, its shell became public garbage. Everybody would judge it, its loss of self. Everybody knew the egg inside-out. The inner life-turned-outer crackled in paralysis and felt unidentifiable. Paired with others, it did not find completion and deteriorated further, and the question rose whether if it had been kept on its own, it could have emerged anew and accomplished self-love. The other eggs inherited the first one's fate and felt wasted instead of recreated.

Severin was plagued by these burdening images. He sensed this branding iron of guilt in his gut. He pondered whether it was legitimate, and yet he took responsibility to the point of obsessing his self-incarcerating mind. He flagellated his health with the affliction he took on, as he was convinced that he disappointed and failed the person he loved the most beyond recognition. He reconnected with a surmounted past and started digging. Everything that was exhumed, he found himself guilty of and demonized himself.

The old Severin was a tactless beast, inconsiderate to Estefania's feelings. Inquisitive. Brutal. Without shame. Exploitative. The self-incriminating list was endless. He tortured himself until his brain made his psychological ordeal a physical one, and his heart became weaker under the pressure of his self-loathing.

The father started to relive his past in his head and nurture debilitating scenarios that imprisoned, dehumanized, and cut him off from the man he had become. Severin's imagination and memory became two butchering and distorting forces. He was hunting for reasons within himself why Estefania's state was worsening and why his presence had no rehabilitating effect on her wellbeing like it used to. He slaughtered his self-esteem, which froze his motivation to paint. He totally submitted himself to Estefania to make up for what he thought he did wrong.

Due to the couple's enervated state, two housekeepers, a receptionist and a guide for the museum, and two caretakers for Gabriela and Gunnar were hired. The voices in Estefania's head were very receptive to sensitive energies around them and they would feed on guilty consciences. When Severin fully devoted himself to her and cared for her the way he did, she rejoiced, taking advantage of his selflessness and letting him believe the horrendous scenarios he rendered, making them even more atrocious when he offered a solution meant to make her better.

As he read her participation as a chance to reach redemption, he started to paint again, which was the turning point for his more alarming and upsetting art. Estefania was found innumerable times in Jacqueline's memorial room, sleeping on the bench in the morning after she sleepwalked the entire night and waking up in shock that only in her dream-state was she reunited with her daughter.

The voices that surfaced during her sleep and gained total control of her movements, unsupervised and autonomous, guided her heartbroken body toward the sterile room of her dead infant, the one who would not get on her nerves anymore, the silent one, the absent one. In the presence of Jacqueline's death that filled this dismal room, the deprived mother could sleep peacefully, stripped of maternal responsibilities. She was the perfect mother to a deceased child. In this room she could totally dedicate herself to someone who was not there, who made no demands. This child would let her rest in peace.

A Utopia for the Insane

G ABRIELA AND GUNNAR DISTANCED THEMSELVES FROM
their deceased sibling. The twins were inseparable, always
holding hands and encouraging one another. The only obvious
physical difference between them was that Gabriela had red hair
like her mother and Gunnar had blond-brown hair like his father.
In the first four years of their lives, they were neglected by their
mentally ill parents. Two nannies took care of them during those
formative years. Innumerable photographs were taken of the siblings, and albums were filled for the Zweighaupt parents in case
they wanted to go back in time when the moment was right.

The two nannies, Beata Klangstock and Ludivica Reimsumm,
became infatuated with each other during their four-year-stay
with the Zweighaupts, and their twisted happiness grew with the
twins, who felt like their own. Gunnar was a sensitive little boy
who always looked up to his sister. His impressionable eyes sparkled when Ludivica made flower-crowns for him, and he was the
proud fairy king next to his sister, the queen of weeds.

As their parents mostly stayed inside to drown themselves in
their misery, the siblings spent their time outside with their nannies. They spent hours in the breathtaking garden. Every weather
had its charms and adventures. Exhausted from their playtime
endeavors, the twins always fell asleep in their nannies' tender laps
and spent the night without a worry in the world.

When Gabriela and Gunnar were four and a half, the
Zweighaupts pretended they had recovered. The parents discharged

Beata and Ludivica. Heartbroken and unwilling to leave the twins in the sole care, or rather mistreatment, of their parents, the nannies protested. They tried to reason with the Zweighaupts, offering to extend their services for two more years for even less money. To vanish from the twins' life so abruptly would be harmful and damaging to them. They would not understand, and they had all their routines and games that made them so happy. If the parents really cared about them, they would not do that to their kids, the nannies pleaded unsuccessfully.

In truth, this mansion was the only place that would keep Beata and Ludivica safely together, and they were ready to fight for it. The nannies did not believe in the Zweighaupts' recovery, as their physiognomy had deteriorated over the years. They looked like atrocious versions of their former selves, bitter and dissolute. The endurance of both women to change the Zweighaupts' minds molded the parents into a strange unity, even more so when the nannies tried to manipulate them into thinking that they were incapable of taking care of the twins without their assistance.

Rhubarba, the housemaid, and the two housekeepers Richard Nelkenwasser and Salomon Mondhitze, emptied the nannies' chambers by the first sign of argument. They entered the salon, facing the nannies with their packed bags. Ludivica and Beata held onto the children, wailing and begging for their positions and, on a subliminal note, their relationship that would fall apart outside of these premises.

Severin's upper lip beaded sweat, his fingertips massaging his temples. He sat down in an upholstered armchair next to his standing wife, who bit her lip and stared threateningly at the two impertinent and nerve-wrecking nannies. While the two women squealed and yammered, Estefania grew impatient because they made her feel disrespected. She didn't even listen to them. She pressed her sharp nails so hard into Severin's shoulders that it made his face twitch. He jumped up like an infuriated animal, fists clenched, and screamed in the nannies' faces to get the hell out of his house at once.

Estefania interlocked her gaze with Gabriela's, whose blame cursed her mother's gut. Revolted and offended, this child was fighting her mother in her head and did not even blink. The daughter caught Estefania's appalled interest. This had been the first exposure to Gabriela's true inner state for Estefania, and for the first time in years, she discovered that there had indeed been a residue of life in this house, even if it was grueling and set against her. Fury she could work with, and this little body was so full of it, it was damping.

Gunnar was crying as the nannies kissed him goodbye, and he tried to latch himself on to them but was pulled away by his father. Gabriela was so focused on her mother that she completely missed the last time she would ever see her nannies again. Severin took Gunnar in his arms, calmed him down, and carried him away. Rhubarba and the housekeepers disappeared into several rooms again to resume their tasks.

Estefania was exhilarated by her daughter's persevering stare. Their ill-willed visual exchange needed no words. The mother suddenly burst into a grotesque laughing fit, and the daughter, as provocative and nonchalant as she could, walked gracefully out of the room without looking back at her antagonist, which made the latter frantic.

Estefania was an observant mother, but not for the sake of her children. She had a firm grasp on Gunnar's character and used her understanding of his needs to manipulate him to increase his sympathy toward her. Gunnar needed deeply rooted affection, physical contact, warmth, and emotional safety. It didn't take long for him to embrace his parents and drift away from the adorned memories the nannies had left behind. Estefania had a keen sense of the intense bond between her twins, and yet she was excluded, because it was an inarticulate one. Their silent relationship made the mother envious and suspicious. The love they had for each other led to Estefania's rigorous efforts to compete with her daughter for the affection of her son.

Estefania thought of herself as the original part of the triplets, as they all sprung from her life-giving womb. They had been the reason for the receding love between her and her husband. She claimed a substitution for her sacrifices, an amendment of her situation. They took something from her, and now she wanted it back. She apprehended the twins as a mere extension of herself; she was the true heartbeat of her children. Thus she consoled herself and tried to increase and reclaim her authority over her bewildering daughter specifically. The independence and rejection that Gabriela expressed from a very early age scared her insecure mother and made her feel useless. She might as well be dead.

Complacency and matricide is what Estefania deciphered from her daughter's eyes, which seemed so unyielding to her. Gabriela's pupils were immoveable tempests, dark tunnels spiraling down into invisibility, terrifying the mother. They sat still amongst the greenish-brown puddle and attacked Estefania in total muteness. No one could decrypt a mother better than her own children, who had shared her body and therefore knew all of her secrets, anxieties, shortcomings, and buttons to push. Estefania feared nothing more than the betrayal of someone she accommodated and gave life to with her scarce resources.

Gabriela began to talk much later than Gunnar, and her silently judgmental presence in the house was disturbing. Estefania interpreted her defiant daughter from her own twisted perspective, imagining the worst, apprehending her most despicable self in her daughter's slaughtering gaze.

When the twins were six years old, Estefania wanted them apart to develop their individuality. Their proper space was key, she preached. In truth, her intent was to weaken their unity. Gabriela and Gunnar were ordered to decorate and furnish their separate rooms according to their proper interests. They had always played more physically than with objects, always in monotonous coordination with one another, existing more in a fantasy world they both evoked in their minds.

Gunnar excelled as he was faced with all the different toys in the store. Sometimes he looked over to his sister, but then he quickly followed his mother's impulse and pointed at trains, wagons, little figurines, trees, and rail tracks. His room became stuffed with an entire miniature railway world, little villages, fine dames walking around with their sun umbrellas and fluffy yellow dresses, dogs walking around in parks and food markets where people would mingle and taste multicultural dishes. On the walls were bright-colored paintings of him and his sister that he had drawn; they were very immature and lovably innocent.

Estefania presumed that if she bought her daughter dolls, they would end up with their heads cut off. She took her to a variety of boutiques, but Gabriela showed no interest in the typical toys for girls or boys her age. After two hours, Estefania wanted to scratch the child's eyes out. She thought she was toying with her, exasperating her on purpose, wasting her time, mocking her motherly intentions, but then Gabriela stopped in front of an antique boutique. Estefania thought she was kidding, but after some consideration, it didn't surprise her that her daughter chose a different path; after all, that's exactly what she had intended in the first place. As mother and daughter entered the old store, Estefania gave the little one space to discover the vintage furniture and retro knickknacks.

Although Estefania felt uneasy, she remained in the corner next to the front door and examined the movements of her child, whose steps were directed toward an opulent *paravent*, a room divider. Gabriela closed her eyes, magnetized by the object, letting her fingers glide over the old fabric and wooden texture, uninterested in its esthetic. She connected to its energy and history, acknowledging the possibilities.

The shop owner, Marcelian Piaffus, approached Estefania joyfully, telling her that he was quite astonished to see such an extraordinary young girl with a heart for the abandoned and invaluable wandering around in his boutique.

"This octagonal *paravent* is rather unique, I might say."

"Why?"

"Well, I always tell my customers the truth about the objects that I sell. This one has a special history, a rather devastating tale, to be completely honest."

"Care to elaborate?"

"The *paravent* has been in my family's possession for decades now. Its last owner was a Marchioness, what was her name again, ah, the late Marchioness of Blutkutsch.

"As a young woman, she worked at her father's funeral home and was considered the belle of the village. Her silhouette was always visible through the two huge front windows as she walked among the disturbing emptiness of awaiting caskets and exposed coffins, her hands straightening the soft white silk, her dust tissue polishing the glistening black and walnut wood of her merchandise.

"The townspeople always joked that if death ended in her hands, it wouldn't be so dreadful after all. During their lunch breaks, the workers of the town sat outside the old coffeehouse and bakery opposite the funeral home and stared at her, drinking their espressos in the sunlight. The Marchioness, who was an ordinary young woman named Clémentine Kernteppich, always made sure the fresh flower bouquets around the entrance were welcoming and the inside smelled of bursting red roses that alleviated the mourning senses."

"I get it, belle of the countryside, yes, yes. You are quite the narrator, but I'm impatient. Could you fast-forward to what I want to know, please? What about this *paravent*, then?"

"As you wish. One day, the Marquis of Blutkutsch was looking for a coffin for his deceased wife, Lavandine Delamortelier. There were a lot of iniquitous rumors surrounding his wife's death, but gossip didn't matter in the Kernteppich funeral home, and it generally quiets down when the body reaches the privacy within the casket's clean-white bed of satin.

"The Marquis was completely besotted with Clémentine, this young woman who worked so harmoniously with death, who was so familiar with it that, through her vivid presentation of coffins and flower arrangements, death lost its infamous reputation and almost became alluring.

"The beguiled widower recovered rather quickly from the loss of his late wife, and the memory of their marriage was lowered into earthly nothingness alongside the coffin he had chosen for her. Infatuated with the vision he had embellished of young Clémentine, he tempted her to step into the glamorous role of a prosperous Marchioness. They married several months after the funeral of Lavandine, which was the ill-natured scandal, of course."

"The *paravent*, sir."

"In contrast to what people believe, you cannot get to the bottom of a story or a person by jumping straight to the ending. It doesn't do you any favors or justice. Everybody's in a hurry and misses all the necessary information to get things right. Who knows, your life might depend on a story.

"The superstitious Marquis sold all his former wife's belongings, everything but the *paravent*. The servants in the house murmured that it frightened the widower and he wouldn't touch it. They thought it was cursed and brought only mischief upon its owner and would only bond with people it could steer toward demise, seeking out their swallowed weaknesses and torturing them beyond imagination, leaving no scars, no outer wounds, but complete psychological obliteration and never-ending furor. One servant called it an octagonal corset that tightened with the years and gained intensity upon contact. Another claimed that the *paravent* highlighted everything already wrong in one's life and deteriorates the circumstances. Another stated that it encouraged the process of becoming one's worst self.

"The old Marquis had a morbid taste for young women and death, established especially in his art collection. The *paravent* had never been moved from its position in the bathroom, and of course, young impressionable Clémentine embodied its perfect victim. Her comfortable aura around death defied the *paravent* at first.

"And if you ask me, I believe in certain energies contained in the objects surrounding them, that the dead embalm their prior possessions. These energies are manifested in them and expel their intentions out of the furniture's very imperfections. Some people like that and are avid collectors of impregnated furniture, if I may say so. An object is never without a history. These pieces are radiant and convey images and feelings the same way a painting or a portrait does; they are a window into a different world or sphere. I mean, if you were dying against your will and readiness to go, would you not seek out what you loved most, something material that outlives what you're made of, and cast yourself onto it so that even a little piece of you, a story, a sensation, a feeling of who you were, contaminates life?

"Anyhow, Clémentine went completely insane. She claimed she could suddenly smell an alien odor when she got undressed in the arms of the *paravent*. A fragrance that was not hers and first smelled fruity with a hint of lavender, and then deteriorated into a stench of foul eggs and burned flesh, engulfing her body. The odor latched itself onto Clémentine's skin and plagued her as if it wanted new life, as if it craved to possess her and turn into itself again. The Marquis became furious when they had sex and all of a sudden, in the heat of the moment, he smelled the perfume of his buried and forlorn wife. Terrified, he asked Clémentine what she had found or used that belonged to the deceased. Clémentine was perplexed and at a loss for words.

"*Le panier aux fruits embrassés par la lavande* was the perfume of his dead wife, and he forbade Clémentine to use that very same scent, which of course she had never heard of. Many other tales of inexplicable transgression happened, and every time the *paravent* stood accused by Clémentine, but no one dared to listen to the beliefs of a madwoman.

"Clémentine insisted that the wife's ill-will was infesting the premises through her god-forsaken *paravent*. She would scream that all the staff members were afraid of it and yet were incapable of taking action and reclaiming their power. Indulging in Clémentine's beliefs only dragged them into the vicious grasp of death and doom, they thought. She stood alone with her acceptance of the truth and will to conquer it. She tried to destroy the *paravent* on several occasions, but was cuffed by her husband and medicated to such an extent that she would sleep for hours, which weakened her determination and resilience every time. She was ultimately sent to innumerable sanatoriums. She finally came home to him, a changed woman. But the very first night of her apparent recovered homecoming, she was found at dawn, pregnant, raped, and hanging from the *paravent* in a collapsed and strangled doll-like position, facing downwards in her lilac nightgown.

"That's when the Marquis swore off women, dead or alive, and mustered up enough courage against his excessive superstitiousness to call my grandfather Gustav. The despondent Marquis gave precise handling instructions to my grandfather, insisting that his workers wear thick leather gloves when retrieving the *paravent* and not think about things they care about. The widower gave it away for free, and my grandfather had it cleansed and blessed by three priests before it entered our boutique. Never had any trouble with it. Poor Marquis though, eh?"

"A real salesman, aren't you?"

Gabriela listened avidly the whole time, almost trance-like, completely captivated by the story as if someone had just leaned in and experienced an epiphany, feeling deeply acknowledged. The girl then looked at her mother, begging for the *paravent* in a way that felt unfamiliar to Estefania. The mother was convinced that the purchase of this piece of furniture would facilitate the bond she so hungered for with Gabriela, although she hated the unnerving history associated with the *paravent*. But, she thought, what could it possibly do to a child?

Marcelian Piaffus adored the heirloom's macabre biography, she could tell. Strangely enough, he had a disregard for its severity despite his beliefs, especially in the hands of a child, and even though Estefania had always been aware that darkness could latch itself onto objects, having grown up among unspeakable atrocities, she decided her daughter had too much grit to decline into madness.

Gabriela's eyes sparkled, and for the first time Estefania saw euphoria, ambition, and triumph on the girl's little face and felt heroic herself. Gabriela was jumping around saying she wanted this paravent, it was made for her, she loved it, but Estefania felt nauseous. Yet it fulfilled her to hear her daughter's engaging voice, for once. Estefania approached the *paravent* in a standoffish manner, inspecting its impeccable condition and sniffing it but smelled nothing out of the ordinary.

"I'll even give you a discount because you were so kind to listen to an old shop owner's dusty stories, and of course because you have such a little *appassionata* here for high-quality time-worn furniture that has its unique character and tales to divulge."

Gabriela smiled and her cheeks blushed. Her facial expression softened, and she appeared charming. Estefania swallowed her doubts, looking at her daughter's gleefulness, and was suddenly quite proud to be the mother of this radiant young girl. She stepped up to her daughter, put her arm around her shoulder, and said they would take the *paravent*. Gabriela hugged her mother's hips and thanked her. Estefania said they weren't nearly done and as she now knew that her daughter had a knack for antiques, she was free to choose more pieces, because the *paravent* couldn't fill up her entire room like Gunnar's trains did. They spent hours in the shop that smelled like patchouli, clary sage, and sandalwood.

As the *paravent* had eight walls, Gabriela, who seemed way beyond her years, selected eight light oval mirrors to go with each robust wall of the *paravent*. Estefania and Marcelian discussed how this could be done to attach each mirror to the wall without causing damage, the technicalities, and the price, of course.

Gabriela would receive her personalized antique in a week. She didn't care that it wouldn't fill her room; that wasn't the point. She possessed something priceless that belonged only to her and only she knew the true value, timelessness, nature, and power of it. Mother and daughter left the boutique hand in hand, as if transformed, both joyous, but for completely different reasons.

The Saddest of Showmen

OVER THE NEXT YEARS, ESTEFANIA'S AND GABRIELA'S relationship improved, and they found an emotional balance for themselves. Gunnar couldn't quite grasp what had happened and felt left out and inadequate. While his father was busy recuperating lost time and work, Gunnar spent hours sitting in the corner of his father's atelier, two wagons in his hands and observing the artist's movements, seeing almost nothing that he could identify with, nothing that he could ever live up to. When he wasn't pretending to play inaudibly in Severin's atelier, he attended whatever his mother and sister were doing and ended up being upset and jealous. He felt that Gabriela was not quite herself when their mother was around, that she put on a fake face, that she was very spiteful and distraught, yet he was puzzled by her artificially cheery performances that fooled everyone, her ungenial high-pitched voice and controlled body movements. He could sense her discomfort in her own skin and tried to study her transformative behavior.

Gunnar's misery mellowed his features, his hair faded, his almond-formed eyes were more inclined to closure and were downward-orientated rather than forward-steering. His chubby cheeks gradually pulverized in lifeless color, and he sought shelter in his own smothering skin. It seemed like there was only room for one child at a time in his mother's heart, that all her love could only be focused on one single object, and that everything else needed to learn how to survive and cope without her guiding hand.

Sometimes Gunnar fell asleep in his daytime clothes on the floor of his bedroom, among the illusional world he himself created so passionately, and awoke in the same unthought-of position in the morning, in the same clothes, hearing the ferocious giggles of his sister and mother in the kitchen as if he had ceased to exist.

One day, he got up, weeping noiselessly while undressing himself, and walked naked into his sibling's room. He wasn't afraid of Gabriela's room. He knew about her hidden malevolence and, in his eyes, there was nothing secretive about her.

Gabriela's room had a heavy and sultry atmosphere with eggplant-colored walls, yellow curtains, and ornaments. Gunnar approached the wardrobe with her clothes. He sobbed as he picked out a flamboyantly red dress and an Alice band and put them on. He walked down the stairs that led into the hallway and directed his steps toward the kitchen.

As he entered the kitchen, his mother's and sister's laughter stopped. Tears rolled down his face. Gabriela wasn't bothered to see her brother in her clothes or that he had rifled through her privacy because she was aware his intentions weren't directed at her. She remained quiet.

Estefania stood there like a gaping corpse, glancing quickly at Gabriela then back at her son, irritated and slightly perplexed. She waited for him to say something. He acknowledged her expectation and launched himself into the self-deprecating comedic. "Surprise," he said, shaking the ruffles of the dress, pirouetting around and making kissing faces and posing for his mother.

Relieved that this was nothing serious, Estefania started to laugh again, applauded her son, and encouraged him to pursue his act. Gabriela was laughing too, but her nose and mouth twitched. Only Gunnar could decipher the emotion in her face; she was boiling with rage, her pupils stuck in the corners of her eyes, piercing through her mother, yet smiling like a nice little girl.

When Gunnar bowed, Gabriela wanted to whimper. She couldn't stomach the humiliation and disaster, but controlled her urge and bit her lip in contempt for the adult in the room. Praising the feminine grace of her son, Estefania paraded him around the kitchen as if there were an invisible audience in the room, completely oblivious to her boy's reasons for putting up such a good show. She lifted him up and sat him next to his sister who, as their mother turned her back to get eggs, clasped his little hand in solidarity.

From that moment onward, Gunnar knew how to extract his mother's attention during her period of favoritism toward Gabriela: to ridicule himself and play the impoverished clown in girls' clothing. He took his inspiration from his atypical sister, exaggerating her fake mannerisms and pretentious characteristics, bringing an unfortunate caricature to life and masking them both. He made his mother laugh with his charades that jabbed his self-esteem, but all that mattered was that he was not alone; he was included.

Gunnar never loved his mother more than in those moments when she laughed her heart out and never hated himself more than after her applause. He let his hair grow longer so that it could be braided or brushed by his mother before bedtime. For Gunnar, the trains stood still at the station, in front of traffic lights, isolated and spread across the entire sedated town where nothing would ever move again.

As he grew fonder of the image his mother now fostered of him than the truth behind his self-ridiculing mask, he repressed his real personality and pushed it further down his soul, buried himself in his own body and let his performative superficiality surface to ease his mother's life. The wounded voice inside of him became a dead mass, evaporating its toxic fumes across his mind, signaling him its fragility and that he needed to save himself before it would be too late. The trauma had now spread from his soul to his very body. Now was the time to stop hurting himself for his mother's amusement. Estefania was proud to have such a delightful young entertainer in her family, and his future looked promising to her.

Gunnar's room was merely used to sleep in, for the rest of the time, nothing was touched and nothing ever altered.

After a year, Severin, who was so consumed by his work that he ate breakfast at four in the morning, lunch outside with the local benefactors, and dinner alone in his atelier to stay focused on his art, rejoined his family's routine and resurfaced as they were preparing dinner in the kitchen. The twins knew he visited them every night while they were sleeping and whispered kind words to them and told them what he had accomplished during the day, but that evening when he rose from the intoxicating sphere of art and entered the kitchen, he was catapulted right back into the dysfunctional insanities of his family, which felt like an all too well-known punch in the stomach.

Still unnoticed by everyone, Severin stood statically on the edge of the door and observed his son behaving in a desperately effeminate way, trying to please his mother and excel at an incompatible showmanship. The estranged father had trouble recognizing his male offspring now that he was awake and instantly felt guilty, appalled, and responsible for this travesty that he deemed so harmful.

In Severin's eyes, Gunnar's smile seemed shallow, not childlike. He could actually see how alarming his son's mental state was. The reasons for his masquerade were so obvious that he couldn't possibly understand why Estefania had been encouraging this obscene and self-destructive behavior. It was easier for Severin to stand up for others instead of speaking up for his own sake. The fact that his wife seemed to find her boy's hunger for attention hilarious and his despair diverting infuriated Severin. While he fought to keep breathing calmly, he got entangled in Gabriela's glance and intervened.

"What is going on here?"

"Severin, darling, we were just making dinner. Should be ready in an hour or so. I'm glad that you're done for today. Now we can eat together again."

He tried to pull Estefania away to talk in private with her because he didn't want to fight in front of the children. Gunnar looked as if his world had crumpled and he knew this would be the end, his father would bring his mother to her senses. The boy fumbled his fingers in anticipation of renewed abandonment, looking fearful and shattered inside.

"What's the matter with you? Don't touch my arm like that," Estefania hissed.

Although Severin felt submissive toward her, the absence and distance had given him momentary courage, especially when it concerned Gunnar and the abhorrent state he found him to be in.

"Are you blind? Have you looked at this boy lately? Do you even see him clearly? Do you have any idea what you are doing to him? Is he a joke to you?"

"It's just Gunnar putting up a good show, making us laugh, he has a natural talent for it, and God knows we need some comedy around here. Since when is laughter a crime? Lighten up or go back to the hole you came from."

While she sloppily uttered those words, she didn't even look at her son, who was fidgeting nervously with his fingers. When she said his name, she made a belittling hand gesture that hit his heart like an engulfing fever.

"And don't you dare accuse me and portray me as the monster here. You're not even here. You are a ghost. You come and go as you please, and when no one is looking, you offer some half-assed affection. What kind of father are you? Standing here, pointing fingers, you pretentious moral apostle. At least I'm here."

"Maybe that's what made things worse. You cannot be left alone with your own children."

Gabriela sensed the storm erupting in her mother's bones. She took Gunnar by the hand and left the room with the chopped vegetables. Estefania composed herself and approached her husband in a dominant and calculating manner. She leaned in and put her thunderous lips next to his ear.

"Severin, don't talk to me like this. I'm trying to keep this family together at the cost of my sanity, and you know that. Everybody sees that. I'm doing my best, and I'm undeniably on my own. You should be ashamed. If that poor boy is so important to you, then why don't you talk to him, nourish him, clothe him, and feed him? How would you describe your relationship with him? Tell me, I'm curious. Do you even know him? I spend all my time with them, do you hear me? The bad mother-wolf is always there for her children. Do you really think people will buy it that you are the good guy here? If you don't improve your attitude toward me, I will maul you like an egg in a frying pan, Severin. The things I know about you. Do I need to say more?"

"Don't lean so far out the window. You might fall out."

Dinner was not been served that night. Gabriela and Gunnar sat in the middle of her mirror-*paravent* and played with lights in the gloom. At some point, Severin walked in with some cheese, nuts, and grapes and sat among his children, putting the plate on the floor and holding both of them in his arms as they chewed.

"You know, you don't need to please anyone but yourselves. The most important thing is that you can look at yourself in the mirror and not be despised by what you see, but be happy to see yourself there, smile and not stare away in rejection and shame or whatnot. It won't be possible every day, but try your best. Be yourselves at all cost. You are the utmost priority in your own lives, don't forget that. Listen to your vocation, don't let anyone interfere. Commit to it, don't compartmentalize your capabilities. Stand behind your convictions. Remember my words. Maybe I should too. Dedicate yourselves to your purpose. I hope my words will resonate with you one day. I love you both and I see you for what you are. There is so much potential in you, and I believe in it."

During the next year, Gunnar and Severin spent a lot of time together in nature, bonding anew. But Gunnar never stopped wanting to impress his mother even though she failed him constantly, like a wave cracking against the rocks. Severin made an effort to steer his son in a self-affirming direction and Gunnar loved him for it, but somehow he craved to be accepted, praised, and loved by the parent who treated him so dreadfully. Severin took the boy out of the house as much as possible in the seasonal air and let him play in their wide garden that smelled like jasmine and rosemary.

Gunnar tried to lose control and conquer the self-depreciative hole that his mother deepened whenever they were alone with her contempt, remarks, and phrases commenting on his feebleness and oddness. Then she had moments of physical tenderness that felt so genuine on his skin, but were then dismantled by the skepticism that prohibited him to dream and embellish her lies and mind games.

Sometimes, when Gunnar's father went out for lunch, the boy felt vulnerable and panicky, ending up face down on the floor just crying on end, and nobody would come to soothe his anxieties. He disappeared on the cold hardness of the floors, hurling in proximity to his mother's whereabouts. She heard him every time and yet resumed to hum her songs, ignoring his pain and letting him get sore, dancing to the tune her crying son produced in sheer desolation.

One day, Estefania was in a pleasant mood and bathed both her children in her giant black bathtub full of rainbow bubbles. It was a very hot day, and after the bath the three of them went to the en suite master bedroom. They lay on the bed in their white towels to dry and took a nap together. These peaceful moments were very rare, which made them even more precious. Gabriela, exhausted by the heat, fell asleep after fifteen minutes.

Estefania, a usually light and troubled sleeper, dozed off and finally fell into a fortified sleep. Gunnar felt so overwhelmingly appreciated and euphoric that he wanted to show his mother how much he worshipped and adored her. His heart was beating vividly, and as he watched his mother half-asleep, slowly inhaling and exhaling, calm and soft, she seemed so lovable and caring, so innocent and gentle that he wanted to hug her endlessly.

He put his little hand on her arm that had a peachy texture and caressed it. He felt so close to her and safe, now that she was asleep, and he could prove his love to her. Her towel was hanging lose around her body, and his fingers traveled slowly up her legs in circular motions, dreamy little movements, child-like endeavors, until the boy's little fingers reached his mother's labia. Still caressing her smoothly, he glided his fingers between them and let them dive into his mother's sex.

Awakened by the erotic sensation and seeing her son next to her quickly retrieving his hand, Estefania froze and stared at him, completely shocked and alerted. Gabriela was still sleeping, and Estefania didn't want to make this a big thing. She wanted to confront Gunnar and then forget about it, teach him a lesson and never speak of it again, so she started to whisper. She knew she couldn't be aggressive to resolve this issue and needed to get the boy to engage in a lasting conversation, so she sweet-talked him.

"Gunnar, what made you think you can touch me there?"

"Did it not feel good?"

"Why did you think it was appropriate, Gunnar?"

"Because it is good to do that. It feels pleasant. It makes people happy. I want to please you."

Estefania's mouth hung open, her eyes not blinking, her throat dry and her fingers trembling. She didn't know what to say and where to begin even. She refused to look at her confused son, and an acid disgust disturbed her vocal chords. Estefania remained silent, her face revealing her nausea.

"I can do better, Mother. I know it. I'm sorry. I love you. I just wanted you to know. I just want to see you happy. I don't understand. Please, don't be angry with me."

"Stop talking."

Gunnar's chest looked like a rooster's body before getting its head chopped off. The boy came close to a panic attack because he didn't know how to resolve the situation. He wanted her to understand but was at a loss for words. He put his hand over his mouth, his eyes filling with tears, his face turning into a self-loathing grimace of guilt and confusion.

As soon as Estefania saw the child's hand on his mouth, under his nose, she slapped it away from his face, but she wanted to hurt him so much more. Punish him for what he had dared to do. Touch his mother's sex and then put his nasty little hand on his mouth. That's all she could feel. She was repulsed and wanted to release her rage. Instead she took a deep breath and tried to find out Gunnar's reasoning. She held his hand prisoner in hers.

"Gunnar, have you done this before? To somebody else? Who told you this?"

"They showed it to me."

"Who, Gunnar?"

Gabriela lay in a fetal position, her back turned to the pair of them, wide awake and petrified.

"Bea and Ludi."

"Your nannies?"

"Yes."

"How?"

"We were all playing together."

"Gabriela as well?"

"Yes, that's how I learnt."

"What? Tell me."

"They made Gabriela happy and Gabriela made them happy. I could only watch and learn, they said, because I am a boy."

"They did the same thing you did with me?"

"Yes."

"Did they tell you this was a secret?"

"They said you would be disappointed if I said something and think that I'm a nasty little boy that lies and you would punish me."

She held her son's hand the whole time, and her tension and ferocity had increased to such a degree that she hadn't noticed how much she squeezed it. He didn't dare complain, though it had almost turned purple from the pressure. She couldn't swallow. These statements made her heart pump in such a way that she felt it just dropped to the bottom of her gut, unfindable and yet tearing her innards apart on slow-burning coal.

Something deep inside of her had awoken again. It stirred in her stomach and rumored through her deeply repressed veins. Her complexion was pale and yellowish, her hands shivering. So many various recollections, memories, and flashbacks rushed through her mind that she almost didn't dare look. Every sense-making corner of her mind exhibited a new sensation of the past, and after fifteen minutes of silence, she had lost herself so much in her recuperating apparatus that she couldn't tell fact from fiction. Her storytelling brain had all the means to present and merge both equally believable.

Trying to toughen up, she again turned her glance toward her son, who was biting his inner cheek hard to ignore the anguish she caused to his hand and holding back his tears to not agitate her further. She immediately dropped his hand and directed her motherly gaze at her presumably sleeping daughter, away from his trauma, reinforcing it with every step she took away from him. She stood up, naked, the towel dropping on the floor, and walked around the bed toward her daughter.

This moment of rejection and dismissiveness would scar her son beyond remedy. It carved itself in his mind forever, causing emotional tumors that would never leave his body and his thoughts, branding their toxicity through the very essence of every organ like acid.

As she reached Gabriela, she saw that she was awake, eyes open like two glacial mirrors, a broken statue, covered up like a larva that didn't dare move. Gabriela had drooled on the cushion, her visage gone stale. Estefania fell down on her knees and shouted and knocked her fists against the mattress that held her children.

She took her daughter, making sure she was all tucked up in her towel, and hugged her as tightly as she could. The child just stared into the nothingness before her and was heartbroken by the tragedy she felt behind her back; her brother Gunnar, sitting there like misery impersonated, in total abjection, drying his own tears. Gabriela sat up on the bed and felt her mother's pretentious enlightenment, how she put all the pieces together and understood her daughter now, why she was how she was. All their conflicts were explicable now that she was aware of the two scapegoats. Of course her daughter couldn't be normal under the circumstances, and now she could put herself in her daughter's skin. Now she could act like a mother, do what she had to do to prove that she was a good parent, a protective one, and express all the necessary emotions. Estefania would bow before her child onto whom she projected her younger self, lay her head in the daughter's nap and holler in such a way that it hit every wall in the house. Gabriela felt tempted to apply pressure and suffocate her mother's gaping face.

Rhubarba, who was stirring through the soup for dinner that night, ordered her subordinates, Richard and Salomon, to keep cutting the vegetables and mind their business. As the museum had always been a very functional and rather public part of the mansion, the five o'clock tour group of twenty people were frightened by the incessant screeching of the invisible woman upstairs.

The receptionist, Attaca von Rubinklotz, pretended not to hear anything and chuckled merrily at the customers as she awkwardly cashed in their money at the gift shop. The tour guide, Damascus Dâte-à-Drâpe, however, had a bit more difficulty narrating his usually eccentric way through the art museum with this harrowing noise disturbing his five-star-rated tour. (On a side note, if one paid an extra sum of money, one was allowed beyond the scarlet velvet rope that barred the entry to Jacqueline's memorial chamber, which was heavily accessed by sects and spiritual subcultures while the Zweighaupts were asleep. One had to take one's shoes off as if in prayer and worship. Damascus had elevated Jacqueline to an ethereal creature that was nurtured by the comings and goings of fanatics and believers.)

Just as Rhubarba decided to tend to her caterwauling mistress, Severin came back and immediately rushed upstairs with the housemaid right behind him.

"What on earth is wrong with you? There is a tour going on! What is the matter with you all?"

Rhubarba took one look at Gunnar, and she knew. She waited until the kid returned her gaze, and as he glanced back in terror, she winked her left eye at him and put her long bony finger over her putrid lips.

"Here, put something on you." Severin took a bathrobe out of the closet, dragged his wife away from Gabriela, and put it on her naked, pastel blue body. He was soaked in sweat and after looking shortly into the bathroom, he ordered Rhubarba to let the water out of the bathtub and open the window to get rid of the humidity and dampness. As Rhubarba followed his orders, Severin sat his wife down on the bed, stared at his two silent twins, and was enraged that peace and quiet were unattainable, faraway ideals.

"Estefania, talk to me. What happened here? You're scaring me." Estefania caught a glimpse of Rhubarba's face in the mirror. She stood up, walked straight to her, took her by the neck, and forced her head into the dirty water. She dunked it once, twice, thrice, longer, longer, shaking it as violently as she could underwater.

"The help! What a help. A blind help. Don't make me laugh! The help, thank you for your services!"

Estefania was out of control. She screamed maniacally until Severin pushed her away to save the coughing and hyperventilating maid. The distraught mother's bathrobe disentangled itself, and she ran down the stairs like a madwoman. Barely breathing, she grasped the first big object that she could find, a broom, stormed into the tourist group, and started beating Damascus with it. Her breasts wiggled back in forth, and foxtrotting pearls of sweat ran down her legs. The tourists, who were fascinated by the entire family and their known manias, were highly entertained and started taking pictures of the free fiasco. Like a wrathful queen in her revelatory robe, Estefania kept pounding her employee with her broomstick in a reverberating cloud of dust that sprinkled her body with a gray texture.

"Abusing my children! Not my children! In my own house!"

The drama and the scandal were a firsthand feast for the tourists, who recorded Estefania's incriminating behavior. Then she rushed to the gift shop and smacked Attaca's cheeks, which turned from a pastoral pink to a ruby-red tone. After Attaca had urinated on her chair because of this unexpected violence, Estefania moved on, still hollering her slogan that no one abuses her children. The tourists followed her like a parade of flashing scavengers.

As she moved out of the museum area and toward the kitchen, she was stopped by her husband, who ordered the tourists to leave, guaranteeing reimbursements and apologizing on behalf of his disturbing wife who, he said, was ill. After the house and garden had been emptied of every single tourist, Severin assembled his assaulted staff and wife in the living room.

The twins were kept in Gabriela's bedroom, as their father didn't want them to be a part of this, which made Estefania snort ironically. The infuriated mother took up an entire ottoman, sat there like an all-powerful empress, leaning back, arms stretched on the upper length of the sofa, head steadfast, legs crossed, revealing her naked body. She was quite comfortable now, repudiating unuttered reproaches toward her and a sense of her own guilt. Severin stopped trying to talk sense into her and let her be a neurotic exhibitionist. He just wanted to know what happened to his kids and why she attacked the staff.

"I'm trying to remain calm here to solve the chaos we are in now."

Estefania interrupted him with a mocking grunt. The tension amongst the personnel was excruciating. Rhubarba, all wet, couldn't refrain from smiling in the corners of her mouth.

"Housemaid almost drowned in bathtub, tour guide smashed with a fucking broomstick, incontinent receptionist slapped, I mean, those are colorful headlines that I will have to deal with. Not to mention, my maniacal wife, the broomstick attacker, the naked basket case who will not tell me what the hell happened! You incoherent mess of a woman, I should lock you up! Do you have any idea who you remind me of? More and more as our days pass? Do I need to say it?"

"You always ask what happened, but you are always too late to see it for yourself, aren't you? And then I am the lying, fantasy-creating wife who drags every sane person into her derailed world. Of course I am. In your eyes that is exactly what I have always been, but I'm slipping away from you and your interest has turned into mistrust, fascination into a lack of control. You should see and know the things that I feel, and you would break into silence and awe of me, Severin. I will not stand condemned by an absent husband. You only show interest after all hell breaks loose, then the hero Severin comes, the man of the hour, the good Samaritan, post-factum, and you pretend to deal with the situation. What happened, you ask? Are you deaf or are your eyes closed again as you look at me?"

Estefania's reverberating laughter chilled the personnel's spine. She threw herself into a fit, and her nipples hardened as she shook her loose head.

"You are the one who doomed me into exile," he said. "You shut down while pointing a million fingers. You let me beg, and starve, and freeze, hollowed out by unanswered questions. And how could you even look at me like that, how could you even go on, this unnerving passivity of yours slithering down the hallways, underneath the bedsheets, this cold dead air of yours, the coma-inducing aggression crawling beneath your skin rubbed against me. You make a parasite out of me so that you can live, and then you accuse me of not being here and inquiring about things that

involve my children? Stop rolling your eyes at me, you narcissistic loon!"

Severin's nerves electrified.

"Today, mama's sex got fingered by her six-year-old son, how do
you like that daddy-the-dimwit, daddy-what-the-fuck-happened?"

She imitated him mockingly, almost charmingly, and didn't
blink as she looked him straight in the eye. The employees tried
to hide their judgment and discomfort.

"Could you please leave us alone? You are all done for today. I
am truly sorry about this. I understand if you want to give up your
position. I will write references for each and every one of you.
Once again, I sincerely apologize. Thank you for sitting through
this."

Estefania got up and smashed a lamp against the closed door.

"Thank you for the sexually educative services you've equipped
my son with, thank you, thank you, much appreciated. I will write
you a reference, but excuse my wife, she feels unwell and I can't
relate, she feels unwell and I make it up, she makes it up and I
don't ask why."

Estefania parodied her husband and blew a raspberry.

"Shut your vile mouth. I don't know what's true anymore. I have
lost my instincts when it comes to you, you have numbed them,
and since then you roam freely. You hit me with your insanity,
woman, but I am no part of your reality. Rhubarba told me the
nannies are responsible for this atrocity. You attacked my staff for
nothing. This doesn't concern anybody but us. Leave, all of you,
please. Rhubarba, you stay."

Estefania pranced around the room, winged her arms, and imitated a chicken.

"How does she know? Now, that, my dearest husband, interests me. Nobody knows. Nobody sees anything. It is happening
below their noses, but everything is okay. There is nothing to hide
because nobody pays attention."

Rhubarba interfered. "I overheard Gunnar's confession today as I walked past the bedroom to get some linens from the closet in the upper hall. I eavesdropped for a moment, I apologize."

The maid crossed her hands in front of her stomach.

"So you did pay attention indeed. For how long, I wonder. Have you been watching, secretly, participating, encouraging even? Is this really the first time that you have breached the privacy in this household, weaseling your way in to take advantage for your sake, Rhubarba?"

"Estefania, leave her alone. This is our fault. I need to think about our next steps," Severin said.

"My six-year-old fingers me, and you need to think. I would break your neck if I had the strength. They are all in cahoots with each other, the aids, the help, the entire staff. This is ridiculous. Let them set the house on fire, steal our invaluable artwork, or rape me in the middle of the night, see if my husband cares as long as they make one hell of a soup. Yes, let's keep the lot."

Rhubarba approached Estefania and whispered softly, "Mrs. Zweighaupt, you're exhausted and I understand your wrath, but you need to calm down and think what's best for your children now. Put yourself in their skin, imagine what they must be feeling. I will draw you a fresh bath with lavender oil and make you some chamomile tea. It will appease your nerves. Let me be of help. Everything will be sorted once you've got a clear head. Trust me."

Estefania grabbed her upper arm, drew her in, and replied, "What have I done to you to deserve this?"

"No disrespect, Mrs. Zweighaupt, but that question could easily come out of your children's mouths."

A Little Death

IN SEPTEMBER, THE ZWEIGHAUPT TWINS STARTED SCHOOL. Rumors and controversial blather about their fanatic mother had kept the jam-packed newspapers going during the summer months and had established their dishonorable reputation by proxy. School was easy for Gabriela as she was so talented at fooling everyone, acting out numerous roles without losing her thick-skinned credibility. Gunnar aspired to appear as confident as his sister, especially in times of uncertainty and instability, looking up to her like a thirsty animal to a mirage of water.

Gunnar failed to vanish behind his face like she did, unable to contain his emotions behind a veil of skin, and thus he stabbed himself in the back and allowed himself to be an accomplice to pretense for everyone else's sake again. He was certain that his peers could never like him for who he really was, and now he stood in direct comparison to his sister. In order to survive with the fittest, he became extremely cautious not to expose himself and thus seemed more like a shell of a person, which froze potential relationships with girls and boys his age.

Every time he attempted to be something he was not, he felt caught in the act and derailed into the hyperbolic, the phony, and exaggerated mimicry, which excommunicated him from the prospect of making friends and performing well at school. While his twin shone in the middle of cheering circles, making sycophants laugh, Gunnar grabbed his lunch, retired to a toilet stall, and ate it, away from everyone else. His tasteless sandwiches were always sprinkled with tears. Then he rocked himself back and forth on the toilet seat, staring into the void of the shut door in front of him for more than an hour, and hummed unwholesomely until it was time to attend the next class.

In the middle of the school year, the baby sister of a classmate, Twinkle Maupin, who liked Gabriela very much and always talked about her at home, died. Mrs. Maupin was so delusional in her grief that she called all the parents of Twinkle's classmates to ask for a favor that was very dear to her heart. Every single one of them expressed their heartfelt compassion and condolences, but respectfully declined and cursed her most vividly after they hung up the phone, regardless of her circumstance.

Then Mrs. Maupin called the mother everyone had been bad-mouthing over the summer, and the one that because of her own experience, Mrs. Maupin thought she would understand and comply.

Estefania was alone with Gunnar the entire weekend, and the call from Mrs. Maupin came on Friday evening. Of course, Estefania identified with the woman's pain caused by the loss, speaking from mother to mother, and yes, no one should go through that, and it was life-shattering to experience such an unspeakable tragedy.

They chitchatted for fifteen minutes about grief, mourning, motherhood, and how different the mother's process of acknowledging the bereavement of a child was from the father's. They agreed that it felt like an incomplete amputation, that they had a dead and invisible limb, hurting like hellfire, non-existent, and it was up to them to take care of the wound or let it infect the whole organism, even though it would always be painfully missed, reattaching itself in their minds because they could still feel it. Thus a mother is left alone with her body that reeks of visible death.

Estefania had conquered the phantom pain, but Mrs. Maupin had yet to go through that. A part of Estefania's body had long gone, and some people argued over whether it was her heart or her mind. So Mrs. Maupin asked if she would be so kind as to let Gabriela, who was such a wonderful girl, by the way, do her this tremendous favor, which would mean the world to her, and she understood if it was too much to ask of a child, and yet she did.

"No, of course not. Gunnar is going to do it, not an issue at all."

"Ah, yes, of course, Gabriela's twin, I forgot. I would be happy with either one of them and extremely grateful. It's good, really, two children." The mother burst into tears, and Estefania thought of her as quite a dramatic woman.

"When is the funeral? When do you want Gunnar to be there, dear?"

"It's on Sunday, at ten in the morning. It would be greatly appreciated if you could be in front of the chapel near the cemetery at nine forty-five."

"Naturally, you can count us in. See you then."

Estefania hung up the phone and grunted, "Theatrical housewife."

That night she walked into Gunnar's room and told him that they were invited to attend a funeral on Sunday and that he should look very presentable, as he had a special appearance to make.

"A funeral?"

"A celebration for a dead person, really. It's a ceremony, people bury a body, they weep, and then they drink, you know, say good-bye."

"Who is dead?"

"Trudy Maupin. It's the little sister of one of Gabriela's classmates, already forgot her name, so, yes. Poor thing, only a few weeks old."

"But I don't know who that is. Wouldn't it be better if Gabriela went with you?"

"Honey, can you see your sister anywhere? No? That's right, that's because she is not here, so she can't attend the funeral on

Sunday now, can she? We will go in her stead. We don't want to disappoint the poor parents, right? Don't they have enough to go through already? Think of them and your own parents, and that poor little girl who lost her sister. And what would people say about you if you rejected a mourning mother's last wish, bearing in mind that we are both invited guests and that she chose you to contribute a special kindness and service? Only you were chosen for this role. Do you really want to say no to this family who thinks so highly of you?"

Fearful of other people's harsh judgment and his mother's fierce discontent, Gunnar decided to please her and nodded, not really knowing what was expected of him. On Sunday, Estefania woke her son, shaking him, then she washed him, brushed his hair, and dressed him in a most exquisite silver suit and tie. He looked stunning, which was exactly what she intended. With this deed, he would erase those horrid and debauched rumors that had infested this silly town and reprimand her rotten reputation.

Happy to spend time with his proud mother alone and seeing her in such a cheerful mood, Gunnar walked hand in hand with her to the cemetery. When mother and son arrived at the little white chapel, they could see all the funeral guests standing on a nearby hill, next to a dug-out hole. Mrs. Maupin, veiled, walked quietly out of the chapel, closing the door gently behind her as if she had just put her infant to sleep, and squatted down to see eye to eye with Gunnar.

"Thank you so much for doing this for me, my little jewel." She kissed him on the cheek and sobbed, clinging to him for an arduous moment.

Mr. Maupin came down, staggering, to accompany her up the hill. As they both walked up the path that led to the graveside, Estefania bowed down to Gunnar and told him in a sharp whisper, "You are going to carry the little one's casket. Don't embarrass me. Just think about Jacqueline."

Gunnar knew what a coffin was, but not what a casket was. He thought he was supposed to carry a bouquet of yellow flowers, like in baptisms or wedding ceremonies, where girls threw rice around or heads of roses. He knew, however, that his mother's subtly threatening tone had never been a harbinger of good news.

The doors of the chapel opened, and the first thing he could see was not the priest and his beautiful robe, but the tiny white coffin that the priest held in his old hands. Gunnar's fear increased as the priest walked toward him with the coffin, making direct eye contact, as if he expected something from him. That's when Gunnar understood what he was supposed to do, what he had agreed to do, what his mother had tricked him into doing. His little tie almost couldn't maintain the fearful beating of his heart, his eyes widening, and he felt like he would faint any second now. But then he felt a slight hidden pinch in his hips that came from his mother's frantic nails, which catapulted him back into reality.

Now the coffin with the little dead baby inside was right in front of his face, ready to be grasped and carried up the never-ending hill. Everyone was waiting for him, and with shivering hands he reached out for it, although every fiber in his body screamed and revolted. From one moment to the next, he held it in his unsteady hands.

"After you, young man," said the priest ceremoniously and stepped back, right behind Gunnar.

Estefania leaned cozily against the chapel's wall, and everybody looked at the empathetic young boy who had consented to fulfill a mother's last wish for her dead child. Gunnar had never walked smaller steps, although he felt like running away. As he was uncontrollably shivering, the little white coffin shook in accordance with his frightened body. He breathed quickly, his heart pumping harder with every insecure step, trying to combat his anxieties and shock. The boy walked up the hill repressing his tears, aware of all the solemn people up there who were staring at

him and the sobbing mother with the black veil and the mono-
grammed napkin under her runny nose.

Gunnar's silver suit shone like a fish's skin in the sun, and he had
been so proud of how his mother had made him up and prepared
him, but now he felt cheated and hideous, nauseous in the heart.
He pressed his lips together. As he walked up the hill he shook so
strongly, he felt the dead baby's body roll back and forth against the
walls of its tiny confinement. He heard the sound of the infant's
head, this muffled sound, like a little potato rolling off a cutting
board. His teeth clattered, his nostrils widened, his eyes squinted,
and when he arrived at the atrociously gaping hole everybody was
giving him a sympathetic "well done" smile. Then he was ordered to
put the casket down. Gunnar would never forget the word. Casket.
He was soaking wet and wore the suit only once more.

When Severin and Gabriela returned, they went to the salon,
the only room that had a light on. Gabriela sensed a heavy torment wandering across her ribs, and she was sure that something
was wrong. As they stepped into the salon, they saw Estefania sitting in an armchair, drunk and reading. She held the book upside
down, and yet her eyes followed the lines, and she turned a page
as they approached her.

"Is everything all right?"

Gabriela took a close look at her sickening mother as her father
talked to her.

"Yes, darling, I'm delighted. I had a fantastic day." Estefania was
still holding up the book right in front of her face, and the room
smelled terribly of alcohol. Her right hand shook.

"Really? Tell me then."

"I went to a funeral. A baby's funeral." She chuckled, and Severin felt the impact of her insanity hit him again. He sat down
in the armchair in front of hers and asked her to lower the book.
After a few suspenseful seconds, she threw the book right across
the room, past her husband's head. Her face was rundown with
smudged black shadows of mascara.

"He ran away, our dear little boy. Our son who has no apprecia-
tion for life, no compassion for bereavement and no communal
sensitivity. I can't find him, and I don't know what to do anymore,
Severin. I'm trying, you know. He just ran away. Like he couldn't
care less about my worries. He could be anywhere, and I'm here.
The audacity that child has. The disregard for me. And now it's
night time, and who the fuck knows where my son is."

"Gone for how long? He wouldn't just run away. You know that.
Did you fight? Did you take him with you to the funeral?"

"A few hours or so. Of course I accompanied him."

"He is the child, Estefania! When was the funeral?"

"We attended it until ten-fifteen, and then he just looked at me
like a madman and ran away without saying a single word."

"And you didn't follow him?"

"No. He needed to vent."

"Are you kidding me?"

"Everybody was already staring. It would have been incredibly
rude to just disappear. There is something called etiquette and
manners, you know. And Gunnar vomited all over the grass. The
boy was lucky that he was a good distance from everyone. Imagine those acid stains on those fancy suits. That would have cost
me a fortune to pay the dry cleaner's bills for all those imbecilic
hypocrites from the funeral. After that he just walked toward me,
wiped his mouth off, frowned, and left hysterically."

"The protocol is to excuse yourself and follow your son no matter what. Who cares what those people think? Who are they, even?
Do we know them at all? And now our son is missing because
of your crippling people-pleasing worldview and shallow societal
codes. No one would have cared if you left. You're not the center
of the world, Estefania. Tell me you've informed the police."

"No. I thought he needed a little space to get a grip on himself.
He knows his way back. He should have learned his lesson by now.
I don't know what is taking him so long. My door is always open,
but he needs to repent and apologize for the mortification he put

me through. I bet he's sitting on a rock somewhere. Brooding. It takes guts to actually run away without looking back. It's good that you came home because it's really getting late now."

"Can you hear yourself? It's sickening, Estefania. You didn't even look for him. He could be anywhere, and that's on you. How can you sit here and drink yourself into oblivion? I'm calling the police. Look at you. What an infuriating disaster."

"I know what you did," Gabriela said. "I know what you made him do today. How could you? I know where he is. No need for the police. I'll get him, and you stay far away from him. You've done enough, Mother." Gabriela scowled from where she stood in a dark corner of the room. She walked through the lights and out of the house to get her brother. Estefania hissed behind her back like an accursed nutter. Severin barricaded her body in the armchair and slammed both of his fists onto the sides of it.

"One day you are deliriously happy. You want to cook, you want to dance, listen to music, bake or sing aloud. And then the next day you have such an animosity in your gut, such madness, I've never seen anything like it. Not even from my mother. This has been going on for years now. You have become two extremes, and I don't recognize the good in you anymore. What is happening with you, Estefania? Are you a danger to our kids that I downplay? Are you really this cruel and vicious? Or can I find the mother of my children, my beloved wife, and my soul mate in there somewhere? I won't go on like this. It is too intense, too nonsensical. I can't relate to it and frankly, I refuse to. I don't know how to deal with it, your temper, and your abusiveness. I don't understand where it's coming from, but I can see it's also harming you. I don't know how many times I've told you this over the last years, but we have two very fragile young kids who need proper parents, and we're incompetent together. This is a two-person job, but under these circumstances, one functional parent is better than two dysfunctional ones. I'm sick of saying this, but I feel like we're going in circles. You're not getting better, and I'm just letting things happen. I need to draw the line soon and make a decision about you. You can't tell me you're happy and healthy. I've tolerated this behavior long enough. You're sick in the head."

"You don't know your daughter at all. They both detest me. They have abhorred me since they were born, even before that, you know that. I could feel it. Do you even fathom how they look at me? Like I failed them beyond repair, like I should be dead, like it's my fault that Jacqueline didn't make it, like I abandoned them as soon as I became aware of them. I don't want to be like my mother. Or like yours. I don't. They can feel it too, and that scares me. They will exterminate me, Severin. I am on trial every single day. I'm judged and found guilty, and yet they let me roam around freely. What is my punishment, exactly? I don't know who my mother was, but I'm afraid I'm getting closer to her truth. I don't know who I am. I won't go to a sanatorium or an asylum. I won't become a divorced caricature behind bars, dependent on pills and electroshocks. I'm a good mother. Why can't you see that? I won't be psychoanalyzed and locked away from my home and my kids and my husband. Those doctors only see what they want to see. I won't be a human experiment. I won't be sliced open or perforated like an olive in a martini for everyone to look at. I'm fine. You should look at yourself, you attacker. Clean your own doorstep before you come a-knocking at mine with all your brooms. I know how your views of me have changed, spiraled down the toilet, but at least I'm not stuck in the past."

"You never let anyone in. Qualified professionals could help you. Maybe you suffer from something that causes all of this and you're not aware of it. Maybe you could be easily fixed. I don't know, a chemical imbalance perhaps. Something in your brain. Imagine if we could find the reason and take care of it. And we'd have wasted all this time with ridiculous fights, and neither one of us was at fault. Have you thought of that? I don't know who you are most of the time, it's alienating."

"You demonize me and I alienate you?"

"We are all invisible to you. You make sense in your own world. And you feel threatened all the time. You're defensive. We're all exhausted. We can't beg anymore and plead for togetherness. It should be natural for you to let us in. We're your family. Now tell me. What did you make Gunnar do today?"

"He just carried the baby's casket, for heaven's sake."

Reappearance

I SAW JACQUELINE," GUNNAR TOLD HIS SISTER, WHO FOUND him on the brittle dock over the black lake near the house.

"Where?" There was not a hint of disbelief in his sister's voice.

"Up on the hill. She was standing behind the baby's tombstone." He fidgeted with his shoelaces and anxiously stared down.

"Then she must be our age."

"She scares me. Don't talk about her as if she were alive."

"What did she look like?"

"Very different from us. I think she just wanted to help me."

"Why were you scared?"

"Because I know that she shouldn't have been there. Only I could see her."

"Did she say something to you?"

"No, she can't speak."

"When did she leave?"

"She didn't."

"How so?"

"See there? She is floating over the middle of the lake. It's her favorite place. It's the deepest spot. She wants me to think that she's taking care of me, that I'm safe with her."

"Why can't I see her?"

"I don't know."

"Has it always been the three of us, then?"

"I don't know what she wants from me. I don't trust her."

"She's our sister, Gunnar. Always has been, but she's dead. This only means something if you let it. We need to go home now."

Gunnar disregarded the heavy presence as he turned his back on the lake, feeling cornered, and took Gabriela's hand as they walked off the dock in unison.

After Estefania silently acknowledged her son's presence in the house again, she went to bed and slept off her drunkenness. Severin carried Gunnar to his room where the little train village still stood and had become a material whisper of a vanished and tortured childhood. Covered in blankets, Gunnar still wore his silver suit, as his father had only taken his shoes off.

The moon shimmered right over the lake, casting its rays over the mute water that could be seen from Gunnar's room. Its beams penetrated through the glass of his windows and enlightened his miserable face. Severin looked wordlessly at his son and caressed his cold and deserted cheeks.

Gunnar's hands quivered beneath the blanket. Severin's face was clouded in darkness. Gunnar could only see the silhouette of his father's face as it became one with the background of the room, the tapestry, and the dead sister who stood in the corner of the room and revealed her face slowly to him. After Severin repeated that he loved him, to reassure him, be a father to him, Gunnar's focus was drawn away from his father.

Severin's love felt like a taciturn wind that reduced itself to a mere breeze once it arrived. His father had always been an uncharted mystery to him, and yet they weren't that different from each other. They both had the same weakness and self-destructive love for a woman who treated them as prey.

That was the night Jacqueline started to sleep next to her poor brother, breathing down his neck as she tenderly held him and satiated the sheets with a strange scent of white lilies and runny eggs.

While his family gradually fell asleep, Severin was wide awake. He felt a cotton wool, entangled breathing in his lungs, heavy, gluey, crackling and sizzling inside of him. On impulse, he went to the storage room where all kinds of old stuff and hand-me-downs lay around. His gut urged him to look for something specific. He opened the door and six albums immediately caught his eye, the photo albums that the nannies had filled with pictures of his children when he and Estefania were both indisposed. He took one by one off the shelf, sat down on the ground, took a deep breath and opened the first one.

On the first double page were six photographs in which the nannies' grinning teeth had been blackened and their faces branded with an inscription to not dare to smile, to close their rotten mouths and hide their corrupt fangs. Page after page was filled with an aggressive handwriting that disrupted the presented harmony within the photographs, galloping over them all, a motherly stampede that came too late to the rescue, the pressure from the pen carving itself onto the material.

Estefania had superimposed the pseudo-utopic pictures with her havoc-wreaking handwriting and lamentations. She had stabbed the nannies to death on paper. She had been reusing these albums as her diary to vent and attack her children's abusers, who were never found nor accused. The proof of her motherly fury found its only outlet on these pages, where she felt like the one destroying what had seemed to be a perfect world for her children and a compilation of adored memories for molesters.

As Severin fiddled through the album, he read all these diabolical curses filling every single page, this agonizing frustration and uncontrollable internal persecution. He opened up his wife, her silence and introversion. These massacring words stood side by side with his children's smiling faces. After a while, the combination of those disembodied headless shells of the nannies, his kids' disturbing faces, and his wife's alarming diary entries forced him to face his own parental and marital ineptitude again, how he had never been good enough, how he failed everyone, and how helpless he was against the tyrant of the family. There was too much to bear and digest. He ended up with anchoring thoughts of suppression and breathtaking denial. He couldn't muster up the courage to get his wife the help she needed, to confront her, divorce her, love her, stand up to her, and thus he made himself smaller for her comfort and well-being. Severin had discovered the truth and remained silent and motionless. He noticed a repetitive pattern in almost all the pictures. Gabriela's eyes were closed in most of them. She looked as if something twitched or badgered her, or she looked focused and evocative. Her entire body looked as if in disgust or avoidance, but there was nothing to be seen except that she was held in Beata's or Ludivica's arms. Their arms sheltered her from something no one else could perceive. Severin also detected that in numerous pictures, she was wrinkling her nose as if unwilling to inhale. There was often a big empty space next to her which rendered many pictures disproportionate, especially when Gunnar stood at the edge instead of close to his sister.

Gunnar never seemed happier than in these pictures, Severin thought. He looked so lifelike, energetic, bursting with joy and curiosity. He looked like the little boy he should have been, but Severin couldn't understand how he could be so jovial, considering the circumstances. The nannies were abusing them, physically or mentally. How could his eyes sparkle so much? How could his boy latch himself so intimately onto these women's bodies and feel so comfortable and safe there? How could that happen, this illusion and misconception? How could he not see that both of them were taking advantage of him? Would the triggering consequences only evolve much later in life? Would he, as the father, be the scapegoat or future recipient of their wrath? What made them think that the affection they received was love and the sexual treatment of their little bodies was what they deserved, and perhaps all they needed or asked for? He read guilt and shame into Gabriela's postures, but he couldn't even go there, it would make him furious. Severin knew Gunnar had been a passive observer of the physical abuse of his sister. Gunnar must have felt disqualified, worthless and rejected, which could be easily seen in the pictures, because he was desperately craving contact and warmth, clinging to every embrace and holding on to whichever hand he could find. And he found them, and the response was all that mattered, the little piece of affection. And yet. *Why my sister and not me?* Severin let his thoughts elaborate further, and the more he browsed through the albums, the sadder Gunnar became, the more jealous and needy he looked. Gabriela ended up stoic, secretive, eyes open, staring rigorously into the lens, almost belligerent, determined and completely introverted like the gaze of a statue, frowning accusatorily.

Severin closed the album and concluded once and for all that he, as the father of this boy, had failed and would never do him justice. The love Severin felt for Gunnar was simply not enough, their bond too fragile, and thus his own father came to mind and how he had existed beyond his wife's limelight and manias. All Severin had craved was to end the harmful family cycle, but he found himself shackled by his upbringing and cards dealt to him in the past, feeling his father deep inside of him, maybe for the first time. Bitter and disillusioned, Severin locked away the albums and left the room behind. He went back to the master bedroom to watch his snoring wife sleep, rejoicing in his situational dominance over her while her eyes were closed and imagined what it would feel like to smash her airways.

Gabriela woke up in the middle of the night, soaked and horrified. She felt breath on her face, a shadow over her lips, her cheeks, her eyebrows. She was blind to what had moved in her room, as her curtains were drawn. It was sinister, and the only silhouette she could detect was that of the mirror-*paravent* that looked like an enormous hunchbacked, cloaked witch in the middle of her room. Usually a place of sanctuary and solitude, it frightened her now and caused tremors. She sat up in her bed, unable to move a finger, and just stared into the obscurity, trying to get her eyes accustomed to it, but there was simply no difference between closed and open eyes. She heard a few light steps in her room, feet glossing and clicking over her carpet, on the creaking wood, running around, mocking her, teasing her, slow, then quick, then stopping, one stomp, one tap, and then there was total silence.

She was shaking, she wanted to inquire who it was, but she was too scared to get the answer, to hear a voice from the dead. She could feel that this was not a living person torturing her in her sleep. Her entire body froze and she began to scratch herself, hurt herself to numb her fears. Still she couldn't muster up enough courage to stand up, scream, and walk out the door, so she waited.

After a few tumultuous minutes of silence and murkiness, Gunnar's revolving nightlight with trains shone inside her *paravent* and drove across its mirrored walls, doubled, tripled, quadrupled till infinity, quicker and quicker, the bright trains wrecking themselves into the reflective shadows of the mirrors. And now Gabriela knew where the presence that haunted her had taken a rest stop. Whoever it was must be sitting there pretending to be prey, waiting, luring, and pumping the reluctant adrenaline of inquisitiveness into Gabriela's blood. She got on all fours on her bed and stretched her head over the end of it in order to get a clearer view of her *paravent,* as if awaiting the ax to fall down on her neck. But she knew she had to get up and set an end to this nightmare.

As she set her foot on the floor, a shift in the atmosphere occurred, rumoring through the walls. The nightlight stopped revolving and stood still, waiting for her to move toward it. She set one foot in front of the other, head inclined to maybe catch a glance, even though she always closed the *paravent* before she went to bed and therefore had to unhook it first in order to disclose what lurked amid its walls.

When she opened it she almost fainted, because she saw her proper reflection in the mirrors, pasty and speechless, distorted and unfamiliar. Then her gaze wandered to the ground, and there it was, the poltergeist obsessed with her, Gunnar's nightlight and Jacqueline's heart in a jar, adjacent phantoms stumbling after her.

Gabriela didn't ask herself how the objects got there. She refused to conjure up thoughts in her mind that wouldn't depart once imagined, so she dropped them like a dead fish and threw them back into the murky waters. She felt like the objects were staring at her, eating and pecking her skin, accusing her and trying to diminish the distance she had set between them. She sensed the all-too-familiar guilt lashing out at her, a bitter energy, a plea of some sorts. Gabriela, mustering up her courage, reinforced her power over these objects until a dusty and luminously gray face appeared next to hers, like unheard mutterings from a past long vanished.

Startled, she stared at it in the mirror because she didn't dare to gravitate toward it in reality. The hovering presence felt irritatingly familiar to her, unwanted, unclaimed, like something that she was ashamed of, a piece of herself that she had lost and never recuperated and that kept growing apart and away from her, with poisonous fumes and unearthly dimensions, and became autonomous even without her nurture, stronger and offensive even, metamorphosing itself into an elusive being close to her yet disintegrating in its independence. Gabriela decided to touch the face that was breathing through her hair, to feel whether they both had the same texture and find out whether it would disappear across her inquisitive fingertips.

Frightened, Gabriela's right hand wobbled its way up to the air above her shoulder, still only staring into the mirror, and right when she was on the same level as the face's mouth, it bit her finger.

She shrieked excruciatingly. The mouth didn't let her finger go, but sucked on it and held onto it with its teeth. Severin, Estefania, and Gunnar rushed into her room, turned on the light, and immediately saw Gabriela's bleeding finger.

As Gabriela held her injured finger up to her face, pointing upward, she caught a whiff of the transmitted stench. It smelled of white lilies and runny eggs, which resulted in her vomiting all over her carpet, and the only one who seemed able to stomach the imprinted aftermath of the odor was Gunnar because he had already grown immune to it. Gabriela felt cheated, scared, and insecure, but she didn't expose her emotions to anyone that night and slept in the living room with all the lights on. Nobody noticed the two transitioned objects that were haunting her room like dark omens, so she decided to sink into her sleep as far away from them as possible.

A Birthday for One

On gabriela's and gunnar's eleventh birthday, the flamboyant garden looked majestic. The mesmerizing perfume of dew lay in the air, an ornamental wetness massaging its way through the body of flowers, grass, and leaves until it nourished the macaroon ground. A hesitant, pastel-colored sun pierced through the moist sequined fog and brightened the lively shades of each flowery quilling.

While Gunnar's family slept, his unwound parents in post-coital bliss, he put on his silver suit that still smelled like his unforgotten trepidation and anguish, and exited the mansion he grew up in. In his hand, he carried several ropes. He walked through the sensual odors of the garden and the idyllic palettes of nature and smiled.

Gabriela was asleep in her bed, turned on her back and breathing in the fresh air streaming in from her open window, her pillow lightly engulfing her head. Gunnar stepped down the pebbly path toward the black lake which, in contrast with the blazing sun that shone on it, had never seemed so thickly sinister. He stopped in the middle of the way to pick up a large rough-edged rock and kicked it down the path with an almost effortless determination.

Gabriela started to sweat in her sleep, her sheets becoming stale and feverish. When Gunnar arrived at the end of the old dock, his little hands dropped the rock into his father's boat that floated right next to the woody construction. The fleeing prince stepped aboard, ropes and rock present. He sailed over the heavy blackness beneath him, the impenetrable kingdom, the hungry gloom that was unimpressed by the evolving sultriness in the element above it. Magnetized by the moving boat erupting on its surface and awakening its texture and inner life, the muddy waters awaited the boy's every step with impatience and gluttonous delight.

As Gunnar reached the deepest spot of the lake, he rested his chunky arms, rearranged his suit, and glanced at the ominous mansion on the hill where his twin sister lay in her bed. He took off his shoes, placed them neatly on his right side, and interwove the rock with the ropes. Afterward he grasped the remaining end of the longest rope and circled it around his ankle, humming a carousel melody, tightening it, and finishing it off with an impenetrable knot.

The boy sat there in silence and introspection, touching his arms, belly, and legs. He looked at his hands and swore to himself that he loved himself dearly and indeed, in this very moment, he found his peace. Gabriela's ankle started to itch, and her other foot rubbed against it to stop the annoyance. Gunnar closed his eyes, and tears squeezed out of the shut eyelids, moistening his eyelashes and joining the glittering beads of perspiration on his face. He squatted in the boat, and with all his strength and endurance, he lifted the rock and the loose rope across the wood of the boat and shoved them up the side. Just as it hit the edge of the boat, it dropped rigorously.

Gunnar's body catapulted down with it, and the shoes drifted apart in the abandoned boat. As the boy's body filled itself with throttling water, his deserted shoes looked like bumper cars crashed sideways. They were sprinkled with fresh blood that dried quickly and became a pattern on their fabric.

After Gunnar's body had been smashed against the palate of the lake and landed in the wet underground, he floated like a trapeze artist in a still life above the muddy bottom while Gabriela's body started to tremor under her blanket. Succumbing to the taste of algor, her bladder pressuring her, she had the first orgasm of her life, inexplicable, and as her muscles decompressed, she wet her mattress and woke up in a cold delirium. After she had calmed down, she lifted the blanket to get up and froze again when, instead of urine, she saw a magenta puddle on her sheets. When she got up, she checked her nightgown with her fingers on the back and found the same moist color on her fingers. She felt cramps and a sly motion sneaking down her legs, and as she saw that it was yet again that same stigmatizing magenta, of pain and pleasure and delight and shame, she rolled it back up with both of her hands, barely erasing its traces, and kept them like folded vessels beneath her bleeding crotch and ran to her sleeping mother.

"Isn't it a bit early for her to get her period?" Severin whispered as he stood in front of the bathroom with his excited wife, who was happy to see that her daughter had sought her counsel, hoping that this would solidify their female bond.

"Everything happens at the right time. Nobody can predict it," she chuckled.

"She scared me to death when she came bursting in, all bloody. I thought she actually killed someone."

The couple fidgeted with each other's hands.

"Her body certainly picked a fabulous day to do that to her. I hope she'll remember her eleventh birthday for more than just her first period."

"I'll go wake up Gunnar so we can congratulate them at the same time. Make sure she's all right. I'll prepare breakfast. I don't think anybody's up yet."

"I'm coming with you. She'll be fine. I told her everything she needs to know."

The Zweighaupts knocked on their son's door a few times, but all knocks remained unanswered, and they barged in. The bed was made and after they looked around the room, Severin found a little note in the dusty ghost town that never moved, clammed in between two trains.

"Severin?"

"Oh my God."

"Severin, what is it?"

"No, it can't be. Christ, no, Gunnar. We have to—"

"What, Severin, what? Give me this damn thing!"

Severin fell on his knees, his eyes swelling with tears, his throat dry and his nose running. Estefania read the note that captivated the last words her son would ever express: *I'm with Jacqueline.* She swallowed the thick realization of his death like the rock that diffused her son like a tea bag and let it be shredded to pieces by acids in her stomach. Her eyes became glacial with contempt for her son's action, and she mumbled, "I knew you would do this to me, Gunnar. I made you. I knew. Where did you get the guts to do it? I hate this date, you knew that from the very beginning. What an attack. What a simpleton tombstone that will make."

"Maybe he didn't succeed. Maybe it's a lie. We haven't found him yet. Maybe he just ran away. This doesn't mean anything. Maybe he couldn't do it. We don't know. We have to find him straight away."

"He's dead, Severin. Can't you tell?"

"I refuse to believe that he's not alive anymore. I haven't seen his—"

"Corpse?"

"We have to go look for him now. Move it!" He wiped off his tears, shook his face, and tried to compose himself to think clearly.

He left the room to search the entire house, waking up the workers, interrogating them hastily, and as he wound up with no knowledge of his boy's whereabouts, he called the police. Estefania, absentminded, stumbled toward the window. She exhaled on its wet transparent surface and wrote "*Happy Birthday*" on the moist cloud.

"Mother?"

"Happy birthday, Gabriela." Estefania turned toward her daughter, smiling obnoxiously and holding out her arms in expectation. As she told Gabriela the news, holding her, sitting on the floor and caressing her temples, the daughter imploded without making a sound.

"Everybody mourns in their own ways. Some cry, some scream, some kill themselves, some drink, some meditate or wear black forever. Some engage in irrational and erratic behavior, the list goes on, you know, but you're a woman now. There is no need to be startled by death. You can be your own person now."

"Gunnar hasn't been found yet."

"But you know, don't you?"

Gabriela's nose started to bleed, and her lips turned purplish-blue.

"Oh no, doll. Not the nose as well. Everything is happening all at once. No, don't tilt your head back. Close your mouth. I'll grab a tissue. You'll need a big breakfast. I don't want you to get any ideas or fall off your feet. I'm so sorry, I'm very confused."

Severin came back into the room, completely out of breath, and told his wife and daughter that the police would be there any second now and they would find little Gunnar. He couldn't have gotten far, he had done this several times before, he just needed to vent, Severin hoped. Suicide would be too drastic a gesture, too final, too brutal, that simply wasn't our Gunnar's nature. He couldn't have done it, he couldn't have, he is a good gentle boy. As Gabriela bled through her tissue, Estefania shoved her into the adjacent bathroom. She let the blood drip into the sink, and Estefania turned on the faucet to water down the blood.

"You dreamer, Severin. That is exactly our Gunnar's nature, the pomp, the drama, the mystery. Don't you think a mother feels it when her child is gone? Can't you take me seriously for once?"

"What about me? You will not discard me. I'm that boy's father. I remain hopeful. They will be here soon, and I don't have the nerve to fight with you now."

"Gabriela, I'll fetch Rhubarba to assist you and help you get back into bed and make you breakfast. I'll come check up on you after we've seen the police. Don't be scared to ask her any questions, all right? Everything will be good."

Estefania's voice broke, and she held her hand over her mouth as she walked down the stairs with her husband to wait for the police. At some point, she let herself fall down the stairs, farther down until her body reached the bottom. She wanted to be bruised, turned inside out. She slammed her head against the balustrade in disbelief.

"You coward. You made it. I am still your mother, Gunnar. Do you hear me? I will always be a part of you. You will never get rid of me. I can't believe you did this. I can't believe you did this to me, to your own mother, Gunnar. Haven't I suffered enough?"

"You're going to pull yourself together, now, or I'll swear you won't know what hit you, woman. Do you understand me? Stop this blabbering nonsense, this is not a joke and it's not about you, do you hear me? For once think about your son, who is missing!"

Severin held her arm tightly and pulled her up. Estefania straightened her spine and pranced in a heartbeat. The police rang the bell a few minutes later, and Estefania placed herself in the living room, as if she was in a tragicomic theater play. She sat down on the left side of the sofa and felt uncomfortable because her hair was messy and unmade and she had an unclean impression of herself. Severin guided the police, a man and a woman, into the room and introduced them to his wife, who refused to stand up and shake hands.

"I know good old Rufus. We go way back, not a big help, if you know what I mean." Estefania winked at his female colleague.

"Please sit down, officers." Severin positioned himself in the armchair right in front of his wife in an attempt to control her.

"Think again, Rufus." Estefania barked at the male officer who intended to sit next to her, but then wandered off like a beaten puppy to the next sofa, and his irritated yet severe colleague took a seat next to him.

"You really think this goofball is going to find our son in time, Severin? When I was the victim of complete defamation in this small-minded psychotown, who did I turn to for help? Yes, Rufus, the police. What a big fucking help he was. I was the laughing-stock for months, but 'dearest Mrs. Zweighaupt, that's not my area of expertise, we cannot do anything about that, that does not fall under my obligations and responsibilities, you don't have anything concrete,' and all that, while every backwoods newspaper in town had my face on the front page, 'anything concrete' my ass."

She imitated Rufus and laughed bitterly, which turned to des-peration in the microexpression of her mouth's corners. Rufus' col-league, Justine, caught a glimpse of the mother's true state and took over.

"Mr. Zweighaupt, what's your son's name? And when was the last time you saw him?" Justine's head was turned toward Severin, but she scrutinized Estefania. As she pretended to look at him, she secretly analyzed Estefania, who was shaking her head, not making eye contact with anyone, staring into the void inside her mind, her fingers twitching, her feet touching each other at the level of her toes.

While Severin provided all the basic information and was asked to hand over Gunnar's note, Estefania shrieked, appalled.

"No, no. This is my note, this is my last note from my Gunnar. He wrote this for me. This note is mine and I'll hold on to it till I die. Do you hear me? It was meant for me. Freaking Rufus. They want to steal the last memory my kid left me. My last—"

Justine grabbed her arms and blocked her from interfering with the transfer of the note. She knew exactly how to handle her after having observed her.

"How old is he again?"

"He is eleven years old today, Rufus."

"Still using the present tense," Estefania murmured mockingly. She sat on the sofa again, blocked by Justine, who dragged a chair toward her to sit closer to her.

"Unfortunately, this note is pretty clear, but no body, no

conclusion. I'll call for reinforcement. We'll scatter the woods and turn the town upside down. Get our dogs on it. I know he ran away before. Maybe he changed his mind. Maybe it was a cry for help. There's always a possibility. And maybe he is too ashamed or scared to come home now and face the situation. Is there a particular place that he would go to be alone, that you may or may not be aware of?"

"There are so many. He didn't really have a lot of friends. He would always wander off by himself, always to places where he wouldn't come across other people, I reckon," Severin said. "He has anxieties and he can't bond easily. He would always seek refuge in nature."

"There's plenty around here. Anything specific, perhaps, that comes to mind? Anything could be useful in cases like these. Just try to relax and think, please."

"The lake," Gabriela said as she entered the room, water oozing out of her ears, her eyes, her armpits. It came out of every pore. She was dripping wet and stank of mud and water plants. The blood in her nose was replaced by runny mucus, and her menstrual blood was replaced by secretion.

"My mouth tastes fishy. It feels like I'm choking. I keep coughing up water. My gums hurt and my nose feels swollen."

Justine and Rufus looked at each other attentively, and the closer Gabriela came, the more her nauseating smell contaminated the room.

"Do you know where your brother is?" Rufus squatted in front of her, trying to read her face as she answered.

"He died. He's in the lake." She stood there, disembodied, stoic, this watery girl, held prisoner in her brother's body.

"She must know." Estefania yelled as if intoxicated.

Justine walked up to Gabriela as Severin came to sit next to his wife. She looked very sternly into the girl's old eyes and studied her facial physiognomy.

"Gabriela, that's your name, am I right?"

"Yes."

"How do you know your brother is dead? It's a very serious thing to say."

"Look at me."

"I am. He is your twin, is that correct?"

"He is my twin and he's gone. He's not breathing anymore. He's still in there, in this cold disgusting water. Get him out! This dark place, get him out of there. Bring my brother back to me. He never liked to be all alone. Please."

"Why would your brother want to kill himself, Gabriela?"

"It was the hen, sitting in her well-made nest, who sabotaged the eggs in secret."

A shudder ran through Severin's backbone, and both parents stood up and stared at their daughter, terrified.

"He did run off to the lake once before," Severin stuttered.

Justine gawked at Gabriela, trying to figure out why she spoke in riddles and what was going on inside her head.

"She just got her very first period. It's her birthday," Estefania declared proudly. Justine lifted her eyebrows, bit her tongue, and got up.

As they all got ready to walk down to the lake, Gabriela was instructed to stay put. She sat on the sofa and stared at her sister's heart in the glass jar that had always been the centerpiece of this room. Justine glanced one last time, irked, chagrined, and mystified, at the eleven-year-old's odd demeanor, and then followed the rest out of the house.

When they arrived at the dock, they all saw that the boat had been removed and was floating lifelessly on the lake. Far away from them. They looked at the heavy dragging traces on the old black dock. Reinforcements arrived with cadaver dogs and divers.

"If, and we don't really know anything at this point, Gunnar has drowned himself and he is in there, only one of you needs to stay here to identify him. I'm sorry, but I must warn you, even though this is only a matter of hours, if we find him in there, he will not look like the son you knew and saw for the last time. The sight of him might be even more traumatizing. So, I suggest, and I don't want to be disrespectful, that Severin should stay here with us." Justine and Rufus acknowledged all the signs and knew that this was bad.

"Oh, Rufus, how tactfully honest. I always have to enlighten your dimwitted villager's dilettante brain. You really think I can't stomach the sight of my son's body? Me, who created and pushed him out, all nasty and dirty in the first place? My son, who threw the life away that I bestowed upon him? Is that what you're thinking, Rufus, that I, the mother, can't take it, the woman, the sensitive, fragile soul who went through hell to get him out of me?"

"You've just proven my point, Estefania. You are beside yourself. Understandably. And yet, here you stand making this about yourself again in all your narcissistic glory. Do you even realize what is going on here? What I could find in that lake? You are acting out, like a little child, proclaiming your motherhood and ownership of this boy. Do you have any idea how bad this looks? All eyes are on you. I don't like what I see and hear."

"Don't you dare threaten me! He was an autonomous boy. I did not make him do this. It must have been some chemical imbalance, hormones, everything in uproar. I didn't do this. I gave him life. They are all running away from me." The divers disappeared into the water, the dogs sniffed across the lake, and a handful of news vans headed their direction, shortly followed by hectic coffee-pumped reporters with their escort of cameramen and technicians and makeup artists. Justine and several policemen barricaded the dock for minimal privacy against the invasion and contamination of the scene.

"Oh, fuck me. Keep them at bay. Enough bullshit for today. There's a kid missing, for Pete's sake." Rufus screamed and waited for the divers to pull the boat back to the dock.

"The maggots are here, swarming again. I can't take the maggots, the vultures. They will take pictures and write, bits and pieces and lies, all the scavengers. They're haunting me, following me. They distort this family's reality, and I haven't even showered yet. The propaganda against me will restart, defaming me once more. Can anyone hear me? It's not the cemetery that I dread the most, it's the empty house, the deep hole it puts me in, the soundless room full of memories." Estefania whimpered. Paranoid, she pulled her husband's arm, who was concentrating on the horrifying approach of the empty, ominous boat.

"Leave."

"There's no way."

"Leave. They will let you out. Go to Gabriela. I don't want you here."

Estefania was just about to walk toward Justine, but then she looked straight at the mass of reporters, flashing and clicking their cameras. She was thrown back into her past. Every soul-devouring click was a cut through her flesh, and she was once again the frontwoman of motherly horror, the optimal target for bestselling finger-pointing headlines. The exposed skin of a demented woman is a blank platform for outsiders, easiest to perturb, defame, and sully. Nobody had ever seen a mother in her, not even now, not with two children gone.

Estefania decided to stay on the dock, still in her nightgown and boots. When she saw Gabriela walking toward her displaying a serene unearthliness, an apparition of beatifying womanliness in the mother's eyes, Estefania's loss-infected heart pounded enviously. As soon as Gabriela stepped on the dock, all the cadaver dogs raced in her direction. As soon as they reached the girl, they howled and barked, not leaving her side. She stood still. The dogs didn't bother her, as she only had eyes for the ill-omened boat that gradually reached the shore.

"His shoes," Severin whined.

Rufus studied the abandoned shoes closely without touching them, noticing the blood sprinkles on them and two teeth in the corner of the boat. His gut got heavier, and he felt a hot tension in his airways.

"Step back, Severin. I can't let you touch anything at this point. Anything could have happened here, so it is crucial, listen to me, that you don't touch anything. Let me do my job putting the pieces together. This area and especially the boat need to be secured and kept uncontaminated no matter what, do you understand? Somebody shut those dogs up."

The dogs were taken away, and Gabriela sat down on the dock. Estefania slowly moved toward her husband and stood behind him, put her face on his back and grabbed his hands. Severin was tense, composing himself, tightening his upper body. He looked up into the sky and clenched his jaws to not cry. His gaze was pulled back to earth as the divers announced they found a little boy. Severin wished to dissolve on the spot, to dissipate, to be elsewhere, gone, not here, not awaiting to see this. The wind and arms of the divers cracking the lake's surface to extract his dead son and bring him back on land blew right through his blood cells, airing his soul out forever. Not again.

"This is not your fault," Estefania whispered.

Severin didn't reply. At this point, he didn't care that Gabriela was going to witness the whole thing. Now everything had gone to hell. Now, there was nothing more to save or live for. The two women in his family were so incompatible, they dragged everyone else down the gutter, he thought. Now, he, the most dispensable link, was left over, like expiring meat that nobody was going to eat anymore or had ever had an appetite for, totally unseasoned, tasteless from all the grief, self-loathing, and uselessness. The family man had been sucked dry.

The approaching corpse felt like a smothering snowball coming his way, unwanted, in need of claim and identification, a fiery sandstorm perhaps, something elemental, something that would engulf him, conquer his fatherhood, defeat him upon contact, something undeniable that was out of his control, a pain that he needed to acknowledge. Defeat was heading toward him, dragged toward him. All he could do was stand there and look at his son's self-extinguished eleven-year-old carcass.

With a paradoxical delicacy, the divers lay Gunnar's body on the rotten dock.

"Of course he's wearing this suit. This good silver suit. Passive-aggressive. Such pettiness," Estefania muttered as she took a peek at her son.

Rufus put on new gloves and lifted Gunnar's upper lip to check whether two teeth were missing, and they were. Gunnar's face was swollen and purplish-blue. Rufus looked into the nose to detect any residual microscopic sign of a pre-mortem nosebleed unaltered by the water and noticed that his nose was broken. The divers told Rufus that the child's foot had been attached to a rock, the size of which was compatible with the rolling traces on the dock and that the boy made sure his suicide would be a success. Rufus stood up, approached the family, and asked Severin if he could identify this cadaver as his only son, Gunnar.

Severin didn't need to step closer; he could see it from where he was standing and nodded.

"Why are his teeth missing?"

"I've come to the conclusion that the way he fell off the boat was rather unfortunate. I don't think he predicted this, but to get a rock that size overboard, and being attached to it and looking at his light weight, the way he would be dragged into the water would be out of his control. As far as I can see, his nose was broken in the abrupt process and two teeth were chopped off. He must have hit the side of the boat with his face. He might have been unconscious when he hit the bottom and drowned. This pre-mortem injury would explain the blood on his shoes. I will get his body to the morgue as soon as possible for further examination to confirm my theory. I'm pretty sure at this point that there is no foul play, and looking at the big picture, taking all the circumstances and context into account, I'm convinced Gunnar committed suicide. I'm incredibly sorry for your loss."

Rufus walked the parents away from their son. When the coroners approached the cadaver, Gabriela asked them whether they could give her five minutes with her twin to say goodbye.

Gabriela leaned over her brother's obliterating corpse. One eye was half-closed and the moldy odor that had previously traveled across her own skin clung to him. Her steady hand glided over his wet hair. This was it, he wouldn't be there anymore. He had given up, left her alone. He wouldn't be heard nor seen anymore. He had already abandoned his own body. She could feel she was just caressing his dead matter, his degradable remains. His young face looked so deprived of life. Anger arose in her, as it didn't do him justice anymore. Tears filled her eyes, and she held his unresponsive hand. She didn't want to let go even if he felt like frozen labyrinthine flesh to her.

Suddenly, Gabriela felt an unusual hand on her shoulder, branding itself through her clothing. Someone leaned against her body. A head now lay on her shoulder, and blond-reddish strands of hair that were not hers fell over her chest. The hand was glisteningly white with a hint of gray and overflown with blue, halted seams, and rested on Gabriela's hand like a stone on sand. She knew who hovered behind her. She could smell the runny eggs and the white lilies, and yet she couldn't move to see her fear confirmed, as the head on her shoulder blocked her from taking a look at her twin sister, who was smiling at the sight in front of them.

"Comedy and tragedy are one step away from each other."

"Now that he's dead you can suddenly speak? He told me you would do anything to trade places because you love her so much. What did you think would happen?"

"Why wasn't he allowed to live? Don't deny him his peace. I gave him his happiness."

Gabriela could feel that there was no jaw movement, no facial expression, nothing. She knew that she didn't hear her talking aloud; she was hearing her sister's voice in her head.

"Why did you do this to him? You could have given him courage. Instead you murdered him. You should have known better, shown him a different way, his future, that life will change and that it won't always feel so extreme. He was everything I had, and you took him from me, from himself."

The delicate white hand pinched her, the nails carving Gabriela's knuckles.

"Why are you so vindictive and merciless?"

"I am a part of you. Ask yourself why. The past is a tricky thing. Sometimes we don't see it clearly. Sometimes that's for the best and sometimes it's for the worst. The past is a perspective, a subjective mirage. What really happened doesn't even exist anymore. A second later it is gone as such and then it is forever transformed. Is it still the past, then?"

"I didn't do anything. I loved him."

Her hand was slapped.

"Why are you hurting me?"

"You pretend. You see things for what they are. You have a very sharp eye, and yet you look away. You don't use your courage to help others who are struggling. The pain of others fills the void inside of you. When injustice is committed right in front of you, you remain passive and safe. You are an accomplice. You receive the pain of others more than anyone else, and yet you stand still. Do you think that's enough? Brooding on the inside, you opportunist, carrying the thunder around without releasing it, and turning it into a rainbow? You could have prevented this. I came instead."

Justine noticed Gabriela's odd crouched body posture and grotesque proximity to the cadaver and observed her as she moved closer.

"Look at him. Look at all his pain. He needed you. Why do you think I'm still here? Why do you think I've grown? How could you let her do this? How could you let him become such a burden to himself? You were aware of the everyday injustices. Where was your spirit of siblinghood? Your heart is in the right place, and yet you didn't stand up for him and tell her how you really feel about her as a mother. You let yourself be paralyzed by fear. You felt safe as a mystery to her and secure as long as you were the one scaring and intimidating her.

"As long as you were safe, everything else could go to hell. Plotting against her in your brain, losing time that could have saved him if he had known that he wasn't suffering alone, that it was real what he went through, and you, and her and everyone else. You know who she is and what she's made of, and yet you shy away from her. You don't want to conjure her up, infuriate her, be on her bad side. She is a sick woman.

"Why is the known always chosen over the unknown, even if it's killing you? It's comfort that makes rats out of us all. You've chosen your side. He's on mine, now, forever. I will take care of him. Happy birthday, sister." Loose and underdeveloped lips that felt like tea bags gave Gabriela a departing kiss on the cheek.

Gabriela collapsed in Justine's arms and was swiftly carried away from what was left of her brother.

Madame Infanticide

AFTER A DISTURBING SERIES OF POST-MORTEM PHOTOG-raphy was taken of Gunnar, Estefania screeched that she wanted his body to burn, that he had erased himself and that she would cleanse them all from his self-murder with the opposing element, with fire. She kept his urn on the chimney piece to exert some delusional control over his final whereabouts.

As two of Estefania's children had now preceded her into the forum of death, the bereft mother thought it was rather adequate to decorate her deceased children's artifacts with a golden plaque indicating their names, birth, and death dates. After Gunnar's suicide, Estefania's sense of humor drastically deteriorated, and she constantly reminded her daughter not to dare kill herself on her birthday or nine days after because she had had it with the ironic anecdotes.

The wife's gaunt face had started to sink in amongst her bone structures. Gunnar's death had been the ultimate catalyst of the Zweighaupts' relationship's downfall. Severin couldn't look his wife in the eye. All those years of verbal abuse, passive-aggressiveness, intrigue, provocation, her mental illness, and narcissism had fatigued him into a state of lethargy. She empowered herself further, as a reaction to her powerlessness over her children, by thriving in effortlessly taking her misery out on her husband.

There were times when Severin mustered up almost enough courage to call a psychiatric facility and have her locked up for treatment, but her character had been too compelling, too persuasive. His wife's manipulative instincts and moods, worsened by his imagination, her underlying threats, subtle microaggressions, and her influential and scheming nature to fool everyone were too convincing to have her institutionalized. Being her own worst enemy, she mastered him completely, and he was too intimidated and interwoven in her manic oppression that only he could distinguish as such. She wounded her husband in such a way that no one could see it.

In Gabriela he detected traces of his own mother, the emasculating force, the grudge-holding absurdity, and the deep frivolous silence, which all led to an unbearable longing for Gunnar's lost warmth. Severin knew that this resourceful woman, even if incarcerated and institutionalized, would not stay long behind bars. Eloquent, quick-witted, and charmingly versatile, she persuaded all the psychologists and psychiatrists that there was nothing wrong with her that she, a woman of power, could handle herself, and at some point Rufus stopped appointing them.

Severin slipped away from life and his family. During the day he helped his employees in the museum, and during the night he drank and painted himself into oblivion. He considered himself of no value to anyone. Gunnar's suicide had pushed him over the edge.

The mourning artist's paintings had become excruciating and unwholesome. Nobody had permission to access his atelier after Gunnar's suicide. He locked himself up in his sanctuary of art and carried the keys with him at all times. He maintained the social façade for financial security. The more tragedies were shackled to his name, the more demand there was for his public persona to clean up after the family name and showcase his art to overshadow his domestic disasters. His prominent reputation in the limelight of the town kept buzzing while the man behind the infamy withered in privacy.

Gabriela scorned the decline of her father. She needed him now more than ever to prove himself wrong, liberate him from his suspicions and doubts, and instigate his unconditional love for her, a love independent from his wife. Gabriela was deprived of a chance to recuperate and preserve the bond with her father, so she stopped knocking on his door.

Estefania reached new heights of insanity. Self-declared dame of the house, her interest in fashion, art, social commitments, and cosmetics was piqued, and she reinvented herself anew: mother of a single child, regenerative *belle du village* and cosmopolitan wife of a renowned and bestselling *artiste reclus*. Rhubarba became her confidante. Always gossiping, drinking, and cheering in the servants' quarters and the kitchen, Estefania blossomed and embodied the sophisticated source of puerile entertainment of the mansion. She would throw little galas and soirées in the museum, guide exclusive tours herself, providing the guests with made-up and resounding *amuse-bouches* in the form of secrets, contexts, and anecdotes when she paraded herself across every single artwork. She repaired her reputation rather easily with her charm, her charisma, her marvelous storytelling, and, of course, her money, which was reflected in her trendsetting couture and groundbreaking attire that blinded an entire village.

While Estefania's husband faded away in the shadows, she became the radiating mastermind of the town that she reclaimed for herself, and no one could ever be reminded that this lady was a mental shipwreck. Her nerves quickly refilled all the holes her life had cratered in her existence. The mistress of suppression and denial, she rouged those gaunt and collapsing cheeks and put on the fakest masquerade of all and had never been more celebrated and adored.

As Gabriela's father withered away in his atelier in a state of cachexia and her mother gallivanted with the local limelight and blew insincere kisses into the cameras' lenses as they were pointed at her accentuated breasts, she became an orphan without parental death certificates.

Severin felt an inner peace when Estefania distanced herself from him. Left alone, he could breathe. He gave her luxury and prestige so that she would stop terrorizing him. It was a very easy give-and-take that he would never recover from. The forlorn husband destroyed himself slowly, dragging himself through every single day until death took pity on him and made the decision in his stead, but not just yet.

Estefania dragged her champagne-gargling guests along the stylized wall that was covered with Gunnar's eleven post-mortem photos. "One for every year he lived," she would holler. The *grande dame* performed the awe-inspiring part of the exceptionally well-maintained and coping female head of family who had gone through the worst nightmare a mother could fathom and silenced every photograph with her deviating master-narrative. She fabricated story after story; her perspective of her son, her point of view of who he had been and never could have been. She ridiculed him to her private self, a heinous cellar that only she had access to. She talked about her son as if he were still alive.

The *femme d'artiste* boasted, thinking of herself as the eloquent and feverous angel of her shredded household that lay entirely in her healing hands. The world hadn't been ready for someone like Gunnar yet, it had only been a matter of time, she preached, it had been out of her poor smothering hands.

Wearing crocodile accessories as her signature look, Estefania commented on her son's post-mortem stubbornness. The Madame Zweighaupt chuckled during the intervals of her sentences, revealing that Gunnar's body had given the photographers an arduous day of work, as his seated body kept slipping away from the upholstered satin couch. Oh, and how she loved this picture, where he is looking romantically at his sister's jarred heart, they even opened his eyes for this one, tricky but doable for the right amount of money.

Estefania's enthralled audience had completely lost its mind in the empty champagne glasses, enchanted by this perverted mother, this self-embellishing heroine, how she glossed over her tragedies, weaving her listeners into her self-orchestrated and confident remake of past events, inscribing it onto the not yet dusty glass pressing the image of her son into a frame that she chose.

Ensnared, the mother's ignorant audience devoured every word she offered as her voice dripped into their ears like syrup. Nobody listened to what this woman actually said because she sounded convincing and awe-inspiring. As they dedicated themselves to the sound of her voice and fake sentiment of celebration, they were blind to the buried heartache of this reality-deprived being.

Estefania went on and on about how Gabriela wouldn't agree to pose with her dead sibling, she's just that age now, the mademoiselle has a mind of her own. The audience focused less on the morbid and frankly unsettling photos and more on the mother's glamorously disguised catatonia. Estefania had become a shallow spectacle that was pitied on the way out and revisited to remind the spectatorship that their lives weren't so terrible after all, they could be worse, they could be hers. But no, she was chosen to live through these tragedies, for which the gluttonous audience always had some money left.

A Girl's Imagination

WEEKS AFTER GABRIELA TURNED TWELVE, SHE FELT abandoned in her own body, as her siblings had ebbed away. In these moments of solitude and misplacement, the sexual urges that had been activated by others resurfaced and promised to cure her wounds. Her sexuality was the first thing that thrived in her after Gunnar's suicide, even though she knew all too well that the dead never ceased to exist. She found life inside her head.

In moments of Gabriela's solitary intimacy, she opened herself up to the sexuality of her own body, a safe haven where she was in control. The girl's frequent daydreams consisted of heated scenarios with blurred faces, unmemorable bodies and herself in the middle of all the orgasmic corpuses making her feel alive. Her fantasies were a net of sensations and psycho-sexual accomplishments that alleviated her pain and made her body momentarily transcend the confinements of her home, of school, of death.

Gabriela treasured the power she had in her dreams as she sensed her skin with her eyes shut. Her energy and aura seduced people into her smoldering arms, and she gained so much confidence from her fantasies that she lost every regard for substantial relationships and focused on extrapolating her desires from their theoretical realm and shifting them into her reality. Her sexual voraciousness drowned her gray sorrows in accelerated heartbeats.

The people that the deserted daughter saw outside of her dream-world became enslaved and idealized surfaces onto whom she projected her desires and identities. Her imagination became the tailor of human bodies, all of them offering themselves as a blank page. She dictated away and had never felt more autonomous and unsupervised, cheating her vulnerability into thinking it had succumbed to the loss of her brother. By superimposing an alter ego over people and treating them as objects of transformation without their awareness or consent, she eliminated plausible dangers and alarming signals that might persist beneath the illusions that she brought forth. Amongst the gulp of imaginary bodies, she felt consolidated.

The people beneath her wallpaper were the same. They did not vanish, remaining strangers, becoming a blind spot in her eye, moving as the ideal image. As she sat on a bench for hours in the town square, watching people and molding them in her head, the possibility that a murderer could pass by never crossed her brain. She put more trust into the fake images she had created than the reality that lay beneath her projections. She still was a fanciful virgin with an immense capacity to imagine all kinds of scenarios that she could derive pleasure from, but now she felt ready to execute her ideas.

Gabriela's sexuality was a childlike hubris. She signaled her readiness away, conveyed her intentions, and showed that she knew what she was doing and what she wanted. Richard and Salomon, her father's employees who had watched her grow up and were decades older than her, were the first men she ensnared. She behaved in a mature and determined way, oversexualizing herself, empowering and bold in that young body so that they thought they had hit the jackpot, having no emotional bond with her and having her right under their nose all the time. Undressing her with their eyes, they totally forgot her age. The way she moved and spoke in ambiguities, innuendos and undertones, they really bought the illusion that this twelve-year-old girl was in charge of her sexuality and knew what would do her good.

Both men, belonging to the Zweighaupt mansion kitchen staff, never questioned the image Gabriela portrayed because she herself believed it to be true. She exposed her skin as she walked past the open kitchen door, luring them in, taunting them, feeling powerful and attractive. Almost no words were spoken between the three of them. She didn't know what to say because it would have cracked the illusion, and frankly they weren't in the least interested in what she could have had to say. They were proud to be approached by such a young nasty thing.

When the time was right and the three of them were alone, Gabriela tried to emerge herself mentally into one of her fabricated and well-known scenarios to control the situation, but as soon as hasty hands wandered ferociously over her body, she found herself walled in and detached from the sensations she had achieved on her own. They hadn't asked her about previous sexual experiences. According to her behavior, she must have had plenty of them. In the room, there was only one candlelight flickering, displaying the three of them as shadows on the cold wall. They undressed her so quickly that she didn't feel her clothes coming off.

Suddenly, she felt three fingers penetrating her mouth, gagging her. She could see their smiling faces and thought she must be doing something right and tried to derive the same enjoyment from it. She learned by observing them, behaving and experimenting with her body and recording their reactions in her memory and setting the standards for her sexual behavior. Her vision, ideals, and emotional safety slowly dozed off into the background and soon were last on her list of priorities as she was hit by a reality where she played an unfamiliar role.

Soon teeth held her nipples captive, savage fingers robotically penetrated her vagina, hitting her clitoris, scratching her labia. Mouths spat on her breasts and her eyes endured what they were doing to her body, and the girl tried not to scream in disagreement. Pretense was the point here, amenability, staying in character, harvesting what she had seeded, complacency, responding to the image that she had sent out of herself and that now came right back to her, slapping her in the face. She was not in her own hands anymore. They occasionally looked at her face in expectation of ecstasy, and she gave them what they silently requested, and thus their fingers penetrated her soft genitals even harder. She teared up under her closed eyelids, but the grimace on her face still functioned in the name of pleasure, consummating the role, lying to the rest of her body that she was still in charge, that this was what she had intended. Gabriela would not be exposed and humiliated. This is the real thing, she thought, this is how it is done, I'm doing everything right because they keep going.

After her buttocks had been slapped and her breasts salaciously devoured, Salomon and Richard put their hands on her shoulders and made her kneel in front of them and immediately stuck their genitals in her mouth. She gagged, and they got off on that. The girl felt a slight taste of bitterness on her tongue that quickly disappeared and was replaced by a hint of urine. They moaned, and she gained ambivalent confidence through those sounds. Their faces, groans, and tastes provided her with a sense of orientation and were guidelines for her success and quality of performance. What she herself had felt faded away, falling into repression and numbness. What she really needed had been neglected and ignored, and she thought that mentioning it or addressing it would destroy her desirability, and that she simply couldn't risk. Her true thoughts and desires had no importance in this scenario unless they served them sexually.

As her neck was grabbed and penises were shoved inside her mouth like baguettes in an oven, she didn't perceive her sounds as erotic. Her hair was pulled, and she struggled to control her gag reflex. The tears rolling down her cheeks were read as a pleasant and ego-embracing facial reflex, their genitalia being too big for her little mouth. She tried to filter the scraps of her own pleasure out of their immense sensations. They lay her down on the floor, and she already knew this would shatter the entire world she had created in her mind and had actually felt was possible while she had been touching herself. Salomon's penis ambushed her vagina with one violent blow that made him growl. Richard juggled his testicles on the girl's lips, pleasuring himself, dripping on her forehead like wax, while Salomon rigorously rammed his way through Gabriela's approval-seeking virginity.

As the men switched positions, Gabriela felt like cattle, grimacing and moaning, and that was all they needed. She didn't gain an immediate awareness of what she subjected her body to in that precise moment. Only age and maturity would grant the revelation of the aftermath of this night and the clarity of it in the light of distance, like unwashed clothing rambling in an ignored drawer. The twelve-year-old was at their disposal by disposing of herself. She didn't know what she wanted anymore and followed their lead because they knew so well what they needed and expected of her. She imitated the image they projected onto her in direct contrast to the image she had of herself.

While Richard pounded her like a battering ram, Salomon pleasured himself, his penis directed at her breasts, alternately grabbing them and putting his fingers in her mouth. That was when Gabriela, her body thrusted back and forth, put her head sideways because she had had enough. *Just finish it already and let me be.*

In that moment of passive resignation, Gabriela discovered an insecure face in the corner of the room. As it moved more into the flickering candlelight, she saw who it was, and her body tensed up and shame enflamed her stomach. It was her four-year-old self, observing her, puzzled, looking for identification, intimidated, incomprehensive, and there again, next to the girl: Jacqueline, with a hole in her chest. Estefania had buried her without her heart. Jacqueline's grudge.

Jacqueline held the child's hand as if to protect her from herself, and the little one's face looked mournful.

What are you doing to yourself?
What makes you think you deserve this?
Is this what you want?
Does this make you happy?

Disappointment gnawed in Gabriela's stomach. She saw her-self cry and Jacqueline covered the child's eyes, shielded her from Gabriela's actions. Jacqueline, suddenly alone, walked away, dis-solving in the darkness juxtaposed by the light in which Gabriela was sprinkled and her ordeal sealed with hot sperm, blemished, stigmatized, ashamed, uncomfortable, and used.

Happiness had been sucked right out of her as she lay there on the floor, half-naked, shoved aside to perish like a fish on land, having lost the empowered woman she had imagined herself to be. Her skin smelled of spit, garlic, and cigarettes, and was sore from the constant rubbing of unshaved facial hair and chapped lips. But most importantly, she felt like she had been torn apart on the inside.

After the conclusive sounds of buckling belts, her body lay deserted in the room. She mustered up the strength to stand up, her legs trembling, and she slowly put her panties back up and scratched the dried sperm off her body. She wondered what had gone wrong, how it could have possibly ended like that, and why they felt such pleasure doing it like that. She felt alienated. She had obviously been able to provide them with contentment and must have played her part well, because they did not seem to notice her inexperience. The more she replayed the event in her pondering mind, the better she made herself feel.

Jacqueline and her younger self soon drained away from her eroticized mind and lost their significance. They were in the past again where they belonged, and she would not allow herself to succumb to self-destruction because she was strong on her own.

I made them come. I am the reason they had an erection, and they both desired me. A new consciousness awoke in her, a new knowledge and vocation. She rejoiced in retrospective when she could mess with reality in her imagination. She lay down in her bed and started to rub her pulsating clitoris rhythmically and revived the act from the past. Only then did it give her intense pleasure, observing it as a spectator, masturbating safely in her bed.

Instead of remaining true to herself, to her corporal self-love, and realizing the richness of her own carnal imaginings, she persevered to accommodate the wishes of her romanticized lovers in secret and derive her fulfillment *a posteriori* when she was alone, free, and not under any kind of scrutiny and intrusion.

Salomon gradually lost interest in the adolescent girl and distanced himself as if nothing ever happened. Richard exhausted her sexual availability without words or unnecessary kindnesses. She quickly learned how to behave, pose, and act in the arena of sex, but remained clueless when it came to connecting with this man she had been so intimate with. He was a house where only the neglected basement was open to her. Childlike and insecure, she cultivated two personae that were at each other's throats instead of taking care of one another and not ashamed of each other. Gabriela asked her lover to provide her with all kinds of erotica, whatever existed out there in the world, everything, a variety, in any kind of form, he shouldn't leave anything out, and he obliged.

As the Zweighaupt girl's gaze wandered over the flat pictures of wildly copulating flesh, browsing through harmless sexual acts, deviant practices, and brutal fashions of intercourse, she sensed that the portrayal of humiliated and abused young women by several men aroused the greatest lust in her. She couldn't quite understand, because when she was not in the mood for anything sexual, this overt and sensationalized maltreatment of women, or rather, girls her age, their portrayal and willingness to oblige, made her furious and disgusted her. It was a paradox that she couldn't fix. All the soft love-making images didn't arouse her. When everybody was treated nicely and comfortably, she was bored.

Against Gabriela's rational will, she succumbed to aggressive and harmful erotica to quiet down her inexplicable hunger for abusive images and the resulting orgasmic intensity. Soon she internalized that she was expected to have lesbian desires but was not permitted to actually be one. Whenever she gazed over female bodies, she became aware of the automatic and unprovoked sexuality of them that her brain had been programmed to see. She stared at a half-opened mouth and thought blow job or worked her way down through the eroticized landmarks and ended up knowing nothing about those women, looking at them in a pre-scribed way that rendered them anonymous and exchangeable, divorcing her own sex.

As soon as Gabriela was done pleasuring herself, she hid away all the evidence of her questionable tastes. The nastiest men, the oldest men, the most unwashed men taking advantage of one humiliated girl all at the same time, using her, degrading her, verbally insulting her, showcasing her and treating her like trash, passing her around like cattle turned Gabriela on, but only if she was an anonymous voyeur, passive, resigned, by herself. Only if she wasn't that girl in those images could she derive pleasure from it.

The erotica she watched and enjoyed the most was the one that she would never engage in herself because she knew the reality of it was abominable, traumatizing, disgusting and hurtful, but maybe only in the aftermath and not in the moment itself. Maybe some of the older women were unapologetic like those men; maybe they had the same lust and the same satisfaction, and maybe as self-victimized objects they were in control because that was how they got off themselves, willingly. Maybe they were done justifying their needs and making their own ends meet. Lust and reason were fiends and influences. Was it possible to always be resilient in a standstill?

What was socially despicable in reality, turned Gabriela on in pictures. She often thought about those girls who performed like circus horses among all these violent and cheating men and father figures and asked herself whether they really were enjoying themselves, being treated like that, and whether they were really having orgasms in such a disastrous environment. Was she malprogrammed? How could she, as a female, sexually rejoice in the maltreatment of her peers who were just as naïve as her, who didn't know what they were actually doing to themselves until much later in their lives? Was her taste the problem, the ignorant unpolitical source of it all? Did those girls have to suffer to fulfill her momentary tastes and needs? Who had reached a higher awareness of it all?

"Kiddo, don't you think I know what you were doing just now?"

Rhubarba burst into the room, closed the door behind her, and looked at Gabriela, whose cheeks turned scarlet. The teenager had always thought of Rhubarba as an all-observant nun who had sworn to allow bad things to happen. A woman of irresolvable depths, hovering in the side wings of Gabriela's home, fearing, at times, for her life, as Rhubarba was the one preparing the dishes, and that gave her power. She had fed the girl silence that brought her threateningly closer to the stillness of her dead siblings.

"Get out."

"My goodness, open a window, will you? The entire room reeks. I will do it."

Rhubarba paced up and down the room, sniffing, partly disgusted, partly delighted, and assigned blame to the adolescent's body with a disgraceful and ridiculing smile on her lips. She did not have to say a lot, as her malicious energy crept into every corner of the room. She was a woman who hid her hands when she spoke, and mostly they landed behind her back, where she scratched the hard skin around her nails.

"Get out of my room."

"Haven't seen your father in ages. Your mother won't open the windows in Gunnar's room either. Nothing is to be touched, she says. As if he was coming home. His trains are surrounded by dolls, that's what she is doing, your mother. It's a train wreck of dolls in there, but I'm not supposed to clean it up and erase his last traces, she says. Instead I get to wash your dirty laundry."

It takes a woman to make a girl feel ashamed of her budding sexuality and condemn her with insecurity and self-depreciation. Rhubarba's weapons lay in her intentions, not necessarily in her words. Gabriela thought of it as fighting with thin air, as she was unable to prove Rhubarba's inflictions. She had shared unfortunate secrets with this woman, who was still a stranger to her after all these years of living under the same roof. The head maid enjoyed the power over this girl, who could not quite understand why she acted so submissively around her. Maybe because Rhubarba persisted in this household, side by side with the teenager's parents, or maybe because she had been the one to refer the nannies to the Zweighaupts.

"Are you not enjoying yourself, then?" Gabriela said.

When guilt was swung at Rhubarba, it made her chuckle. As Gabriela studied the features of this hardworking and depraved woman, she always tried to find a sign of veneration for something that she could use. The maid stopped prancing about and folded her hands over her lap and stared at the teenager. It looked like she was missing all her teeth.

"Washing those nasty panties of yours? Yes, it is a real treat. Who else is going to do it? They really screwed you, didn't they? I know what you're up to, kid, and I must say I have always wondered how everything that happened in this household must have affected you over the years and how screwed up you must really be deep inside. But this is kind of an off-putting direction you've chosen."

"*I've chosen.* Right."

Rhubarba was able to hollow out Gabriela's insides without batting an eye. There was no need for nightmares; the falling off a cliff could happen every time they crossed paths. When they spoke to each other, there were times when Gabriela thought they were on the same page until the maid completely derailed the girl again to confuse and ridicule her.

"You really sound like a twelve-year-old now. Very atypical of you. Are you regressing, little Gabriela? Are you trying to break free?"

Rhubarba imitated a wing-flapping bird with her bony hands and then the breaking of its neck as she clicked her tongue. The maid's eyes were glacial with glee, and she looked like she had evanesced from her body.

"That would make your life easier, wouldn't it? Wouldn't you miss me, Rhubarba? Wouldn't you miss the memories we share? Or the enjoyment you get out of keeping me under your secret surveillance? Reheating the enabling muteness of the past?"

Rhubarba walked toward the window. "Think of the outside as the past." She stuck her head out, dragging the glass down. "This is both of your parents, my dear. They are so enmeshed in the past that they are paralyzed by it. Don't blame me for selling yourself short. It's not my fault you're chasing men for something they can't give you. I didn't push you into their arms. You are falling. What are you trying to find there, anyhow?"

"Disillusionment."

"I knew. Long before I heard them bragging about their submissive piece of meat in the wine cellar like nauseating schoolboys. Wouldn't have thought of them as grown men if my eyes had been closed. I'm the eyes and ears in this place. We both settled that a long time ago, little Gabby."

"I can talk as much as them. Doesn't matter. I enjoy myself. I have no expectations and I initiate everything. My sexuality belongs to me, and I'm in charge."

Rhubarba laughed wholeheartedly, a rare sound, unwholesome, and after she wiped a tear from her eye, her face turned sad and sour, a glimpse of truth rushing over her lips. She looked like she felt sorry for a millisecond. "I know what it feels like to evoke courage in the darkest of places and assume a hint of responsibility instead of accepting shame." She stomped on the floor two times with her heel, biting her tongue.

"That may be the first time I've heard you say a silly thing, Gabriela. You're just making everything worse. You don't even see how much self-harm you take on as a burden that will get heavier with the years and become more impossible to ignore. They will use you up. You seek love in a man's crotch."

"Don't touch me, Rhubarba, I mean it. I don't need your pity. I'm not a lesbian, okay."

"What a dead end after all. You unbearable youths. It's best to keep it in the past. Don't you burn those fingers. Today's delight may very well become tomorrow's damage."

"Then leave me be already!"

"You will never be left alone if you don't take matters into your own hands, Gabriela."

The Broken Heart of an Artist

F OR TWO YEARS AFTER GUNNAR'S SUICIDE, SEVERIN
dragged his body around as if his soul had been attached to
his deceased son. Wasting away and always carrying the burden
of knowing that he had failed at fatherly love and protection, he
punished himself ferociously, only to join Gunnar in death as he
reached not only for the brush but also for a bottle of bleach. There
was no catharsis in sight, and he deemed himself unworthy of it
even if it presented itself to him. Severin's broken heart supported
his loyal endeavor to descend into pioneering self-destruction. The
inner life of the rancorous painter had deteriorated so drastically,
his emotions had long been starved and unheard, his mind tortured by self-sabotage until it had reached apathy.

The coroner declared that the majority of organs had already
sustained irreparable damage prior to the main cause of death,
manifesting that Severin's body had become useless in the fight to
survive the swallowing of bleach. In addition to his failing organs,
a bunch of shards were found in his stomach, causing fatal prior
lacerations and infections not only in his pharynx and esophagus,
but in the entire digestive tract.

It was the gangrenous waft of mist expelled by Severin's unnoticed
corpse that gave rise to suspicion in the household, not his absence
and enclosure in his atelier, as that had become a known routine
for his co-habitants. Severin's scarce visibility in the Zweighaupt
mansion was a pattern in his last years, but after four nights of
absolute non-appearance, the pungent odor caused suspicion from

below. The locked door of his atelier was smashed open, and upon the sight of her husband's dissolving body in his temple of humidity, stuffiness, and moist fumes, the gagging Estefania officially crowned herself with the title of Widow von Zweighaupt.

What caught the widow's attention and surprise more than the remains of her husband were all the paintings surrounding her that she had never seen before. She sent all the employees away to call the police and the coroner. The ambitious and goal-oriented widow promenaded across her husband's last works and asserted that the more he had been falling apart, the better his art had become. By the time of his death, he had completed the most accomplished masterpieces of his entire career. What a *Décadent*, she thought.

A sense of reconnection with him engulfed her and she felt proud and deserving. Severin's family was the focal point of his unpublished legacy and there they were, eggs everywhere, in every form imaginable, the thread running through every piece like a gut-jabbing curse that had punched him into his untimely grave and artistic mastery.

Estefania, fighting against an upcoming fit, talked herself into making the most out of these paintings and strategized how to commercialize them in the most effective way. She planned to iconize her husband for all eternity. Severin's death would hit the town hard, and she refused to end up in a hazardous situation. Even though she was wealthy beyond belief, she could never rid her mind of financial anxieties. She just needed to stage the entire process between the revelation of the beloved artist's death and the town's nostalgic and materialistic grief with impeccable calculation and timing, making the loss of her husband dramatic, pompous, and unforgettable, as if a chasm had hit the village.

The male Zweighaupt line had been halted. Manuka would be raging if she were alive. Severin's mother must have been grunting and chain-smoking in her luxurious grave. Now all eyes were fixed on Estefania, the maniacal widow, who was used to turning grief into a joke that exonerated her from taking part in it.

Gabriela was informed about her father's demise by her headmistress after she was taken out of the classroom.

When Gabriela and Rhubarba arrived at the mansion, word had already gotten out, and the surroundings were buzzing with official-statement-awaiting reporters, saddened fans, acquaintances, neighbors, and devastated fellow artists. Estefania opened the door herself in a vivid yolky yellow dress, striking a bereft pose and reaching out for her daughter.

"Already making lemonade?"

"It's you and me now, Gabriela. That's enough bitterness to make the glass half-full at last."

Covering up the pain that Gabriela had always been able to detect in her mother's lies and pretentious facial twitches, Estefania put her arm around her daughter, which was captured by the tactless cameras, and closed the door again behind them because one shouldn't overfeed the press that had the attention span of a mayfly; one bit at a time would make them keep coming back for more, and that was what Estefania had intended.

"Now you all listen to me. We have a dead man, my husband and beloved artist, in the atelier downstairs. I know these are challenging and unexpected times, but we have to honor him. First of all, his body is not leaving the premises. The coroners will do all of their necessary work here, and so will the morticians after them. They are already installed in the *grande salle de bain* on the first floor. No one, and I mean it, is authorized to go upstairs during their stay without my permission. Of course, Gabriela, you are allowed. Second of all, no one is authorized to speak to the reporters. I will deal with them exclusively; as you know, this is not just some random man who died. Third of all, the museum is closed for three days, but you all continue to do your jobs. My husband's unseen masterpieces will be exposed to the public as a lasting homage, and we need to get the rooms ready and the texts that will go with it. Naturally, I will consult, edit, and supervise the process. Fourth of all, Rhubarba is my right hand at this stage. Any minor issues that I cannot be bothered with are her concern. In conclusion, I need to plan the funeral, which is scheduled for day three. You all shall attend, as you represent this institution in some form or another, and we will celebrate, not mourn, this man's legacy. Off you go, and complete your tasks."

As the staff all rushed off to start their tasks, Estefania turned her minimal attention to her father-deprived daughter.

"This is a house of death now. As soon as the hallway clears, your father's corpse will be transported to the first floor."

"He's still in that hole?"

"He was stuck to the floor. He must have fallen, because he was lying in a puddle of glue and paint and whatnot. Keep your thoughts to yourself. Don't make a scene."

"Don't make me laugh."

Gabriela walked down the stairs and found her father's covered body in his atelier and several men attempting to retrieve his body from the floor. One of them gave her a mask because the odor was stomach-churning.

"Do you think one can be at peace with one's body looking like that? Obviously, you wanted to see it for yourself. You never believe a word I say," her mother said in a whisper, standing behind her and putting her hands on her shoulders, but her fingers felt mothballed and unapologetic.

"I wanted to say goodbye to my father, not the afterthought that you will create. Can you be silent just once?"

"He's silent for the both of us. And what good can come of it?"

"I need to remember this. Untainted by you and your rhetoric. Have you even shed a single tear, mother?"

"That's impossible. You know that. Don't take your anger out on me."

"Not even this can stir something in you. You're unnatural. It's disgusting."

"I'm not your little puppet, Gabriela. I won't cry on demand. Jacqueline was all I could take in terms of releasing my tears. That was it, do you hear me? Ah, see, they've done it. Now they can take him upstairs. Make way for them, Gabriela. You can say your goodbyes once they are finished prepping and embalming him."

Once the men had carried out her father's body, Gabriela noticed all the paintings and walked through the artist's chamber of depression and self-confinement.

"He made these, all of them," Estefania said. "He must have worked day and night, like a madman. Look at all these empty bottles and tubes as if they were one and the same thing. Quite the inspiration he must have derived from his self-destruction. Paint might have killed him quicker, but his art always had a slower way of depriving him from his will to live, make him suffer and create, drying him out first. Not one straight line in these paintings. Severin the Accursed."

"That's not how it works. If you really give in to all the pain, you can't achieve anything, you just waste away. Destruction and creativity need to be balanced. Whatever he drank tamed what had to get out of him, the waste and the toxicity. All of these look so tormented. He must have gone through hell down here, and we are everywhere. This was a detoxification. He got rid of us before he passed," Gabriela said.

"These women and girls all look so distorted, gray-greenish, vile and vicious, don't you think? He never painted me in such a revolting manner. Those monstrous brushstrokes, the indelicacy. They don't resemble us at all. They are so morbid. They feel like a death sentence for us. This is too grotesque, even for your father, but who knows what mental illness he inherited from that sociopathic mother of his to make us be seen in such a horrific light."

"I'm looking in a mirror."

"What sense-deprived mirror would make you look like a seventeenth-century witch?"

"My father's knowledge of me. His worst fear of who I might become, what lurks inside of me in its early stages. There is still time. This is a call for awareness."

"He made me look like a wrinkled crow. I won't identify with that old hag he drew. That is not who I am at all."

The paintings mother and daughter were examining were mostly portraits. A few of them disclosed a more spectral version of Estefania in a moor, blanketed by eggshells, licking the dripping egg yolk off her fingers. Then there was one where she lay in a bathtub bursting with humongous eggs all sunny side up while she picked at them with a toothpick. Another one exposed her hovering over two broken eggs that had lost their liquid and scratching on the surface of the third with a fourth hiding in the background observing the scene, its color suggesting it had already rotted under her penetrant gaze. The uncanny portraits threatened Estefania's self-image, as her identity shape-shifted across every single canvas, showing that her husband had had insight into parts of her to which she was blind.

There were twelve all in all: two of Gunnar, two of Gabriela, one family portrait, two self-portraits, and five of Estefania.

"I was the love of his life," Estefania boasted as she engaged with the inherited artwork alongside her contemplative daughter.

"The eyes of the beholder," Gabriela answered after a few moments, and then she stopped in front of one of her portraits and was startled by what she saw.

There it was, a close-up of her face, lying sideways on the floor, her cheeks wet from all the tears, piercing through the canvas and glancing at her remorseful father. Her expression looked like she hadn't blinked for a while, maybe to halt the moment, to stop the pain, to end her life, to hold on to the vision before her. Gabriela came closer and stared deeper into her own eyes from her father's perspective. Therein she caught a glimpse of a little silhouette holding the hand of a taller one, and she knew which moment her father had captured. She quivered. He had shown her the way. The escape route. Behind the two apparitions was a hint of the *paravent's* silhouette, and she reached a bitter understanding with the deceased. The color Severin had used for the *paravent's* silhouette appeared in a shimmer when held in the light and moved back and forth. Gabriela released the painting back onto the shelf, hiding away its secret.

The skin of the daughter's painted face had an eggshell texture and was covered in cracks and scratches. There it was again, the guilt-ridden and self-sabotaging rotten egg hovering above her womb.

That's when her father's death hit her, when she understood that the one parent who had always cared for her had been too fragile to act, too scared to lose his family, and too broken to protect those closest to him. He had withered away while she had been discovering her sexuality in order to escape like he did, to make it on her own, letting him get devoured by his anxieties and unexpressed grief; all of them had become catatonic shadows to one another.

Gabriela showered the memory of her father with delayed empathy and wounded herself with an all-encompassing responsibility for his demise. She had always known that he wasn't feeling well. Had she ever known a different version of him? Didn't he always feel natural and familiar to her in this miserable way? Had there ever been a different man in him? How was he as a boy, as an adolescent? Did he have other plans or dreams? Had there been people in his life that made him laugh once? Had he ever felt wholesome and happy? When did things start to change for the man who became her father? She knew what a force of nature her mother was and that he was destroying himself under the very same roof where she reigned and raged. How could she ever sleep again? That was the moment Gabriela's feelings for her father morphed into a suffering for him, a misplaced compassion that burdened her own life and would never bring him back.

Gabriela's empathy was totalitarian, and out of it erupted the conviction that targeting Estefania was the obvious solution to an erased problem and to scapegoat her mother had always been the easiest and most relatable task of all.

"That one looks as if you're dying. What in the hell was wrong with him? Painting his own daughter in such an obnoxious way. Of course you can't heal if you paint macabre scenarios involving your own family. Just look at that family portrait over there. I have no feet and no hands. I'm not in the least connected to all of you standing there and holding hands. Am I not a part of this family? What was he thinking? That's my job now. I need to get under his skin, or canvas for that matter, and come up with adequate descriptions. His legacy will not go to waste, not under my watch. Look, there is yolk running out of my chest, and the same thing is leaking from your crotch there. We control the narrative now, Gabriela. Only we know the true meaning, nobody else needs to know."

A Dead Man's Legacy

A S SEVERIN'S BODY HAD ALREADY BEEN LAYING AROUND
for a few days under the worst conditions, the morticians had
a hard time estheticizing his appearance according to his wife's
instructions. The first thing she desired was a death mask, which
are usually done immediately after death and before the physical
deterioration sets in. Severin's eyeballs and cheeks had already
sunken in, and his entire face looked hollowed out. Fix it, fix it.
Estefania bossed them around, reminding them constantly of the
good deed they were performing, art for art's sake, including the
artist, and that their accomplishment would make them famous,
that this was not some ordinary vain corpse case and that she paid
them good money for their outstanding efforts.

As gifted craftsmen, driven by monetary greed, they did everything in their textbook-power, from optical illusion to chemical
injections, from retrogressively arresting fluids to cosmetic trickery,
inflicting the corpse with as much artificial life as possible. The
masters had finished the job under freezing conditions when the
professional craftsmen arrived to manufacture the death mask and
spoil their work. The number of reporters and mourners had now
doubled, pestering the mansion, as they all knew the grand artist's
body had not left the premises that were coated by flowers, letters,
and candles.

The halls of the museum had been remodeled to make space
for the premiere of the maestro's last exhibition and colossal *chef-
d'oeuvre*. In order to work as unhindered as possible, the widow of

the household ordered most of the handymen and staff to wear masks because Severin's smell from the atelier still penetrated the air in the entire house and made them sick. Due to the hordes of people outside, the ground floor windows were kept closed except for the upper ones, being the only source of regeneration. Fumes of bleaching and mummifying chemicals oppressed the air in the mansion, and as the paintings that had already absorbed the corpse's smell were carried to the lively forums of the house, Estefania decided to expose them in thick glass boxes to contain the odor and keep them locked up like her husband. Photographs had been taken of the atelier to authentically reconstruct the scene after it had been cleaned, and henceforth it would become a standstill-museum on its own, a life-size doll lying at the center of it instead of a husband, very much like Jacqueline's sanctuary in the house.

The widow had become accustomed to artificially extending the life of her losses by surrounding herself with dead artifacts confined to her mansion. Years ago, she demanded Gunnar's bloody shoes and teeth back, and without having cleansed them from sorrow and dirt, she buried them in a glass box that henceforth was carefully supervised in terms of temperature and light so the memento of her son's self-murder remained materialized and captivated forever, his teeth floating around on a cloud of cotton supported by a tiny metal pole.

Estefania orchestrated the logical sequence of the paintings, and in the middle of Gunnar's portraits one could find the morbid artifacts she maintained. As everybody worked so tirelessly under the widow's command, no one confronted her obsessive grief that was wrecking her daughter's upbringing. The mother became an avid workaholic, refusing to be devastated, and made the best out of the situation. Her husband would have wanted it to be this way, she preached, multitasking and micromanaging every single detail in her configuration of his death. The voracious saleswoman knew what death was worth and mastered the transaction of selling it to the highest bidder.

The Widow von Zweighaupt organized the most exaggerated funeral procession the town had ever seen. An overt feast for the media and the press, Severin's costumed body was exposed on a golden stretcher and slowly carried out of the mansion by eight veiled women and laid down on a flower bed inside a six-windowed scarlet carriage. Behind the cortège of eight horses which escorted the artist's remains and initiated the pompous procession, Estefania and Gabriela, two unworldly silhouettes, paced in uncanny accordance. They led the entire body of fandom, fellow artists, and mourners, all captured intricately by hundreds of cameras immortalizing the parade of involuntary showmanship.

The villagers sobbed and wept on both sidewalks, throwing yellow roses and handkerchiefs on the street, and as soon as the chariot passed them, they joined the mourning march through the heart of Arracheusebourg. Gabriela looked up to the veiled face of her mother and discovered that Estefania looked as if she was crying, yet no tears were visible, just her gaping mouth gasping for air. The widow's face looked aggravated and distorted, a grimace sealed by loss and overexposure to death. She bared her teeth in implosive despair under the black lace that saved her from another detrimental headline aimed at her character and composure. Gabriela's mother, deepening the cracks in her porcelain attire with every step, displayed vulnerability underneath the cold shade of her veil. In rare authentic moments like these, Gabriela felt empathetic toward her mother and held her hand to inflict her with stability and courage while tears drowned the pores of her own skin. The blasting sunlight pierced through the windows of the carriage, Severin's sterile face illuminated among the cushions and flowers.

When the procession reached the gates of the cemetery, only a pre-selected group of reporters and an intimate circle of family friends and associates were allowed to the Zweighaupt mausoleum that would reach its avaricious capacity with Severin. His body was taken off the stretcher and put into the coffin that awaited him in front of his resting place, and thus the funeral parade proceeded to the family crypt. The fence of the cemetery was bursting with people who disrupted the silence like chirping crickets.

After the priest had concluded his moving speech, everybody was instructed to say their goodbyes to this wonderful man, artist, husband, friend, and father, and celebrate his life and not his death. As Severin's coffin was shoved into his reserved human-sized rectangle, the priest murmured a final prayer, blessing the deceased and his afterlife. Two churchyard workers closed the inhabited hole with a block of marble that had a golden-inscribed plaque on it, and thus Severin was no more.

On the golden plaque, it said: *Here lies Severin von Zweighaupt and the soul of his surviving wife, Estefania von Zweighaupt, which inevitably passed away with him.* At last, the widow found one way of infiltrating the crypt and defy her banishment. The old Zweighaupts wouldn't take her body, but her name would keep them company forever.

Estefania was given a few moments alone in the burial vault to mumble her private goodbyes to her withdrawn husband. As soon as the last foot hit the earthly daylight, she climbed up the stairs, grasped the doors, dragged them down, and shut and locked it from inside with the only pair of keys to the exclusive vault.

"Mrs. Zweighaupt, please don't do this to yourself. This is your family's resting place," said the priest sharply.

"My family," she scoffed, full of disdain for the dead. "Who am I now? With this constant death everywhere? I'm left behind. Maybe nothing of it was meant to be."

"You have a life to live and a daughter to care for. You have to say your goodbyes and pull yourself together. Compose yourself," declared the priest, with scowling eyes and a voice much like Severin's.

"Whose idea was it to immure the soul of an artist?" Estefania's head rested on her outstretched arms that held onto the handles of the closed doors and whispered to herself.

The body language of the intimate circle was so revelatory that the onlookers knew something was wrong. The few reporters present were dying to use their cameras despite the prohibition. Spectacle was the taste on everybody's tongues and fingertips, scandal, uproar, the Widow von Zweighaupt had gone mad again. The reporters told the family friends that they were only forbidden to take pictures during the official ceremony and burial, which were both over by then and that, technically speaking, they could resume photographing. Out of respect they were giving Estefania five more minutes, but then they had to get back to fully grasping the story.

"Mrs. Zweighaupt, I must interfere and appeal to your conscience. This is preposterous and totally unacceptable. This is a resting place. I must beg you to come out at once. I cannot tolerate this indecent behavior at a graveyard. All eyes are prying and waiting for you to act out. This is enough. Get out immediately, Mrs. Zweighaupt. Let his soul rest in peace now."

"I will decide when I leave my husband," she bawled out of the tomb, and thus the incessant clicking and flashing of the impatient cameras began. Not long afterward, the crowds stormed through the gate and ran toward the mausoleum.

"You brought this upon yourself, child. You must resolve this situation now and get it under control. I cannot help you further. I am not one to knock down the doors of the dead to let in the suicidal, and nobody else will either. May God have mercy on your soul for this cruel disruption and unbearable temper of yours."

"You are staring at a wall, mother. This is not the place for contempt. You cannot conjure up a different outcome." Gabriela tried to appeal to her mother as she knelt down on the door to reach her.

"I need him to forgive me," she replied, and her daughter had never heard her mother's voice break like that before.

Gabriela put her hand on the door and bid farewell to her father. That was all she needed to hear from her mother. Gabriela left on her own because she knew the widow would outstay her welcome.

An entire hour passed, a harrowing voice begging for forgiveness from below. The repetitiveness reduced the crowds bit by bit until it was night, and Estefania found herself completely deserted aboveground and underground, waiting for a sign that her atonement had been heard. Her wailing clashed against the cold marble walls and drifted straight back at her in broken waves.

As she sat in the faint light of the disintegrating candles, she realized that in places like these, where there had never been life, no tragedies, emotions, hopes, or dreams, just death and immoveable bodies and the static reality of it all, everything came to a halt, to silence, and she would not find what she wanted in there because life had happened in her mansion. That was where all the energy would persist forevermore. Their home was the place that Severin had desperately longed to escape from, the ghosts and images and memories were all there, and he chose to bring it to a definite end, to himself and the pain. He had never been more lucid in his decision-making, which broke Estefania's heart once more. She asked herself whether it wasn't him who needed her forgiveness.

The mansion was on lockdown, the museum still closed. Everyone waited for the mistress of the household to come home and resume her role. Estefania spent two nights and two days next to her husband's vault in the family mausoleum she had always been excommunicated from. No one ever knew what happened in the confined resting place. No one heard what words were uttered. Some reporters came back to check whether she was still there to add new details to their newspaper stories, articles, analyses, and character studies, but then she was as quiet as the decedents themselves.

Some magazines badmouthed her, writing that she had insulted Severin's parents in the crypt, cursing the mother in particular, blaming her for her son's inarticulateness, depression, and his weariness of life. Others wrote that she shattered the photograph of Severin's mother and ultimately fought the madwoman who failed to raise her husband in such a way that he could survive himself, that she could finally stand up to this beast of a mother-in-law and make her liable for what she had done to her son by choosing art over life and death over motherhood, that she had initiated a vicious circle that kept infecting all branches of her family. They wrote that she couldn't bear the scornful gaze of the dead woman from within her small oval frame, not within the vicinity of Severin's photograph.

When Estefania decided to leave her husband in peace and vacate his final premises, having locked the mausoleum and all good memories and old unspoken grudges beneath her, she was confronted by a storm of maddening reporters. The resulting image of the inconsolable widow walking out of her husband's crypt branded itself into the brains of every single inhabitant and voyager.

Crushed, stale-smelling, tearlessly sobbing, the dark widow walked all the way back home. Through the vivid streets and tattling crowds, the veiled widow stumbled like a deserted creature from the underworld. As she walked by, loud voices became whispers or died away completely, then resumed even more harrowingly as soon as she had passed. At some point in the middle of the energetic marketplace, she halted in front of the Zweighaupt Powerhouse statue and punched against Manuka's hard womb, shouting that she should never have procreated, women like her should never have children, that only harm and evil could come out of their wombs and now look at her.

All the carnivorous people orbited and stared at her, and in pure exhaustion she stopped and fell on her knees. The crowd didn't move a finger. Waiting, immobile and tense, they gathered and feasted their eyes on this horridly desolate woman. Estefania clenched both of her fists, looked up to the sky, and howled with all her might, with all the capacity her strong lungs had to offer, with all her assembled wrath and bile, frustration and fury. No one had ever heard such a beleaguering scream, one that echoed through everybody's spine. Her entire body shivered, her sinews stretching and outgrowing their coat of skin, and her throat looked like it was about to burst.

Women had tears in their eyes, men covered their mouths because they didn't know what to say or do, and children just watched and listened. That was when Estefania, who had made her pain the world's pain, stood up, her knees dirty, shaking, her tights torn. She took a distanced look around and then she started tearing her tights even more. She kicked her expensive shoes through the wind, then she ripped off her dress, screaming as if it were burning, her second skin, her role as an actress, her one-woman show, as if she herself were on fire, as if her clothes were drenched in acid and abandoned love.

The widow undressed completely. The bra landed on a child's head, the panties in a nearby well, and there she stood amongst the titillated crowd, naked and slamming her fist against her chest. The veil had not come off; the face, yes, the face had always been the most intimate part of a person, of her, the most exposed and the most secretive. She didn't care for her nudity, but her face was an entirely different matter. It could be read, interpreted, and defamed. She felt what her face looked like, what it expressed, and she had no control over it on that day. Her sorrow had engraved her facial features. Her face had been carved like moldy wood left unsheltered in a thunderstorm and was the breeding ground for vulnerability and dissolution.

As the widow let the veil glide off her head, her long thick red hair loosened. Everybody looked at her appalling grimace, the smudged lipstick, eyeliner, mascara, the old made-up face all over the skin. Her fingers, covered in back and red, had done the non-existent tears' deed. Her eyes were red from sleeplessness and her incapacity to cry, her lips quivering in agony. She looked around without seeing anything, like a lost child looking for its mother.

The widow perceived only herself, what was going on inside of her, her adult composure collapsing into a disoriented childishness, shoulders down, arms down, dragging the long black veil along the cobbled road until she dropped it. Without looking back at what she felt she had slowly killed, she walked home, lacking the love that had once sustained her.

A Daughter's Trauma

THE CRESTFALLEN MOTHER RETURNED TO HER HOME. ALL her wishes had been completed to perfection. Rhubarba immediately offered her a bathrobe, which the widow refused. She walked straight into the museum, followed by her housemaid's anxious steps. Estefania strolled across every glass-boxed painting in admiration, feeling that she herself could never escape. She read bits and pieces of her self-written descriptions and gave Rhubarba a satisfied nod. The chief housemaid was told that the museum would re-open the next day as soon as the widow was ready and that for tonight she would retire to her chambers.

"Is it there?"

Rhubarba nodded with refrained tears in her gray eyes.

As Estefania entered her room, the first thing she saw was her husband's hardened face on the pillow next to hers. Detached from the living mechanism that she shared such a history with, the face stared at the ceiling, and she remained unacknowledged. The energy of his death mask enveloped the entire bed more than it had in life, the longer she observed it. The face lay there with its eyes closed, and yet they felt more open than anything else, staring, peeking, curious of the onlooker's next move, depriving the room of tenderness. It didn't feel like a deceased face to the widow. It resembled her husband too much to be dead. She was used to this dormant face already, and on this pillow it would always appear to be asleep, comforting her and erasing the nightly loneliness.

Unwashed, Estefania slipped under the fresh blanket and sensed the weight of her husband's body next to her, sinking into the soft mattress, warming it up, now more than ever. She leaned in, putting her face next to his, mistaking the hard texture for warm skin. She wanted it to feel polished, soft, and sleek, and it was. It had every detail of Severin's face, and she kissed his manufactured lips, obedient objects to her every whim. The mute head of her husband became her vessel for despaired desires hitting a dead end, an emblem of her failures. As she caressed her husband's cheek, her fingers reaching a life-retreating hallucination, she fell asleep as if nothing had changed in these sheets.

In the grief-stricken darkness before the sun rose exhaling into the clouds, the widow rolled around turbulently in her bed, hitting her forehead against the hard mask, and woke up startled. Only a weak grayish ray glazed over the sinister room. The mask lay on its side, directed at her, and looking at it, she saw two obnoxious pupils returning her glance. She moved closer toward the face, detecting a foul smell. Then she put her finger on the slightly opened mouth and felt a thick, runny wetness. A cloud unveiled the natural light from outside, revealing that the mask's lips were covered in yellow liquid. She shrieked until Rhubarba stormed into her boudoir, and as she turned on the light, she saw the wound on her mistress' head and blood on the mask's mouth.

While Rhubarba cleaned the wound and the mouth of the mask, she looked at her absent-minded mistress.

"Mrs. Zweighaupt, may I say something?"

"All he left me is his disappointment. He cleansed himself before he died."

"Maybe it would be better to let the loss sink in before jumping into the next stage of your life and maneuvering the business all by yourself."

"Everything that was good about me he took with him. Who am I? I have to be there for Jacqueline. I have to take care of Gunnar. I have to be strong for Gabriela. Be a good wife. An outstanding mother. An obedient daughter. The perfect neighbor. Who did all of this for me? I cannot just sit here and let incompetence, injustice, and loss overwhelm me and take me back into a past that I don't even remember. Do I want to see things clearly, acquire resolution? I prefer to move on. I refuse to let the dead Zweighaupts make me insubstantial while I am alive."

"You are miserable, Estefania. We have known each other a long time now. You are gutted, and you torture your body with this image of yourself that you compose instead of healing old wounds to begin with. You are not looking forward and pretend to be able to combat trauma in less than an instant and move on. You don't do what your body truly asks of you. You have to grow through it.

"You do exactly the contrary. You do everything in your power to counteract it every time you get a chance. You cannot win this struggle in the long run. When your body aches, you condemn it to work harder. When it needs to cry, you overtone it with a hundred smiles. And it abides by you, but for how long? How long will the dams take to break? How long can you maintain a collapsing system? You cover yourself up. You are a master manipulator. You never accept your body's real state. You derail it and lead it astray, conducting it straight into the abyss.

"You have been trying to avoid it all your life, but you are not fighting it right. You are evading discomfort. When did that happen? Or has it maybe always been this way without your realization? Can you be uncomfortable on your own? Making a spectacle of your wounds will not heal them. You need to let the pain affect you instead of ridiculing it, belittling it. If you put your pain on the spot, into the intimidating limelight, it will seek refuge in the very depth of your own shadows and duplicate itself until heard, until your real state divulges itself to you once and for all, Mrs. Zweighaupt. To shut you up and overrule you."

"I am the victim, here. I lost my companion, the only person who knew that I was lovable. Why did he look so serene when he was dead? Lying in those nasty colors, engulfed in disgusting smells, glued to the dirty floor, and he was smiling. He left me with a smile, Rhubarba. Do you know what that feels like? And now he's lying cozily in that silky coffin inside those calm walls, in this mural of peace and quiet, far away from deception, silly little games, and the trivial mob. I'm unprepared. I'm surrounded by glass, Rhubarba. I can't move."

"A victim you are not, Estefania. It almost sounds like a wish. Self-pity is hard to shake off when it hits you. You don't need anybody to take care of you. You must love yourself first and foremost; that's enough, that's self-sufficiency. Reach your potential. You have been unprotected as a child, but now you are a woman. Now you need to stand up for yourself, and don't you crawl back into a child's skin, begging for sheltering authority figures. You are making yourself smaller than you are, and you know that. You're intimidated by what you could be. Victimization doesn't suit you. Gabriela is punishing herself and succumbing to the whiplash of the past, where the reasons for her father's demise are hidden. Take her back. She mustn't look for clues if the conclusion has already been reached."

"It hurts to look at her. I get so insecure and torn between my blemished love for her and my rejection of her because she reminds me of myself, my weaknesses and my failures. She upsets me. I've noticed her arisen sexuality, and it frightens me. It has a bad seed. What good can spring from it? She welcomes every opportunity to prove to me that she is not like me, that she is the sane one, unaffected by all of this. Does that make her healthy and self-loyal? Does she define herself in contrast to me? I can't teach someone how to deal with grief. Everybody handles it their own way. There is no universal method or cure."

"Be in the same room with her once in a while and let her know that you're there. That counts for yourself, too."

"I think it is the awareness that both of us are here that drives us into separate rooms. We take up too much space and collide."

Estefania looked into Rhubarba's concerned eyes, then at the blanket in between them and drew a continuous round of circles with her finger.

"Sometimes I want to reach into my closet, grab all these heavy layers of colorful clothes and extravagant dresses, put them all on as if in a sacrilegious ceremony to contain me, roll down to the black lake myself like a fattened peacock in the footsteps of my poor homosexual son, and just roll right into the embracing water, a pompous balloon of bullshit. The layers soaking up like the deck of a sinking ship, weighing my useless body down, the material getting heavier than my gullible human flesh, my head floating then throttled by the wet clothing materials, a dead flower closing itself in regressive retrospective, becoming a beautiful closeted bud in the midst of vanishing decay and grandeur. And then I would join ranks with my son's bodily fluids contained in the black water that would become my shared grave with my own flesh and blood. My final resting place, a colossal element. How poetic, at the very bottom where no one will ever regain sight of me and my poor, poor son. Endlessly drowning in ourselves, intimately, in complete solitude freed from vicissitude."

Rhubarba's hand stopped the bereft mother's never-ending circular motion, holding her mistress' hand in hers. Both directed their gaze at Gabriela, who stood at the door. The daughter had a perturbed expression on her face, stuttering and mumbling.

"What is it?" Estefania inquired impatiently.

Rhubarba got up and put her hand on the teenager's forehead. The housemaid had a hunch of what was going on, yet remained silent.

"I—"

"What? Can't it wait? I really need more rest. Today's a big day for all of us. It's all arranged with the press."

"I lost it."

"Lost what?"

"I think I lost it. I'm not sure. I don't know what it looks like."

Only then did Estefania rise and walk toward her daughter.

"This makes no sense. I don't understand. What are you talking about?"

"It just fell right out of me, almost painlessly. I was just sitting there. I had these weird cramps. I thought that I got my period, but it was very different, and it just came out. Dropped in the toilet. I didn't know. I couldn't flush. I couldn't and it's still floating in there."

Rhubarba held the girl's shoulders while she sobbed.

"You were pregnant?"

"Estefania, there is no need for commotion. The pregnancy is no more. It has been vanquished. The child is already agitated enough. Let's go have a look, call a physician to check her out, and send her back to bed to regain her strength as soon as possible."

Upon reaching the bathroom, the two adult women inspected the content of the blood-sprinkled toilet.

"You can be relieved," Estefania said. "Now you don't have to abort it. What the hell were you thinking? Going this far, so soon, so quickly, and obviously without protection? What does that stupid school even teach you pubescent imbeciles? I want to have a look at those pseudo-biology books. What are you studying in there, that koala bears only eat eucalyptus leaves all day long? I can't believe it. You live with your family under the same roof for years and you never know what someone is really thinking or doing. It's terrifying. Do you want to be badmouthed in town? Get a heinous reputation? Do you think this creature would have ameliorated your life at this stage? Sometimes these things happen, and it's for the best. It ended itself. The unfinished fetus had more of a clue than its creator, apparently. I don't even want to know who the nitwit father is. It can't be a good sign that I've never seen him around."

"Come to your senses, Gabriela," Rhubarba said. "If you're ready, I would like to get rid of the fetus now, all right?"

By the time Rhubarba said those words, Estefania had already pushed the button, flushing the unborn down the toilet, and brushed the bowl and corners clean.

"And another one lost at sea." Estefania giggled as she rubbed away every sign of the occurrence.

Gabriela slapped her mother's maniacal face.

The widow dropped the brush, knowing that she had crossed a line, but she couldn't cave in like that, be dominated by her teenage daughter. She was the authority figure, after all, the rule-making mother in charge who knew better. Despite having read her daughter's intimidating and accusatory face, Estefania couldn't bear it. She threw herself into a calamitous fit, grabbed her daughter by the neck, and pushed her head into the toilet. She flushed twice before Rhubarba could tear her away from the erasure of the past.

"You want to go chase the dead, girl?" Estefania said. "You want to go after them? Be with them? Do you miss them that much? I put you straight through. Mark my words. You are alive, now get over it. It has gone, it has never been here, take your head out of the water. Nothing good ever comes out of it. But believe me, if you keep hunting the dead, I will put your tangled head in the current, girl."

Gabriela coughed and spat into the toilet bowl while the rest of her body tremored uncontrollably. Immobile and shaken, Gabriela said under her breath, "Sweet dreams, Mother." She stared into her void face reflected in the wet puddle beneath her head that was now illuminated by the rising sun.

The Exposition of Truth

THAT AFTERNOON THE GRAND EXHIBITION TOOK PLACE with a colossal media coverage. The entry fee for the premiere was almost five times the usual admission price for the museum. People queued in front of the mansion to pay their respects while indulging in the masterpieces outliving their creator. The first group let in was friends of Severin, fellow artists, art critics, benefactors, merchants, and reporters, followed by a constant flock of admirers, aspiring artists, students, townspeople, and art fanatics. Estefania sat down for interviews and Q&A sessions during the entire day as new journalists with new questions came in with every group.

"First of all, my sincerest condolences, Mrs. Zweighaupt. My name is Eleanor Mythola, and I'm an art and visual culture student at the local university. I'm currently writing my thesis on your husband's work, entitled *The Last Male Memory of a Longstanding Artistic Family and the Female Form and Misshapen Identity: Sexuality, Trauma, and Despair in Severin von Zweighaupt's Complete Works.* With your permission, I would like to quote you in my paper. I've followed your husband's career for a while now and studied it intensively, and frankly, this exhibition sheds a whole new light on his conflicted side. It really proves many points I raise about his artistry and style. I'm not trying to prey on your private relation with him, but you stand here now as the spokesperson for his deceased mastermind, and thus only you are able to provide us with some clarifications concerning the very exposed themes in these paintings.

"I recognize you in quite a few of them, however transfigured or disfigured, and you seem to have taken up most of his mental space. Although on the informative plaques the word 'family' is never mentioned, once I figured out your predominant identity, the general anonymity of the subjects was lifted, I've been familiar with his earlier work for a long time now. It mostly revolved around you as well, so that was not too hard to deduce.

"His vision of you in your earlier years certainly has changed, and some would say degenerated into the modern portrayal of you. The tone of your initial collaborations stands in clear contrast to the depiction of your influence on him before his death. Furthermore, in his early years you actively posed for his paintings, whereas in these works, rumor has it that you were absent from the process altogether. And yet, you are right there. My first question is, how do you, as wife and muse, feel when you look at what I presume is a family portrait, and why is it called *On the Edge of Life*?"

"That was quite the monologue, Miss Mythola. Generally speaking, thank you for all your condolences, no need to start off with them. I know, so let's move on. What a miserable person I would be if I hadn't changed in all these years and had remained the same girl stuck inside of his head. His style needs to move on with the muse. What I feel when I look at the family portrait? Deprived. It's called like that because our family becomes non-existent, deletes itself, and he was very aware of us all falling off the frame at too fast a pace. It's quite unnatural really. On this portrait we are all kept together in forced captivity, exposed and inseparable by paint and artifice. Severin became quite aware of his mortality. It made him thrive, creating these last pieces made him accomplish his goal, staying true to our family's pattern, but mostly his own. It's quite obvious, I think. He cut his life short. Next question."

"I didn't mean to offend—"

"You didn't. I answered your question. Use your visual eye, your imagination, your obvious research. I listened to you for almost five minutes and I can say with utter certainty that you know exactly what is going on in that painting. Just for the record I'm not here to give tabloids and gossipmongers food for their simpleton silliness. And I won't give a million answers to the same question, so I hope you have all prepared different ones. I despise boredom."

"Can you confirm that there is an underlying sense of fear, resignation, and self-sabotage in the portraits depicting you?"

"Not from my side."

"That's what I meant. What do you say to that?"

"That's a whisper from the grave now, isn't it?"

"No, I disagree. The consequences of your narcissism in this relationship are right there, in a glass box, for all to see. Would you mind answering my question, Mrs. Zweighaupt?"

"My husband found solace in self-hatred. If you are interested in the roots for his malaise, then do some research on his upbringing and his parents' behavior toward him. Something was not right in their brains. Some people are wired like that and they transfer the damage onto their offspring. I can't love someone who doesn't love himself and so I gave him the space he requested. The only people with the truth are the ones in the relationship; all bystanders and onlookers are merely guessing. I'm not responsible for his actions against himself. This is not a cross-examination; an artist is always guilty of the art he produces. I'm surprised that he could muster up enough creativity in the state he was in and I'm glad he was found with both his ears intact. What would he have painted without me? I'm the sole reason you are able to write that paper and have access to so much material. I kept the flame alive."

"What do you make out of the careful distance from your face, your barred close-up, and the impossibility of touch that the portraits entitled *Mother Succubus* and *Mother Infanticide* display?"

"The face is as close as you can get. There can't be any distance. This is more intimate than a nude. I also think that including the title of a painting right on it is in bad taste."

"They were all done in seclusion. No one posed for them and they were all evoked by memory. Maybe that was the only sphere where he could confront you and not be shattered by your gaze. Canvas incorporated the only way out, the only possibility to control you and face his demon by creating you anew himself or decreasing the harmful impact you had on him by demystifying you with his own means and talent. Materialize the living. Building a barrier. Digest you in a way with his paint. Render you familiar and breakable, humanize you to make his life under your regime more bearable. Empathize with you and all your wrongdoings to protect himself from your active wrath."

"What a vivid imagination you have. An artist's sickness is most visible in the work he brings forth. Everybody has their own interpretation. You obviously came in here with preconceptions set in stone. You based your interpretation on the paintings not on facts which is fair enough. Why do you reduce his art to an autobiography? Once a piece of art is concluded and ejected into the world it changes with every single pair of eyes and becomes an endless object of transformation. The spectator makes it his or her own. Don't decontextualize it and call it truth, call it your perspective. What does that say about you? If you perceive me as a monster, his paintings are certainly effective, but don't forget art works in many different ways. Your interpretation makes room for its very opposite."

"Concerning the egg symbolism. A new pattern that holds the familial theme together in this chapter of his work. What does it represent in your view?"

"I know what it represented to him, so there is no guesswork or pieces to put together. The eggs are there, figure them out as you see fit. I won't divulge this private information and my imagination has certainly been arrested by this knowledge. It's out of our hands now that the paintings hit the limelight. The spectatorship dictates their afterlife and meaning."

"The broken home? Guilt? Abandonment? Remorse? Emotional mutilation? Different forms and stages of all these emotions?"

"I think you should give others the chance to ask questions, Miss Mythola. Good luck with your paper, and try to not demonize me too much."

While Estefania was answering an art critic's questions, she saw a hooded silhouette come into the room, unnoticed by everyone else. The female silhouette in a long beige coat slowly walked along the paintings and halted in front of the family portrait. Estefania moved her head subtly to identify the girl's face, but couldn't without dragging her audience's attention with her and arousing suspicion. She really wanted to avoid another scandalous scene because this was crucial for the survival of her inherited business.

After Estefania fended off questions concerning her public behavior and uncivilized outrage after her husband's funeral and her obscene nakedness on the marketplace, a reporter managed to engage her in a fruitful exchange. The widow still kept her eye on the magnetic and immobile girl who had been staring at the same portrait for almost ten minutes without ever moving her head, which drove Estefania insane. She began to sweat.

When the reporter asked Estefania why (and he didn't want to be indelicate, but this was a personal art exhibition and the question offered itself so blatantly) Jacqueline was not present in the family portrait, the girl turned around, unhooded her face, and held up the heart in a glass jar right in front of her chest, capturing the widow's struck gaze.

Estefania didn't need much imagination to reconstruct the identity of the girl who had shocked her heart in an instant, putting years of life over an infant's familiar face. While the reporter waited for her answer, she immediately stretched out her hand to the girl standing in front of the family portrait exactly in the middle of the room opposite the widow, the tense audience in between.

"Jacqueline!" Estefania screeched.

The agitated audience followed the widow with their heads, wondering if this was another act or whether she was having a hallucination. She kept repeating her deceased daughter's name as she stumbled toward the girl with the heart in a glass jar. The audience started whispering, absolutely perplexed, when Estefania came to a halt and embraced an invisible silhouette, a figure made of air, a body that only she could see, and they didn't know whether this was real or fake.

Estefania hugged her invisible daughter who had always been out of her reach. The entranced mother was ecstatic to smell the skin of her offspring again and didn't question the probability of this moment for one second. Baffled, the audience kept their eyes on the widow, who was kissing the air in front of the family portrait. When the mother stepped back to have a proper look at her daughter, she was frightened by the dead eyes on her daughter's face that butchered her soul.

The daughter closed her eyes, dropped the glass jar, and disappeared from the widow's eyesight.

"No! No! Not the jar. Help! Please, somebody! Clean this up! I need the liquid. A jar, quick. Oh my God, quick, please!" Estefania lost all composure and knelt down to protect the exposed heart. She swept away the shards with her hands. "Quick! I need help here. All the shards, so many shards, shards all over the floor and the heart. I need the liquid, quick! Somebody!"

The invited guests stood there gaping, and others walked toward the confused widow, trying to help yet unable to see what she was cleaning and unsure how to react to her *malheur*. There were no shards to reassemble, no liquid to replace, and her cut hands were holding nothing. The audience just stared at the fumbling widow and her disoriented sweeping movements. The museum staff called Rhubarba, and after she arrived and walked up to her mistress, Estefania stood up with the heart in her bloody hands and said to her housemaid that they needed a substitute jar and new chemical liquid for its maintenance, and that luckily she was able to save it and keep the shards at bay because she couldn't survive without it.

Rhubarba looked at her mistress' hands. There was no heart, but they were injured and bloody. She looked at the floor where Estefania had been kneeling when she entered the room. No shards were to be seen, just a swooping puddle of blood in front of the family portrait, like a reflection. Eleanor Mythola grinned. Rhubarba glanced at the puzzled faces of the guests who scribbled savagely in their notebooks, excusing her aghast mistress for half an hour and guided her to her boudoir.

As soon as Estefania was out of sight, Gabriela entered her mother's limelight platform and started talking, as she had the spectators' undivided attention.

"My father was a deciphering capturer of masks before he met my mother. He tore hers down with great effort and perseverance because he did love her once. And what a find that was. All these paintings express what he lost in his lifetime. He witnessed the destruction of everything he had ever created. These are the crippled pieces, the faces that he was stuck with; a puppet show that he could not get out of, all the strings tangled, the dead attached to the living.

"My father's empathy for others drove him mad. He was the recipient of everybody's pain, a recycling body without an exit. There was too much input and no support from within. He remained silent and perished. The love of his life, for whom he sacrificed himself, drained him of his will to exist and made it impossible to keep their love healthy.

"My father slowly became a transparent figure of contortionism. What an inimitable talent lay beneath each stroke of his hardened brush, in the detrimental colors, in these insane faces and bodies. The truth hits you. These are his reflections, and my mother is the whipping trapeze artist, the big undeniable circus animal that crushes them all. The decoder of masks, losing his integrity and identity to such patient shallowness, was starved by unmasking the greatest threat to his life; he himself became his own liability.

"If you are wondering where my twin sister is on the family portrait, just look at the color of our clothes and skin and link it to his omnipresent egg symbolism. Her death tainted our lives forever. We are running away from each other without making a single move. We never spoke of the tragedies that befell our family. I didn't know my father more than you did."

"Gabriela, that's your name, right?" Morgane Astrid Meterosin, an intern at a local newspaper, was eager to talk to the remaining daughter of the artist and push her first major and career-deciding article. The teenager nodded and stared at the aspiring reporter.

"Gabriela, would you mind telling me which painting is your favorite and speaks to you the most?"

"The one where my father captured the moment I lost my virginity."

The room buzzed with appalled excitement and intrigued controversy as an incestuous relationship was presumed.

"Which one is that?" The intern tried to remain as professional as she could.

"Number three, *Truths of the Inner Child*."

"What makes you say this is the moment you speak of? How could he have known?"

"Because this is exactly what I looked and felt like. What he painted in the reflection of my eyes is exactly what I saw. I underestimated how close he was to me and what he was capable of."

A few people walked toward the painting to get a closer look at what she referred to.

"Capable of what, dear?"

"Of seeing the dead and the souls of us all."

"I beg your pardon?"

"He must have had an intuition, a sense for the beyond, some kind of transcendence while he was painting; that's when he could connect with us. All I know is that he was not in the same room with me that night. He never said a word."

The last answer that Gabriela gave was overheard by her mother, who had entered the room again with Rhubarba and knew this situation would escalate. Everybody's eyes were fixed on the terrified widow.

"All these years you've been lying to me? You both? You communicate with my dead daughter, with my beloved Jacqueline, and you don't tell me? Leave me out of everything, don't tell the evil mother-crow, is that so? What kind of daughter are you? Dropping a stillborn in the toilet yesterday and now standing here, all dolled up and knowledgeable, thinking that you understand your father's cryptic work?"

"You saw her today, didn't you, Mother? Is that how excluded you are? You are always in the very middle of things."

Estefania looked at the bewildered reporters and didn't know what to say because she didn't want to sound like a lunatic. She secretly feared them. She wanted to remain in control at all times and be taken seriously at all cost. If she admitted to seeing her dead daughter, she would be judged and misunderstood. She couldn't let another defamation happen, not now, now that she needed to rebuild the empire and run the business all by herself. Gabriela was mentally challenged, yes, exactly. Crazy people have the most confident voices.

"No. I must be rather unfortunate to not be blessed with this gift you and your father shared."

Eleanor Mythola dared to interrupt the conversation by reminding the widow of her calling out her deceased daughter's name earlier and the blood on her hands.

"Yes, I tend to get these horrible migraines mixed with light sensitivity and visual distortions. It can get very ugly. Everything is fine, ladies and gentlemen. Shall we resume our Q&A?"

"It's because of cliché-perpetuating women like you that our real illnesses are not taken seriously," Gabriela said. "You denied her when she was alive, and now you have done it again for your sake instead of accepting what role you have played in all of our short lives. You of all people should know better, don't you think?"

"It's because of girls like you who get pounded in backrooms by my staff, faking orgasms with squeaky moans and praising the endlessly ineffective pseudo-stallion hammering that our real sexual identities keep getting insulted and ignored. Our needs are not taken seriously and are continuously discouraged, always placed second, as if all we needed is a little one-man-show-thrusting. Not speaking your mind plays a part in the chain reaction," Estefania fired back. "Don't you underestimate me."

"It's because of maternal failures like you that abominable daughters like me get abused by their fucking nannies during their infancy."

"Don't you dare put your traumas on the scales next to mine. Rhubarba, send in the next group. I think these people have gotten their money's worth."

Estefania pushed the teenager out of the room, and with a demonstrative smile on her pretentious face, pinched Gabriela's flesh on her back while she escorted her out.

"Pinch all you want. I'm resistant to you and your terrors," Gabriela said calmly.

Out of Reach

THAT NIGHT, WHEN EVERYBODY WAS SLEEPING IN THE mansion, Salomon and Richard broke into Gabriela's room. Salomon sat on her stomach, his legs holding her arms down while Richard put his hands on her mouth.

"You told your mother about what we did. Do you have any idea what harm that causes us?" Alcohol-breathed, Salomon hissed at her cheek, squeezing it tightly. They wouldn't let her reply; she just shook her head.

"We'll get fired. Because of you. You are not even worth it, you dirty little tramp. If you weren't her daughter, I would rape your guts out right now, believe me, and you would never dare say my name again in your entire screwed-up life. But something tells me that you would like that, you little fuck-up."

"Sal, you can't threaten her like that. We agreed to fuck her, remember? We could have said no, all right? Nothing has happened. She heard you, so let's get out of here," said Richard.

"Are you kidding me? That nutjob of a mother will not let this one slide. For fuck's sake, man. It's like you've never seen what that woman is capable of. That bitch can get away with anything in this town. We're fucked. I have nowhere else to go. This has been my home for as long as I can remember, and because of a little fucking around, I'll lose my whole life here. She'll drag our names through the mud. Do you know how much influence she has? Forget it, man." He bit his tongue to ease his aggression and started to squeeze Gabriela's throat.

Gabriela, against her better judgment, felt that she was getting wet, that her pulse was pounding and that she had never been more lustful than now, in this moment of sheer panic and danger. She felt ashamed and exhilarated. Her self-defensive mind couldn't arrest the inexplicable pleasure her body derived from this detestable treatment. It felt so familiar to her body that her sexual instincts felt safe and challenged. She didn't care that they thought that she had betrayed them; it only brought this intensive interplay to life. The more distance her mind reached, the more her body reacted with ignorant pleasure.

The pressure of Salomon's buttocks on her sex reactivated her muscle memory, and then she saw it again, the botched human being that fell out of her, that she had not known about and lost without establishing a connection. She felt the weight of that discouraged life in her, of her own choices and personality that were both fading away in moments like these where she listened to the abused parts of her body in the worst way imaginable.

Salomon's hands tightened their grip around her throat. As she moved her hips to loosen his vile force, her upper body jumping up, he misinterpreted her counteraction for sexual excitement. The more blushed her cheeks became, the more he thought that she was embracing his violence against her. He misread her body in every possible way.

"You could at least let her say something. Maybe it wasn't her. I mean, we weren't that careful around here. I will take my hands off."

"She'll scream. I won't be messed with anymore. I'm sick of this shit. They all act as if they have nothing to lose. They don't care who gets hurt in the process."

"It looks like she wants to say something, man. Just let her, for a second, come on." While still holding her arms down, Salomon lifted his hands from her throat, and Richard freed her mouth.

"Dissect me not," Gabriela said without flinching.

Richard's primitive and compliant body was oddly aroused by

the togetherness of sex and death, by the image of a completely submissive female body, motionless, in sheer carelessness to what could be done to it. His mind imagined her approval, her consent, convinced that she kept track of his thoughts.

Salomon unbuckled his belt, bit her cheek, and slapped her. He stuffed her mouth with her hair, spat on her eyes to keep them closed, and thought that morals didn't apply to a corpse. As he was about to penetrate the girl, the light in her room turned on.

"Out, you sexually deprived, child-abusing scumbags!"

Estefania stood by the door with an ax in her hand. "Get out of my house at once!"

"What the hell?" Richard was terrified, and Salomon got off her daughter, holding his hands up.

"We'll leave. No harm, no foul. I just need to say one thing, Mrs. Zweighaupt. Please, stop bellowing for a moment. It was all consensual. We all knew what we were doing. It was just sex."

"A thirteen-year-old has deviant ideas about sex, and you should know better than to jump at the opportunity. Get a fucking conscience. Do you think she has a clue about what a scarring and self-esteem-depriving effect primitive men like you have on her later on? How much you define her sexuality along the way? 'Just sex' you say; that girl there was pregnant and lost the baby.

"Fuck women your age who understand who they are dealing with, you lousy, lazy opportunists. Don't even dare justify this; even if the girl is willing, you refuse the sad ego-boosting offer. And what exactly makes you so proud that you could persuade a naïve girl to jump into bed with you? She had no idea what she was getting herself into and you know that. You're not that stupid, just too irresponsible and prurient to give a rat's ass. Out, now! Rhubarba got your luggage ready this afternoon. You're both fired, and if I ever see you with my daughter again, I will sue both of you criminals."

"Stop swinging the ax, Mrs. Zweighaupt. We're leaving. Thank God she lost that baby. This family is a fucking madhouse,"

Salomon replied, and they both rushed toward the door to disappear forever.

Estefania barked like a thunderstorm, lassoing the ax, ready to strike Salomon, who escaped the attack by milliseconds. Both men ran down the stairs as quickly as they could. Estefania ran after them, still screaming and swinging the ax. As they got out of the house, she dropped her weapon and bellowed, "This is my house, my family, my household, mine! This household has been raped! I curse you, you poor excuses for men." She sank down to her knees, hurling, and whispered repeatedly, "I hate myself, God, I hate myself, so much, hate it, everything."

Hesitant steps came down the stairs, and as Estefania turned around, she saw her daughter holding on to the bannister.

"Mother, why are we like this?" Gabriela's eyes were swollen with tears, her lips quivering, and her face had turned into a whimsical grimace that needed genuine affection more than anything else.

A child, as far away from womanhood as possible, the daughter was supported by the bannister alone with nothing else to keep her upright as she fell apart. After she had cried in the company of her hunching mother, paralyzed by the sound and ignorant to its solution, the girl's temper turned to frustration and resentment.

"Why won't you answer me? I am right here. You never follow up on your words. You, the big proclaimer of titles masquerading your immeasurable shallowness. Why are you so uncomfortable with me? You claim to be my mother, and yet you do everything to unmake me. How can I be strong if you have never given me a backbone? How can you be there for me if you try everything to get as far away from me as possible? Why have you never made the world a safe place? What happened to you? Will you ever let me understand you? You corner me and expect me to malinger my way into oblivion and despondence. I'm thirteen and I'm garbage. You harass me every chance you get. Out of the blue. There is no in-between with you. You twist and turn your faces. Operating between two extremes. Why have you never cared enough to find out who I really am? Instead you antagonize me, believing in the daughter you think you raised, but that's not me."

"Why, why, why." Estefania imitated her daughter's outcry and covered her ears as if she had a splitting headache. Gabriela crawled down to get closer to her crouching mother and pointed at her own face.

"Why won't you look at me, mother? Am I so horrendous, so repulsive, that you feel obliged to turn your back on me? I am shattered among the craters of my body. I am disappearing below, drowning beneath my own skin. I want to cut off the surface of my body, everything you created and infected. You made it never belong to me, poisoned my own body against me. It was always others who took it, owned it, claiming it for their purposes. They stole my body, tearing us apart, pieces floating around. You make me feel so worthless and unlovable that I'm losing my will to live. I want to die far away from this pretense, this belligerent silence, these constant embellishments of the past. Mother, you let everything die. Let me join the parts of my body that loved me truthfully and were pulled away from me since you gave birth to us. If you wanted me belittled, then you've succeeded. I'm sick of fighting you. There is no growth around you."

"You listen to me," Estefania said. "You stay alive. I gave you life. You are not going to throw that away. Do you hear me? All the life that I have given has been extinguished, and I won't have it, Gabriela. You stay. You are not allowed to leave my side until I perish. You are here to stay. I always sensed destruction approaching me and I ignored it. It frightened me to death. I froze every day, out of fear. I was powerless, I had to look away. It was too cruel, the awareness of a mother. You will walk to my grave, mourning my death. I can't see your face. It is not revealed to me. Are you relieved or devastated? You will outlive me, not the other way around, not anymore." The mother got up, leaving the ax on the floor. She locked the front doors and vanished into her boudoir.

Estefania had no trouble falling asleep again after the expression of her daughter's vulnerability, which she apprehended as inferiority. The widow's escapades had exhausted her.

While lying in her bed, her daughter tiptoed to her bedside, holding a cushion in her hands. Gabriela held it over her mother's head and whispered in a broken voice, "You made me like this. I hate you, too. Mother of mine. You deny me life as much as you deny me death. This way we both get our peace. I can't get there fast enough. You always prove me right."

Estefania had suffered from night terrors and nocturnal anxieties since her own mother's horrifying nighttime visit to her bedroom when she was a child, and as soon as her daughter's cushion hit her face, she sensed that her offspring did not have the gall to murder her, in contrast to her bedeviled mother.

When the widow found a way to breathe under the imposed pressure, letting Gabriela vent, Estefania's hands slowly crawled up the girl's weakening arms, touching them tenderly. Gabriela responded to the unusual gesture of gentleness by decreasing the pressure. The daughter unclasped the cushion as it lay over her mother's face, looking at the fluffy whiteness hiding it, and slowly slid it away to the side.

Every detail of the widow's face reawoke the ill-omened portraits that her husband had painted. It was the face of a forlorn child who escaped infanticide, the groundbreaking shock that initiated it all, the lullaby of death whispered softly in her ear. First her mother and now her very own daughter had wanted her dead, and here she was. Once again she survived the murderous ambitions of those closest to her whose desire it was to be free of her like a disease. There she lay, the apparent curse of this family. The most miserable woman in the world yet again freed of her own murder.

A few days later, Gabriela asked her mother to send her away to a renowned boarding school and university on a nearby island. *La Scuola Della Profondità Creativa Sull'Isola Delle Anime Affamate* had been an acclaimed institution for centuries. It housed girls and women, boys and men, in two separate manors with the historical school building in between. Gabriela told her mother that she had done some research on the school and that it felt like the right decision to enroll there, especially after everything that happened, the constant shaming, bullying, name-calling, all the out-in-the-open family tree scandals, every single thing that had erupted like a scarring firework between themselves, all the fights, violence, mind games, double entendres, unresolved issues, space-lessness, the burden of being related so closely, and the attempt to finish it all just recently.

The daughter wanted to head in a better direction to figure out who she was, the remaining body of a three-pieced ensemble, instead of being a matricidal and sex-hungry teenager. Something in the mother's gut stirred, and her daughter's reasoning made sense to her. Life needed to become simpler.

At this stage, a murder-suicide seemed more plausible than an effort to make it all work under the same forsaken roof. In sad contemplation, the mother took a long glance at Gabriela and agreed that it would be the best solution for the time being to live and grow apart so that they could each spread their wings anew and maybe find their way back to one another someday. And, of course, the grand Widow von Zweighaupt certainly considered a death by pillow-suffocation inflicted by a family member unacceptable and out of the question. No, she would go out with a boom, not smothered to death like an infant.

A Mother-Daughter Correspondence

Dearest Mother, as you've told me that writing to you as often as I could was one of the conditions allowing me to transfer to this school, I will gladly find some comfort in the act of putting my thoughts on paper. As you said before I left, we've exhausted all the hurt we could do to each other already, so why not indulge in complete honesty from now on?

I'm all settled in. It's been a week now. I have four roommates, and it is almost inevitable that they either become your best friends or your worst enemies. I'm doing my best. I've previously shown poor judgment on matters like friendship or intimate encounters or people in general to the point of secluding myself entirely in order to live in peace. Here I have the chance to start anew. My body feels numb at the moment and I don't feel any kind of passion or physical excitement, I've had quite enough of it, I guess. This will do me some good, to digest everything that happened and learn my lessons even if they hurt so much. Sex seems to be the centerpiece of every school, the energy reigning over every single teenage body at the moment. It's crazy, but I try to observe and listen to other people's stories without judging them.

I really like the program of the school. I selected various literature classes as my most important subjects. I would have loved to subscribe to an art history and techniques class, but I didn't want the memory of father to overshadow my success and emotional stability here. I don't need to be reminded of him constantly, and I refuse to be taught in reference to his art, it would just feel too much like home. The teachers support me in my decision and understand it. I need to be on my own, without him and what he did.

There are a lot of group activities after school which sound really interesting to me: expressive dance, liberating dance, role playing and healing, theater for mental health, classic and modern choirs. There are plenty, and I'm still figuring out which ones to join. I've started to read a lot, for pleasure and because I have to. There is one teacher whose class is called 'The Female Protagonist: Roles, Identity, Illusion, Bodies, and Narrative Liberation.' She really inspires me. The first cycle is about female suicide in narratives written by men, suicide as the only supposed option for women to escape the sentimental and societally suppressed prison they find themselves in. The female body in uproar against itself. Ah, yes, and there is an obligatory class every Wednesday for two hours before supper about Feminism and why it still has a long way to go, and guess what, they make the boys go too which I think is the whole point.

I'm tired now, that's about it for tonight. I will send this letter to you first thing in the morning.

Bye, Mother.

Gabriela, that sounds fine, I think. It's been a long time since I've last written a letter, but it's the only way to be able to stay in contact without being at each other's throats.

The house feels emptied of life, which has always been the case, I know, and yet, there seems to be a lack of fresh air. Everywhere I look life has left its mute marks, it feels like my memory has been externalized and I'm being reminded of the past wherever. I hired two new female members of staff. We all make mistakes and are able to molest one another, so you can never be sure who you really have in front of you. People derail when their sexual self comes out, it's frightening. I've started to redecorate some rooms. They look like perfect still lives, untouched almost, fresh, ready to be lived in, but no one does. They are *so pretty and tasteful. Business is going well, the world just adores your dead father. I know you want to forget about him, but dear, just because you're on an island now you're not safe from the past and the wounds still bleeding from it. Just don't turn your back on all of it.*

Actually, I've had long talks with Rhubarba recently about the beyond. We've come to the conclusion that we both believe in certain energies attached to homes. As you know it has never been easy for me to live amidst all of the judgmental character studies done of me. If you take a look at my family and my upbringing, it might come as a surprise that I've suppressed my netherworld beliefs.

I just wanted to let you know that I'm about to meet some interesting people, mediums and professional practitioners. They will examine the house to determine whether there are roaming spirits living with us, bound to the same walls as I am. Of course, the ideal ghost to find would be your father's, and then I would charge admirers and tourists to attend our séances and through the medium they could ask the maestro anything they want, isn't that neat? The atelier has been opened for tours as well. Don't mention Jacqueline, that's just plain scary and unnecessary. I feel like a magnet for the dead.

Feminism and suicide you say, now that's an interesting combination. If the reasons for suicide would be eliminated, counteracted, or cured beforehand, there wouldn't be any suicides or almost none. Either way, you know what I said, this is it, you and me, staying alive. When it comes to Feminism, I think it just addressed you at the right time, or maybe it would have been better if it had presented itself to you earlier before all this mess. Maybe you would still be a virgin, maybe you would have waited for the right person, or you would have discovered your sexuality in a self-loving and healthier manner. I'm glad that you feel disassociated from your sexual urges and needy body. At your age you feel everything in extremes, and by turning yourself inwards you can focus on what moves you forward without the distraction of the superficial fight for bodily attention.

Tell me more about those roommates of yours. Be a chaste and studious girl. Don't suppress your father because he will always know how to find you.

Awaiting your punctual response.

Your mother.

Dearest Mother, now that I've spent some intimate time with my roommates I can actually tell you something about them.

Léopoldine Dumas is a daydreamer and a ruffian. She is very charismatic and eccentric. In my opinion the most fascinating of four sisters, although I know their characters only from her perspective. She is very generous and comes from a highly respected, wealthy, and politically acknowledged family. All of her sisters are engaged already, or reserved, as she said, to men who had been chosen for them since their childhood and approved of by their parents. Her sisters feel very comfortable in that outdated arrangement, as they lack ambition or rather knowledge of their own abilities, as Léopoldine thinks.

The reason why Léopoldine is here is because she revolted against the prescription of her own life and because her father is convinced that she's a lesbian who needs to be straightened out. As instructed by the despotic patriarch (that's how she calls her tyrannical father), one of the teachers keeps a very concentrated eye on her, which is ironic because that teacher is the most ferocious Feminist in this school and promised Léo's father that he shouldn't worry at all and that his daughter is in the right hands. Léo preaches that there is nothing more important than expressing her inner child; her mother wants it extinguished to blossom in womanhood and her father wants to transition it into marriage, the younger the better.

Agnes Tapissora is an only child and adopted. People on campus say that her family is the head of a feared sect that no one knows the name of. She has an engaging and mystifying aura. She has all these rich perfumes and oriental oils which make her dream. I want to use them myself. She knows six languages and recites from old books before she goes to bed in a language that none of us comprehend. She always lights incense and keeps gems under her pillow to chase away ill-natured energies and nightmares. She used to wake up heavy-headed and with extreme pressure and tension in her temples. She doesn't talk much but her presence feels very soothing, and if she says something it's always worthwhile. She seems older and more mature than her age suggests. She is very contemplative and lives mostly in her head. Everything said in class affects her, and she goes through every piece of information in her mind. She's just very modest about the way she studies and acquires knowledge.

Anais Clémenceau comes from a family that has so many illegitimate children, fathers, mothers, and mistresses that I've lost count and orientation. It's comforting to know that not everybody is perfectly coy and well-behaved. Anais' confidence is bulletproof because she overcame years of bullying. I admire her courage. She doesn't care if she is badmouthed. She only cares about constructive criticism that comes from someone who means well, and as I've witnessed, there are not a lot of people who do. She prefers to have only a handful of good-hearted people in her life, less drama she says, more sincerity and authenticity. She has no time anymore for bullshit. She is my age. I don't know all the stories, but it must have been horrendous for her that she came out this strong. And it is because of her. She's very sexual and there is no shame in her. That's how they get you, she told me, and that's true. She always claims that jealousy and shame are the two most powerful and detrimental emotions a human being can succumb to. At times, she can be rather vulgar and straightforward, but I try not to be judgmental myself, especially because I know what it feels like.

Daphne Macaronatier hates it when people use belittling or possessive terms to call her. Terms that are so engrained in everyday use that they don't seem harmful or influential anymore, she says. Darling, cute, sweet, little girl, or baby, to name a few, and she gets all her extra credit from organizing and helping with the weekly Feminism class. She is very opinionated and fearlessly defends her viewpoints. Her passion is captivating, and she says that she experienced from the very bottom why the feminist cause has every right of existence and as long as there are ignorant people out there, the labels are still needed. She's a bit older than the rest of us. I know she just ended a two-year relationship and cannot talk about it at all. She only wears pastel colors and fluffy collars. Her rhetoric is persuasive and enthralling. I can learn a lot from her.

Daphne never talks about her family. She is the most communicative and free-spirited of us all, and yet after all these endless conversations, never have I heard her mention her family. I think that might just be the right strategy, and who am I to stick my nose into her business which she obviously doesn't want to divulge? She is so helpful and observational. Sometimes she just sits somewhere and stares at people, for hours, and then she just gets up and smiles. Despite her petite figure, she is not to be underestimated; she is very strong. Much of that strength comes from deep inside her, you can feel it if you touch her skin, it's electrifying. It took a while for me to realize she has a glass eye. She was standing in front of me in the sun and I recognized the mismatched tone of green and the slight lazy movement in her left eye. When she noticed my realization, she kissed me on the cheek, and I was so euphoric.

Daphne became even lovelier, and that evening she put her hair up for the first time, and I could see that her left earlobe was missing and her ear was extensively scarred. The more time passes, the more her body shows what a past she must have had and how proudly and intimidatingly she wears her own body.

I'm very well. I'll tell you more in the next letter. Let me know how it goes with Father. I hope you're all right. You're a fighter, after all. We both know that.

Bye, Mother.

It certainly reads like you've already forgotten all about our little family and where you come from. Who are you in this diverse mix? The poor daughter of a deranged mother and a self-destructive dead father who happened to be one of the world's greatest artists? I caution you not to forget us so very easily.

I've hired and accommodated two mediums, Isabella Gnorgian and Adèle Irrestanzia, a house cleanser and spiritual protector, Carmen Copnerkan, and lastly, a supernatural spirit conversationalist and facilitator who is also an academic, a Feng Shui expert and a Reiki practitioner named Dr. Héliopolette Goethan-Vergangier. They were all unanimously terrified by your mirror-paravent and what it projects and communicates, or rather what it hides. They feel the same about Jacqueline's jar and Gunnar's shoes, which frankly disappoints and vexes me deeply. They have also felt a repellent animosity in the exhibition rooms of my parents' work, and that doesn't shock me at all. I'm not ready to let them access the atelier. It's as though my home is set against me, and its hostility toward me is growing continuously. The emptier the house gets, the more powerful it becomes.

My parents encountered the worst stories you could ever imagine. I myself shudder when I merely do as much as cross the room. I've begged the experts to invest great efforts to sense something on your father's death mask, but they touched it, spoke to it, caressed the air over it, chanted holding it up and whatnot, yet nothing, unfortunately. He refuses to open up to me, even now. He's silently accusing me, ignoring me, harassing me with his inertia, there must be something. I'll not let it go until his guard is down. His rejection of me makes me miserable, and yet a man who does not want to be remembered and immortalized does not leave an undiscovered legacy that would redefine him. You cannot judge me as a wife if you have never been one yourself. Only the people in the relationship know best what it is made of, what comes in and what goes out. I'm vexed.

I have to be honest. You confuse me. When I read your letters I already have a transformed image of you in my mind. An image that seems so far away from the person who stood in front me a few weeks ago, leaving me at the front steps, waving goodbye. I already have a sense of disorientation. I can't identify my own daughter anymore. So what's going to happen after five or eight years? Will I even see you once in a while, or would each visit shred your heart to pieces and pull you back into old mechanisms of a dysfunctional past? Is it that traumatizing to revisit your roots once in a while? What are you without them?

Dr. Goethan-Vergangier palpated your letters to me, she smelled them, let them glide over the peach fuzz of her face and even licked their corners just to discover that I'm nowhere to be found in between the lines, on the paper, the ink, nowhere, you've erased me. We are speaking alongside each other as we always have. Will you dissolve like quicksand far away from me, likeness of mine? Does your head not suffer from the consequences of a drastic vertigo, so quickly you changed directions?

Think of me.

Your mother.

Dearest Mother, *sorry for taking a while to get back to you, it's been a very hectic two weeks. Daphne and I have really bonded. My other roommates and I are good friends as well, but I feel very connected to Daphne because she revealed her story to me. She spoke about it for the first time because I caught her harming herself, strangling herself to be precise, just enough to soothe her pain and not quite enough to lose consciousness. She told me that she has indulged in this behavior since her breakup. She said it changed her forever.*

Every time her body conjures up a panic attack and she feels the bubbling explosion burning upwards through her gut, she locks herself into a bathroom cabin (where else, that's the place for teenage tragedies), putting her hands on her throat, tightening her grasp and closing her eyes to exfoliate him from the texture of her lips, her heart, her skin. He had become an integral part of her life's plan, she had it all figured out. With his encouragement, he made her believe in their union until it all collapsed upon her. Her throat is purposefully never exposed, as she covers the marks with a concealer, perhaps as a lie to herself, as a blanket of comfort, to draw away her perfectionist gaze from her imperfections and vulnerability. I've seen her throat. I just wonder what else I haven't seen on this young body that has already overcome so much suffering.

That night, on the cold and heartless bathroom tiles, I held her in my arms, our legs intertwined, and I asked her why on earth she would do that to herself. I didn't understand. She is so bright and successful. Then she told me. Her parents had been at their wit's end. They had lost every sense of communication with her. They didn't know how to handle, educate, treat, or raise her. They always thought she would grow up perfectly, as they considered themselves to be, without so much as making an effort or moving a finger. They took her evolution for granted. She took care of her own education, because for her parents, 'education' meant indoctrination and parroting their opinions without skepticism. Of course, the older she became, the bigger a disappointment she was to them. They sent her to a psychiatrist for two years when she was around my age for hysteria, babbling, incoherence, unreason, melancholia, and egocentric self-pleasuring, which others would have called plain puberty. That's when she met Egon.

Her charming psychiatrist, married with two children, dedicated his extensive experience and curious knowledge to her case. Attentive, caring, engaging, and talkative, he weaseled his way into her refound open-mindedness and trust in good-natured people. He painted with her, shared secrets with her, treated her as his equal, spent after-hours with her playing board games, discussing books and art, and slowly she fell in love, as adequately as a thirteen-year-old can fall in love, and she was convinced that he shared her infatuation. Something good finally erupted from the scratches of her home. They were both feeling this for sure, this couldn't be fake. There was so much she could give him, she thought, that his wife had stopped giving him what he needed as a man.

But now he had found her and cured her from her misery. She became better, her skin glowing, her cheeks rosy again, not life-deprived, and she felt loved for the first time, and it happened during a psychiatric treatment of something she thought she didn't even have and it was plainly ridiculous to be accused of and persecuted for. His love made her believe in her sickness.

Daphne became pregnant, and he foresaw his reputation threatened and his family in ruins. She refused to get rid of the child and promised to tell no one where it came from, but he wanted to hear none of it. He couldn't confide in a teenager and trust her with this, so he had to erase his traces and had no choice but to abuse her therapy and his role in it. He made her understand the true meaning of power and privilege henceforth. Intimidation. Control. He told her parents that she had gotten so much worse, exposing behavioral signs of a pathological liar paired with paranoid hallucinations, and that her state and mental depravity had deteriorated to such an extent that he saw himself forced to apply shock-treatment therapy, which could do wonders in her case, before it was too late. Out of touch, docile, and authority-compliant as her parents were, and hopelessly trusting titles and not characters, they agreed without visiting her.

Egon performed the abortion himself, including the innumerable shock-treatments pounding through her brain until she reached blurry and incoherent memory losses and nonsensical articulation, all performed under a non-disclosure agreement. She had trusted his care for her well-being so much. Nobody listened to her stuttering or believed the words she so carefully shared. Her ability to speak was without value and significance. Her reality was overridden with lies, manipulations, and false memories. Re-organization. Tidying up. When their story had been put back into the realm of the improbable, he felt like it was time to disappear from her sight for a while to close the procedure of his crimes against her and facilitate her obliviousness. That's when he went on a four-week vacation with his family while she was heavily medicated on a daily basis. As soon as her body had recovered, he signed the release papers from afar, sending the brainwashed troublemaker back to her parents, guaranteeing them the gradual amelioration of her condition with a lot of rest and peacefulness in her parental home, and that she would be a new-born woman.

In addition, to perfect the whole medicinal and social image, he added a handwritten reference that would guarantee her acceptance at this school in a few months' time. A period she used to regain her personality, her sensitivity, and reinforce the mind she had lost. That's when she read her way through her mother's secret Feminist collection of literature that she hid from her husband, and that's when she reconnected with herself, what had happened to her, and learned that she needed to be there for herself more than anything because no one else would. She felt that she had been cheated out of an appropriate reaction to what had been done to her, and that the passing of time and the societal concerns were not at all on her side, and so she formed a hierarchy within herself with her at the very top.

Of course, I couldn't contain my tears, and we both cried. It was cathartic, Mother.

I thought you might be interested to know her story. She is my best friend, and I will do my best to maintain this relationship. Daphne, what a beautiful name, isn't it?

Bye, Mother.

What a dreadful tale. Don't believe everything people say to you. It's the age of the Golden I. Everybody is deeply traumatized these days, but you have to move on because the alternatives don't look too promising, do they? I guess you have contributed your own story, and what a monster I must be in your tales.

In my opinion, you are getting too obsessed with this Feminism thing. Not that I disagree with it, how could I, but you know how many misconceptions there are out there about it. I don't want you to get hurt, that's all. Feminism is a stance. Women die for it, but I guess more women do without it. If you're calling yourself a Feminist, you must be ready to face the consequences, be they good or bad. Fear has taken over the world. Where does it take you?

I have a feeling of knowing your roommates better than I know you. Tell me what is going on in your head. You don't hide the fact that you are in awe of them and admire them all with a newfound passion. Be careful not to be dragged away by your sentiments, because the greatest narcissists present themselves as addictive Übermenschen *that you want to please, copy, and live by until you are the prisoner of their multiplying shadows that diminish you and everything that once seemed so irresistibly good about them.*

Sometimes at night, I hear the paintings clatter in their glass boxes and smell the odor of your father's death and I wake up soaked, and yet the sound and scent are reminiscent. He's in the room with me as somebody else, as a facet yet unknown to me, superior and all-knowing, my cruelest thoughts and tendencies and the worst versions of myself, my shame. I feel like prey in my own bed. I cannot penetrate his scheming brain; his afterlife is anything but sterile. I'm on the hunt, Gabriela, but I sense that I'm being teased and persuaded that there is something to chase, a breakthrough from beyond.

You should buy some local magazines and newspapers. I'm in all of them, and I must say for once I'm quite proud to fill several pages in these usually superficial media coverages. Reporters are coming everyday with new questions and angles, even art professors. I get to talk to so many people from different cultures that don't have a preconceived notion of me or call me a fame-seeking witch or a megalomaniacal exhibitionist. I just want to make peace with your father. He robbed me of that opportunity. Our story has not reached its happy end yet, and he knows it. I keep him alive. By the way, after burying myself in the closet full of his clothes, absorbing the last sniff of his dearly missed aroma, I auctioned them all off.

I'll keep you updated with my efforts to reach him even though you already let him go into the depths of death.

That's all for now. Keep up the good work. Your teachers contacted me to reassure me that you're doing well and are properly integrated. Don't become a sycophant.

Awaiting your response,

Your one and only mother.

Dearest Mother, it's interesting that you mention the word 'narcissist.' Daphne informed me about a lot of new research literature that concerns itself with the psychological patterns and behavioral codes of narcissists. They are very common in everyone's daily routine, exhorting emotional and mental violence and microaggressions. They feed on the compliments and praise of good-intentioned empaths and derive their delusional confidence from the uplifting energies empaths provide them with, which in turn drains empaths because it's never enough and they have to fade.

At some point empaths realize that their efforts are not reciprocated. The infliction of wounds happens in layers and sublayers, in an invisible space between the two where violence stops being sugar-coated. As empaths feel smaller, narcissists feel bigger, thus the controlled fear grows and the perverted dependency. Think about a leash. It's very hard to cut the ties and find oneself again. Regain one's energy and reclaim one's worth. Prosecution is a nightmare because the wounds narcissists inflict are not physical and almost impossible to prove, because retold and disintegrated, they don't seem harmful, and yet they scar their victims deeply. At some point empaths are so unbalanced from being the strained puppet of narcissists that they get physically sick.

After Daphne's misfortune, she had to verbalize what had happened to her, she told me. Her psychiatrist sucked the life out of her. Being so irresistible and splendid, she felt fascinated by him, telling him her fiercest secrets, and he engaged so intricately, imitating her mannerisms to enhance his likeability and gain her trust. She felt so connected and understood, as if they were both meant to be with one another. He transported her into a different world where she could be someone else, someone liberated without fear, doubts, or reserve, and she believed the agreeable image of herself that he held up before her eyes. He pretended to be her safe haven.

Everything changed when he found out about her wish to give birth to their baby. That's when he became her worst enemy, using every-thing she had divulged to him against her, always in the nicest and most harmless voice, pretending to care and wanting to help, making her look weak and mentally unstable, parading her issues in front of everyone, masqueraded as a preoccupied darling doctor. That's where narcissists get their support system from, acting, pretending, putting up the most intimidating shows, and only Daphne was able to read the arrowing and undetectable violence. He could have destroyed her whole life, exposed her, humiliated her, dehumanized her, kept her locked up forever, spreading lies and false prognoses, and everybody would have believed him. Egon's true self hid behind his social identity.

Daphne's fear made her bow to him, and she abandoned her self-worth. He had her totally under his control. She wouldn't stand up to him because he would make her look even more insane, and she couldn't grant him that satisfaction. He was so much worse in her head, wreaking havoc and turmoil, because that is where he was truly himself, locked up in her mind. He made her feel so small, dominating her mind, her body, her spirit without being in the same room with her as she conjured him up in absentia to hurt herself for allowing it to happen, so strong was his damaging influence that belittled her on a regular and detrimental basis. She became nothing, worthless, and thus the shock treatments eliminated the person he had sex with and impregnated, for the sake of his family, erasing her mind, memory, and will, destroying her for his own good, ruthlessly taking her away from her own self without so much as batting an eye. Egon couldn't afford to have his glorious reputation end up in flames and ruins.

You say that you can hear my admiration for Daphne, Mother? Well, isn't it justified if you hear her story and how she fought for herself and how she arose from all of this and is able to smile and love herself again? Isn't it truly remarkable? She made sense out of her past, and that's how she can survive and outlive it and the pain it caused her. I could listen to her for hours. She also makes me feel better about myself. I mean, is it really so bad what I've done? Can't I recuperate from it? Am I such a misfit? Doesn't everyone fail from time to time? Poor judgment is something we all struggle with.

Maybe we all look at mistakes in the wrong way. We should hold them up high and praise them as lessons. They let us move on and allow us to become better versions of ourselves if we truly let them sink in and acknowledge that we are not perfect, that everybody hurts everybody sometimes and we cannot have the best intentions all of the time. We have to be truly able to forgive ourselves and one another, because sometimes circumstances are beyond our control. I know that holding grudges makes me sick to my stomach. I have to let go, otherwise I only hurt myself.

*When it comes to Father, I don't understand why you don't take the mask and go sit in my mirror-*paravent*? That's as close to him as you can get.*

Be careful.

Bye, Mother.

*Gabriela, I think that might be the key to my longing, and yet as soon as I read your suggestion, I got the feeling in my stomach that there was truth to it, a truth that I'm still not ready for. I'm too scared, frail maybe, afraid of the definitive in the limitless. I've always avoided your mirror-*paravent *for those reasons. I never understood how you could be so comfortable in that reflective circus, this exposure of all these repetitive and endless selves all staring at one another as if your soul is being kept and barred inside of the glass itself, in the darkness beyond* the light shed in your face as if a version of you is breathing down your neck to drown you in your own underworld. I don't know whether I can face the underworld your father is dissolving in.

I want to remind him of my love for him, but the mediums are skeptical about his intentions. They cannot tell whether he's close, if it's even him. So many things happened in this manor, so many memories and incidents, not all of them wholesome; on the contrary, they stick, and I wonder who it is that I perceive with me in the bedroom. I need guidance, but I'm afraid of the recipient of my request. I don't want to be fooled, because to the dead I'm see-through.

What the mediums are certain of is that my energy is like a magnet to the transient in my manor and more potent than the usual energies of humans. I need to identify your father. I had hopes that the quest would not involve your mirror-paravent, but now that you've uttered it, it makes sense that your father would seek shelter from me there. He knew that it made me shudder and extremely uncomfortable, and that's why, on the other hand, he provokes me like he used to, to leave my fears behind and be uncomfortable. But everything feels ambiguous, and I can't reach a decision yet. I'm afraid of the troubled concoction of previous abyssal inhabitants of the mirror-paravent, because they never left and became stronger through the eerie mirrors but haven't exposed themselves yet, which worries and restrains me.

Follow your heart, wherever it takes you. Be ready.

Your mother.

Dearest Mother,

There was a moment a few days ago when Agnes and I were alone in our room, and at some point I asked her why she never takes part in any school activities or physical exercise. I felt ill that day and couldn't join, but she always stays in our room. When she answered me, I almost forgot to swallow, my throat became so dry and my heart beat so fast that I couldn't believe what I was hearing.

I don't know what it is about this school, if it's a coincidence or fate that brought us girls together. I'm in awe of them, what they are carrying with them at their young age and how miraculously they seem to cope with everything that's been thrown at them. Agnes spoke of her condition to me, and it needed a lot of explanation. She said doctors had been telling her without exceptions that she shouldn't grow too comfortable with life because hers wouldn't last long. Due to the fact that she needs to take incessantly pedantic care of herself, she will never be able to live to the fullest.

The constant worrying of her parents that she might just die any moment under their watch terrorized her insomniac mindset. She needed space, deprived them of their helplessness and begged them to send her here to take her mind off her death with education. She says the school feels like a life-affirming hospice to her, and as she spiritualizes herself every night getting ready for her demise, she loses her existential fears and contacts the person she will be once she is no more.

I don't know what to say, Mother. They just feel so old to me that I can't believe that they are still so childlike. What Agnes revealed to me felt heavy, despite her hopeful attitude. The peace she makes every single day with her death makes me shiver because it's just so unjust. I had to lock myself up in the bathroom to weep. I didn't want to do it in front of her, but I was just exploding. I felt so sorry for her I didn't know what to do. Of course, she heard me through the door. I didn't want to open it. So she sat down on the other side, listening to my sobbing. We put our heads against the door and shared a long afternoon.

I don't want her to know that when she looks into my eyes she'll see that I cannot erase the thought of her impending death. She said just because she was dying every second doesn't mean I have to participate. I should treat her as alive because that's what she is. I only needed to cope with the end result when it arises, not now. Everything before that is on her.

I still feel weird and useless. I need to lie down.

I'm thinking of Jacqueline and Gunnar. I imagine living my life with them, going through the same horrors and paradises with them and mocking the same things, alongside each other like proper siblings, with death not playing a role at all. I've been robbed of our eternity. I'm growing up without them and they left like a favorite toy that at one point disappeared from my hands and showed itself no more, not even in my memory.

Sorry, I can't think about you conjuring up ghosts right now.

Bye, Mother.

This school you've chosen so stubbornly has assembled every screwed-up kid they could find and they really get a kick out of it. How much money they must be making. Decadence wherever you go and all these tragedies you have in common. Do you miss Gunnar? Do you sometimes wonder whether you would look alike were he still here? How tall he would be? What his voice would sound like? It's hard to believe that we never came to that knowledge. I still cannot accept it. I force myself to live with his suicide. Who would he have become, my son? Would he still be alive if I weren't his mother, the creator of his flesh and Weltschmerz? I miss his smile, although it was too close to misery and woe.

I feel like throwing myself against a wall.

The mediums say it's not my time to go meandering through my home.

I'll wait. It's just a momentary impulse, and it feels good to write it down.

I'm too sentimental to write today. What a waste of paper, a mere concoction of useless one-liners.

I can't question myself, it hurts too much. Your father had such insight. I'm lost without it, or am I?

Ennui is taking over my limbs. Rhubarba is convinced that I need new companionship. I'm enough to handle, even for myself. Everything is wasting away around my body, and I can't stop it. I'm paralyzed from the inside, movement-impeded, I can't leave this house, it wants to keep me. I've no idea who I am anymore.

Maybe it's really time to confront your mirror-paravent. *I can't breathe below the weight of my own masks. Nothing fits, I dissipate and abnormalities grow.*

I have a headache. I'll conclude this letter by advising you that you have to be your own best friend.

Bye.

Your mother.

Mother, you wouldn't believe it, but something occurred that I need to tell you.

I heard rumors for a while now that the school houses several secret students that nobody ever sees, except for a chosen handful of people that can be entrusted with their special care. Apparently they are Wunderkinder, *old and young alike, prodigies working and learning under pseudonyms in their hidden chambers. It makes sense; there are so many locked areas in the buildings that we don't have access to. Of course, there are so many theories on campus that one cannot really tell the truth apart from embellished fantasies, but nevertheless my curiosity was triggered.*

Yesterday, I received a note from the headmistress stating that she was more than pleased with my progress at this school and that she had observed me for quite a while now with a sense of amazement, which led her to the composition of this note. She asked whether I was ready to fulfill my designated role at this school, honor its reputation, its progress and my peers with loyalty, servitude, dedication, and trust. There were two boxes, one for consent, the other for decline, and I was supposed to tick one without any further information. I went with my gut and consented.

Beneath the ticked box it was stated that I was urged to be utterly discreet and keep everything I was about to see to myself exclusively and that by signing this note I would bind my word to that of the school's.

I signed it and handed it back to the headmistress' assistant, who was waiting outside of my dorm to deliver the note back to her superior as soon as possible, as the matter that I was now involved in seemed rather urgent.

A few minutes later, the headmistress herself stood in front of me in her cerulean gown, ready to lead the way. In her hands she held a set of keys that would be mine forthwith. Keeping up with her hasty pace, we picked up two prepared packages at the library and the kitchen, both with the name Sybille Mastoornuct on them. As we arrived in a secluded area of the main building, she leaned against the wall, put her cheek against the warm stone, and hummed a distinct melody which led to the unlocking of one of the adjacent doors. After we both stepped through and the door closed behind us, she told me there was no going back now and this was my moment to shine or wither.

She pushed a button with the letters S. M. on it, and I saw we now stood in front of an elevator that looked like a lacy cage. Upon entrance, an off-putting synthetic odor crept up our noses. S. M. was the last button on the highest floor. It was only then that I realized the height of this school through my rioting stomach. I lost my orientation, as I had the impression that the elevator functioned more like a round staircase, pleased to confuse.

When the elevator halted and the silent headmistress shoved its crackling door to the side, I felt sick, and the packages tottered in my hands. She gave me a push from behind and blew at the back of my head. I stepped out into complete and cold darkness and stood there blinded by my environment. The eyes of the headmistress were used to this solemnly lonesome place, as I could hear her confident steps galloping around me, and after a few moments of sheer angst, her face appeared in front of mine as she held up a gas lamp. "You are going to meet someone very dear to me and crucial to this very establishment. Think of her as the spider who is more afraid of you than the other way around, even if it's poisonous." That's what she said to me as she stared into my pale face that reflected the wild pounding in my chest.

Okay, Mother, before I get to the point, I need to see your written consent that you are going to destroy both this letter and the next one as soon as you've read them because I take my duty very seriously and I don't want to disappoint anyone and risk expulsion.

Answer soon.

Bye, Mother.

You are a tease, child. Of course, I'll destroy them both, I swear. Now, who is this mythical persona that you've met by now? My imagination is a savage arena, and I visualize all kinds of things. Your school sure is entertaining, and I'm proud that you've been chosen and that you've proven your worth. You are obviously not sleeping around, buying into ridiculous female stereotypes, polishing your fingernails all day long and only talking about boys. It all ends in the toilet, you know that.

I'm glad you learned your lessons from the past, although I still think you are too young to have one, but it was out of my hands. I'm from a different time and age, or maybe it was all in my head, the way I did things, and I was just lucky with the men in my life and the way they treated me as they saw fit. Or was it as I saw fit? Does one experience count for a generation? I don't know.

You seem like you've aborted your past. While you went for a long swim, or shall I say, a never-ending voyage over the ocean, you've left your garbage memories behind like seaweed festering on a whipped rock. I'm not sure whether I'm on the shore with all those sad deserted rocks or whether I'm limping and suffocating beneath the waves that you leave behind or the anchor that connects your travel to your origin, grounding you and keeping you close to me against all odds or handicapping you, I'm uncertain. Am I still your mother?

I feel like the walls are caving in on me. I feel so invisible and worthless among all these paintings of your father, the works of my parents, the memorabilia, everything, the vile-smelling furniture, the glasses, the dust and all these tidily decorated rooms that death left behind. My lucid skin needs thickening. I feel transparent to the bone. I am in need of a new manifestation, although the money is ceaselessly multiplying, my worries seem to join its dance. I won't condemn myself to be swept under a magnificent rug. Not in here and not now.

I'm familiarizing myself again with Gunnar's room that I've stuffed with dolls amid his trains. The windows are rusty from their constant closure and the air is putrid. I try to seek shelter among his ruins. I won't bow to my fears.

When did your father become so infuriating? Has he changed so much after his death? Will I weaken after mine? Where the hell is he that he ignores my pleas to him so impertinently? Has he locked me away in here forever, to look at what I've done and accomplished?

There are so many requests from authors to compose my biography, but I've declined them all so far. I desire to remain an unsolved enigma. I don't want to be figured out. Feels like a death sentence. Maybe I need to write one myself, but how does one view count when there are hundreds of different facets to every story?

Answer me swiftly, Gabriela, I'm curious.

Your mother.

Mother, before I reveal the identity of the person that I've sworn to care for, I want to give you a piece of advice.

Look around you. You're speaking of death, dust and ruins, of remembrances, ghosts and netherworlds, unaired rooms, lifeless artifacts and paintings that stare back. How can you even breathe in such a vicious atmosphere?

I'm not suggesting that you should sell the house, but you are the one who needs to dominate it and be in charge of all those phantoms, because only with your permission and frailty will they grow taller and eventually outgrow you. You have lost the sense of boundaries. Something is taking advantage of you. The house is draining you. I've felt it myself. I tried to replace all this emptiness, to fill up the void that opened up like

*a moor in my bile. You need to realize where you stand and acknowl-
edge how your surroundings mirror you and what is buried restlessly
in your conscience.*

*You need to face what escaped from your soul and latched itself onto
the* paravent *that decorates your house, mocking you in its unruly freedom. If you feel that way, it's time that you repossess what is possessing
you at this very moment.*

*There I was, in the midst of obscurity led by only one flickering light,
listening to the unsettling rattling of keys, heads turning and mechanisms twisting like throats or dripping wrinkled towels. We entered
another room, even darker than the corridor before, but more accom-
modating. Like a triangular black silhouette, the headmistress positioned herself in front of yet another door. How vast these chambers
were. Suddenly, without turning toward me, I felt her arm stretching
against my hip, handing the keys over to me. Then I perceived the quick
caressing of her heavy cloak over the floor across my clothes, the flight
of light, and I was completely alone with my anxiety. I only held the
two packages and the one key in my hands that she had elevated from
the others beforehand. All I needed to do was to put it in its hole and
see who awaited me with such pressing urgency.*

*After I turned the key and opened the creaking door slowly, I caught
a glance of her. A womanly figure under a cloak whose face was tightly
covered by a milky see-through veil. It enhanced her facial features and
made her look like a churchyard statue of an angel. Her hair was hidden
in a green turban, and I quickly closed the door behind me. The light in
her musty room was minimal. Her mole-like eyes were extremely dark
as they pierced through the veil that was her second skin. All else was
guesswork, as she was incredibly pale. Even her lips seemed more yellow
than red. We stood opposite one another, examining each other's features
and bodies. She appeared very* weltfremd *to me, and as I stretched out
my arms to give her the packages, I assumed she would walk up to me in
comprehension. But instead she imitated my gesture with eerie accuracy
without moving her feet.*

And there we were, both gesturing toward each other, she holding out her hands for the packages I held. The weak candlelight flickered with agitation. I chuckled awkwardly and so did she, but it didn't sound like a stranger's voice, it sounded exactly like mine. It made me feel vulnerable. So I decided to walk toward her to hand her the packages, and as she moved in accordance with me, my pulse rose, and I could barely breathe as I approached her. It was like looking into a mirror, moving toward your own image and yet reaching for the unknown, approaching the bottomless image of yourself that comprehends you better than anyone else. Her pantomime of me deeply irritated me.

As I came close to her, I smelled her. She had a sour odor, but not in a despicable way, like a yogurt almost, a yogurt that had been abandoned in the sun, perhaps. I couldn't really tell how old she was, as her hands were covered by black gloves and her throat by the veil. She took the packages, uninterested in their content, placed them on the desk beside her, and stared at me. She breathed in my rhythm to my face, saying nothing. It was disturbing.

I broke the silence and asked her why she copied my mannerisms. She asked me whether I liked her. I answered that I couldn't tell at this point because we had barely met. Her voice was undefinable and girlish. I asked her the same initial question. Weird, she said, then it doesn't really work. I asked her what she meant, to which she replied that people grow comfortable rather quickly if they apprehend their own behavior in other people, if they see their physicality reflected in others on a subconscious basis which increases mutual likeability, although it could deviate into manipulation of the unaware party, which was not what she was intending. She wanted me to like her instantly, although she admitted she wasn't really subtle in applying her theory because if detected due to obviousness, it can be interpreted as aping someone. This made us both giggle, and yet I had the impression that I wasn't faced with a girl my age, but with a woman beyond my years.

When I introduced myself, talking about my interests and favorite authors studied in class and in private, she looked at me in a fascinated way, genuinely intrigued, studying my expressions and listening acutely, leaning in, not interrupting me at all, just giving me space and time and comfort to speak for as long as I desired. When I finished, she asked me why I changed my voice. Of course, so unusual, I inquired again what she meant by that. She replied that she recognized my natural voice from the moment I spoke even though I concealed it with a higher pitch and increased the sound of my voice, making it shriller, more artificial, and cartoonish. I knew she had a point, but I never noticed it before. She told me women tend to do that, especially when they feel the need to play a role, another persona, when they are uncomfortable and when they fear rejection for exposing their true intention. It was a way of cuting things up, of not sounding too harsh, but it defeats the purpose for the woman as she deforms herself for the benefit of others at the risk of not being taken seriously, which is what she wanted to avoid to begin with. She had a point, because I was still feeling insecure and I wanted to please her.

I began to notice how often I did that and how much I hated my fake voice. We spoke for a long time. Her room was stuffed with books, musical notes, a piano, several armoires and shelves. After a while, I felt comfortable enough to ask her why she was wearing that veil so tightly on her face in this darkness and why she blackened and covered up the windows.

"I am a moon child," she said. I had no idea what that was, I never heard of it. Without explaining it, she said that the only way she would ever leave her chambers was on a stretcher. That would be the only time she would heroically face the sun, survive it, and finally be in the open, if only for a few moments until the very element that had held her captive during her lifetime consumed her entirely. She uttered this with such ease that it felt natural to smile. I understood that she could not leave her confined premises and never let sunlight reach her skin in any way. I suddenly comprehended all these excessive precautions; they were vital.

Wanting to change the subject, I pointed out to her that I was an avid admirer of Maldorosa Compassat, and seeing all the books she had of her, she must be in love with her literature as well. She smiled and replied in a whisper that she could sign one for me if I liked. I couldn't believe it. I tried to read her dark eyes and as she winked at me, I knew. I was baffled and accepted, of course. So she took one copy, opened it, and wrote in the most gallant handwriting I ever saw: 'To Gabriela, my new companion in this somberness, let us thrive on enlightenment like sisters and spirits bound to a wholesome stage where we all perish and blossom alike and yet so very differently.' The fact that Sybille and I met was not a coincidence, and it meant the world to me in a way that nobody but her could ever comprehend.

Mother, this was one of the most empowering and redefining days in my life, and I will honor this role of mine with the greatest passion, ambition, and perseverance, and to be honest, I think this will be the beginning of an everlasting and symbol friendship. It's no wonder that we all landed on this island.

Don't forget to destroy the letters.

Your daughter, Gabriela.

I'm devastated.

You are so lucky. You didn't have to look into your baby's eyes and know of its impending death. I had to bear my baby's curse for nine days, holding her in my arms, and I knew. Yours wasn't even fully formed, it couldn't look at you, feel you, smell you, attach itself to you. It was already dead coming out of you. What does that say about you? Were we ever meant to be mothers, women? Were we made for it? I had to let go of a daughter that I doomed with this unworthy heart that now stares at me every day, victoriously, defeating me anew, the failed mother, the proud symbol of besieging me for eternity. I can't get rid of it now, it's all I have, incompletion and reproval. I held her, Gabriela, and now I'm disaster-prone.

And then Gunnar; how could he? You were triplets, twins, and now you are indeed a single child, how must you feel? Are you dead, my

dearest Gabriela? What did you do to them in my womb? How can
it be that you came out so immune and defiant? Why are you so unaffected? From where did you get this backbone and this mindfulness
that antagonizes me? You transformed so quickly, heading in the most
opposed direction from me. Have you had enough nurturing? I'm your
guidepost to calculate the distance you intend to take. I am everything
that's wrong in your life, a poison. Don't you feel cheated? Don't you
feel like Gunnar just dragged a part of you with him?

Whatever I do, my mind catapults me back to my deepest pits, and
I'm a prisoner. I can't get out. I can't face myself upright and steadfast.
I'm horrified to the core. I can't stomach the dismissive reproach in your
father's face, the knowledge in his brain, the company he might be in.
Judging me. Keeping me from them all as they are together, the devil
finally eliminated. What voices was your father lending his ear to?
Were they begging for their daddy? Did Daddy need to come home to
take care of them? Did he have to drown his soul in alcohol to build up
the will and courage to slowly send his body back to his dead children
who were crying in the mirror world? Don't mind Mother, that old
useless monster. I'm still here. Nobody talks to the devil.

You think that I'm a coward who looks the other way. Your father
rang the bell to my demise. I could have had a different life if he hadn't
insisted. Through all of your excesses I've been here, remember that. You
were this person once, Gabriela. You were. Where did you leave her?
Did you leave that version of you behind? How long does it take her to
catch up with you? How long are you going to keep her limping and
incarcerated, this bad self of yours? Maybe that Anais girl is quite right.
Shame and jealousy are the two most powerful emotions in this world,
and they accelerate like a wildfire when you least expect it and are the
least prepared. Watch out for the smoke, child, creeping its way in until
it bursts in flames like everything that you are trying to build and
accomplish for yourself. Whose face appears to you in the fire?

I feel like that piece of slimy flesh that you barely squeezed from your
source of pleasure into the toilet and that I myself flushed. Am I gone?

Am I a bad memory to you, daughter? Am I coming back or is it the other way around? Have you set yourself free by repression? Are you building up the stamina to face me as an educated woman? Who will I be by then? Will I be old and crippled? Will I even be able to defend and justify myself? Mother, the old hag. Maybe we should keep superficialities aside for a long while and meet again, woman to woman, when we are both ready to put the cards on the table.

Goodbye, if I'm not forgotten already.

Your mother.

Homebound

Estefania gallivanted in a transparent lilac gown through the buzzing garden beneath the glistening sun. She licked the sweat on her upper lip and ignored how bitter she tasted.

She sprinkled the flowers and parts of her dress alike, knowing her biographer watched her as the heat dried her up again. Her hair had grown so long and heavy that her nose was even higher up than usual. She posed as she gardened, positioning herself like a time-traveling statue, displaying her sensual flesh and femininity in broad daylight, engaging in obscene water games.

It was in that moment that her estranged twenty-one-year-old daughter appeared in front of her, separated by the entrance gate, staring at her with those piercing eyes and waiting for her mother to make a move after all these years of silence.

"After seven years you come back to me. To me, of all people. I wonder why."

Estefania stared at her grown daughter's face and shuddered. She merely focused on the young woman's silhouette, so similar to her own, and was thrown back into her childless adolescence.

"W-w-woman to woman, y-you said."

As Gabriela uttered her first words to her mother, her features were unreadable to Estefania. Unhooked from her reverie, Estefania heard her daughter's stutter. She detected a disharmony between the image that presented itself in front of her and what she heard. Her adult daughter sounded like a tantrum-throwing kid in the middle of crying, wheezing, gasping for air; her words mature, her sounds crippled.

"Can't you read between the lines? And now you're a stutterer, too?"

"You look beside yourself, M-m-mother."

"You let me down."

"I've graduated."

As Gabriela spoke those words, it was the first time she took a deep breath and felt calmer. Her studies had granted her an intense introspection, permitting her to revisit her past with a new perspective, an educated one, and rip open wounds that had never been allowed to exist as such. Her mind had been reset. In retrospective, she had suffered re-traumatization but had the clarity and space to free her feelings and thoughts. Gabriela's relived traumas left their traces in the shape of a stutter, something that could only be resolved by stepping back into the beehive and entering into a new conversation with the most dreaded of women. Estefania, intensively scrutinizing her daughter's features and hand gestures, tried to figure out what her returned offspring wanted to convey with that last statement.

"What happened to all those pretentious girls you couldn't stop babbling about? Those sick geniuses you so admired?"

"What happened to the g-garden?"

"All poisonous. Every single plant is highly toxic, most of them deadly. It takes a lot of discipline, experience, and knowledge to care for them in order to survive among them, but it is not impossible. Look how beautiful the garden blossoms now. Exactly what I imagined. I take such good care of my oasis; it's strong and omnipotent, and I'm its sole mistress."

As Estefania gesticulated her ode to her fatal garden, Gabriela tried to distance her emotions from her parent and acknowledge her as an identity independent from her family. Estefania the sadistic potter, with her own ideals and ideologies, molding, hardening, breaking everything she touched. Had she ever spoken about her children or her husband in the manner in which she praised her garden right now? Eyes set alight, her hands nourishing, her attention undivided. As soon as the word "mother" crawled its way back into Gabriela's mind, the thorns arose, and the sharp edges reappeared around her mother's body. The cracked eggshells lurking from the dark nurturing earth. Estefania, the galumphing entity.

"You sure are. Shouldn't you be wearing g-gloves, then?"

"I'm treating my mole plants today, they mean no harm to me. My garden never turns its back on me."

"Today's my b-b-birthday."

"It's also the day Gunnar's death certificate was handed to me. The day Jacqueline's fate was revealed to me. I curse it."

Estefania looked over to the grotesque trees overseeing the lake that her son had chosen as his still requiem and puffed, avoiding her daughter's gaze. As Gabriela's head turned downward in disappointment, Estefania scrutinized her offspring and something manifested itself: this young woman with the stutter had come to her door with an agenda. A lover of mysteries and especially of how to shock people by discouraging them, she slowly gave in to this freshly invented dance her daughter offered her.

"Will you let me in?"

"Oh, I see, dear. You never left, child. Seems appropriate. How very unfortunate."

Estefania's biographer approached mother and daughter with an authoritative boldness that intimidated a lot of women and made him feel like the cock of the walk.

"This is Dr. Aimé St. Irresis. He holds a psychology and journalism doctorate. His work focuses on the symbolism of identity-related language, bodies as non-original but inheritable, the effects of convoluted grief, and the claustrophobia of the arrested psyche. Your father could have used his help, I reckon. I, however, am using Dr. Irresis' journalistic capabilities. He wrote a lot of convincing pieces about artists that I hold dear. I admire his depth and lack of judgment. One day, I found a letter in my empty box and it was from him, making me an offer with an alluring proposal. I was hooked."

A twitch ran through Aimé's eyelid as Gabriela stuck her hand through the gate to maintain social niceties. As their hands touched, a quick smile appeared on the corner between his lips that he crippled as soon as it exposed itself. Estefania's eyes were wide open. Gabriela's frown and disinterest turned into an inquiry.

"Did you get that absolution from Father that you were so d-desperately looking for? I remember your l-last letter very well."

"So Gabriela is still very much alive, I see," said Aimé.

"Yes, this is Gabriela, the daughter who can't live without me. Dr. Irresis, give us a moment, will you." Estefania snapped at his nose the same way she would have chased off an insect that bothered her by coming too close.

"How is it possible that you are still the s-s-same?"

"You should have made up your mind. Am I good or am I bad? You abandoned me here. When I die, don't you dare stand at my graveside and cry. Don't you dare shed tears, because you brought me there. You will see, Gabriela, when I'm gone, how much of a presence I have been in your life. I'm holding on to those grudges. I won't forget where you all put me."

Gabriela read genuine hurt in her mother's features, and yet she could not allow herself to give in, to let go of her own protective instincts and feel sorry for Estefania. All she had craved was for them to be on the same page about certain matters, to have an unfiltered conversation that reached the core of all their rancor.

"When will you live up to life, Mother? You are a broken record, a ch-child. You can't do it. I've known that since I was a k-kid. You needed help, everybody should have seen that, and you weren't g-given any. And you never asked for it, either."

The longer Estefania stared at her daughter, the less Gabriela breathed, and yet her premeditated words rushed out of her. Estefania knew how to destabilize her daughter in a dialogue, running in and out of focus as she pleased and challenged her daughter's viewpoint.

"What are you insinuating? You want me locked up? You want to inherit this house? Fulfill my death wishes? I'm the one combatting all the sicknesses in this family. Outliving my children and my husband. Judged by my runaway daughter. Who do you think you are? Waltzing up in here, talking like you own me, like you know what's right for me. What can you say for yourself?"

"It's not my responsibility to take care of you, but I'm h-h-here, Mother. I came back, for many reasons. I stuck my head deep into the p-past and I see certain things with more clarity. And now that I've looked at you and heard what you have to say, I'm convinced I did the right thing."

Estefania was convinced of the truth in what Gabriela had just uttered, and yet she sensed an ambivalence in her daughter's energy that kept her alert.

"Who asked you to? If you should be so lucky to reach my age, then we'll talk. You and your death-obsessed generation. Growing old is a privilege that you throw away because you don't have the guts to see things through. To look into the future, that requires courage."

"I've h-h-had it. Stop postponing me like that. That's exactly how you b-b-blew me off in your last letter. You will t-take me now as I am."

"That feels like a threat to me, child."

"I want to h-help you."

"Help yourself."

"I did. Have you even looked into the m-m-mirror recently?"

Estefania bit her lip and glanced at the house behind her, a sudden melancholy taking hold of her. She was a woman who did not believe who she was. She embedded the lower part of her face in the palm of her hand, her eyes tightly shut to not cry. Gabriela saw a woman who had aged outwardly, but never matured inside.

"For hours and hours, every day. Nobody sees what I see."

Gabriela looked at her mother with an unidentifiable disdain. Estefania stared at her daughter's folded hands, how she stroke them as if to console herself, reminding her of Severin, who had the same habit.

"I understand you better now, M-mother. The v-vicious c-circle needs to s-stop."

"I locked your father in your room."

"What?"

"I found him."

"What happened?"

"He's in there, in your mirror-*paravent*. I knew it. It was horrible, but I had to do it, I was so afraid of him. He scared me. I barely recognized him. All the mediums had left, so hostile was he. I was almost alone with him in the house. You could smell, taste, and hear him everywhere. I couldn't tell the difference between the visions in my head and reality, they looked the same. I could feel him next to me in the bed, his invisible shifting weight, hear him snoring. I reached out into thin air, trying to catch his elusive body. Your father hunted me down wherever I went. I was the one who never let go. I cursed him forevermore."

"Mother, let me in."

Estefania opened the gate to her homecoming daughter, who glanced at all the poisonous plants and flowers, her mother's biographer amid them all. Gabriela's gut turned acidic as she followed her mother's footsteps. The more Estefania dragged her across the garden to the patio, the more misguided and alienated she felt from her family home. The house emanated a strange lethargy and had accommodated questionable houseguests who behaved like unmanageable beasts that needed remedy more than anything. It was impossible to disassociate all the past misery from the house, and Gabriela felt like she walked straight into a serpent's mouth. The home's unrest and heavy silence galloped back into her heart, and the unspoken agonies found their way back into her disconnected mind. Aimé watched Gabriela set foot into her childhood home and closed his eyes for a moment, then exhaled wholeheartedly.

As Gabriela stepped into the rooms of her past, she felt an internal cloud reside and flare up across her skin. There they were, the walls of her home, not at all like she had left them. Every detail reeked of her mother, her insanity and hopelessness that she could never find words for, that she had always been too much of a coward to caption. The wandering daughter could never be persuaded of the inexistence of her mother's folly. Something had always been deeply wrong with Estefania. Her mental illness had always been so blunt and obvious no matter how well she maintained the house. Gabriela's mother, the proper preserver of the social façade, controlled the functional running of the business, but now all that was shattered. The boundaries were destroyed; it was all in the open, the rotting animal of her soul, the tickling sickness in the tumultuous cacophony in her mother's vibrating skull that spoke only to itself in everlasting distortions.

In the past, Estefania's mental illness had occasionally shone through the cracks that she could neither tame nor control. But now it had become the menacing sunshine radiating through the fibers of the decaying house and her mind that had no clouds anymore. Everything was so brilliant all of a sudden.

The museum looked like an abandoned fair, a deserted playground, the gray afterlife of a circus, the reminiscence of a dysfunctional family life, rooms that ought not to be touched or entered, unsecured territory, heavy with the dead-skinned dust of forlorn hopes. There they were, the chambers of art, the pieces brought forth from the creative souls of this long-standing family, dormant beneath white lightweight blankets that made them look like magmatic statues of ghosts. Gabriela's entrance felt like cracking the crusted shell of a crème brûlée.

Gabriela paced across the dead rooms of her mother's labyrinthine fortitude of mental malady where she lived her daily live with the bravura of a rabid rat, among paintings that hung upside down, stains on silk-upholstered sofas, broken glasses on the floor that had been smashed against the wall, forlorn, pasty lingerie that became one with the reeking rugs, pastry that had gone stale and miserable on golden plates stashed next to rare collected books. She was now more than ever confronted with the outward cries of help that leaped at her like an overflowing bathtub where the water had grown cold and rancid. The catastrophe had caught up with her. It had always been there, a re-emerging siren in scarlet tones, a temptation of the abysmal artillery of the brain, a carousel waltzing with crazed horses, the heel-clicking and tap-dancing back chambers where arthropods lay on their carapaces.

"Found your way back to the madhouse, Gabriela?"

"Rhubarba, you are still here? You frightened me, I didn't see you."

"*I* frighten you?"

"Where are all the others? How could it come to this?"

"Look at you, all grown up. I've been on my own for a while now and I'm beyond overwhelmed. I've wished for you to finally come back home and make peace with your mother's struggling soul. I'm swamped, tired, and overworked. Your mother has started a revolt against cleanliness. The beauty of this house wasted away facing its isolation. I fall more into a coma than sleep at night. My work never exceeds the premises of the kitchen. Nobody else would hire me now, I'm too old, they say. At my age, I've gotten so used to certain systems, habits, and organization in a specific household that new employers couldn't undo or reform them. Of course, I've tried to talk some sense into your mother, but I've lost my pull. I'm exhausted, Gabriela. There are things you don't know about your mother's family. Things have been twisted. Everything to your advantage, apparently. You were misled. We need to have a conversation soon."

"Go to bed, Rhubarba. I'll take care of this m-mess."

As Rhubarba stepped into the light to thank her by kissing her hand, Gabriela saw that her eyes were drowned behind a whitish coat that paled her eye color. She smelled like she hadn't showered in a while. After Rhubarba left for her bedroom, Gabriela walked into the kitchen where she saw the masterful high-cuisine creations that the maid exhausted herself with.

Gabriela straightened her backbone and put her shoulders back. She threw the cheap wine bottles through the window. She threw empty ones, full ones, unopened ones, garbage cans, tins, glasses, full bin bags, old food, and waste. Everything she could find was catapulted through the broken window. Gabriela's hands shook. The shattered glass and the hole in the window had been the first healthy reconnection to the world outside, and she had initiated it. With the mansion dressed in Estefania's mental turmoil, Gabriela's interference was like hammering a hole into frozen water where her mother could finally come up for air and sunlight.

What is wrong with you? That was the question that had branded itself on Gabriela's mind her entire life, trying to overshadow everything she set out to accomplish, destabilizing like her mother's gaze, effervescent, and now it resurfaced as she felt overwhelmed by the proportions of her mother's yearlong outrage.

When Aimé looked over to Estefania, running toward the sprinklers as they turned on, he observed her dancing in the splashing drops, laughing as if in another world, as if it had always been that way. Her tragic way, eyes closed, dress ever more transparent, she pirouetted, hands aloof, sticking her tongue out like a child.

Aimé turned his head to the bewildered woman's daughter, standing on the patio, shaking and raging, breathing as if she had been in a physical fight, holding her arms intertwined in front of her body. She glanced at Estefania with eyes that looked as if they stared directly into the sun. It had been the hardest thing, to come home.

Estefania turned her attention to her daughter and said, "It has always been the three of you. You brought back the past, Gabriela, the water."

The daughter took in her mother from the bottom to the top. Estefania's eyes were more clouded than ever, pressed into the skull, darkened by layers of malevolence and repression, traveling further into the backchamber of her brain, the bottom of a rough-handled drawer burdened with too many clothes. Gabriela knew the depths of her mother's eyes revealed the slow movement of a reckoning. Gabriela always had the ability to stir something in her mother. She walked toward Estefania, holding out her hand, and nodded.

"All right, Mother. I want to m-move forward. W-wait for me inside. Tomorrow I will cl-clean this up."

"Happy birthday, my children. You're all h-h-home," Estefania uttered, snorting with laughter that corseted her daughter's lungs.

Allowance

I N THE LATE HOURS OF THE NIGHT, AIMÉ MADE HIS WAY into Gabriela's room and was surprised not to find her there, as the house was already silent and resigned. All the years of Gabriela's absence gave the room a dark and morose atmosphere. The *paravent* stood tall among the shadows of the moonlight, almost like a thriving tombstone engraved with a spell for longevity.

The air was damp and hot. He could barely inhale it at first, but then he lowered his underarm from his nose and opened a window. Fresh air harassed the dead whiffs and chased them out into the night. Intrigued by the *paravent's* presence, he lit a few candles and forgot why he came here. His senses heightened, his heart beginning to race as he felt surrounded, pirouetted against, a whole crowd of female bodies, young and old, formed and undone, different scents evaporating among the hair that stood up on his entire body.

Dizzy, Aimé leaned against the wooden pillars of the bed until his electrified body dropped on the dust-expelling mattress. In the fog that rose above his face, he caught a glimpse of a notebook falling from the bed's ceiling onto his belly. Innumerable loose papers dispersed over the sheets, covering him up. It took him several minutes to regain proper control over his breathing and tame his tenebrous heartbeat. Then he sat up and assembled the notebook and its disoriented pages.

In his hands he held Gabriela's collection of paraphilic pornographic drawings, images, texts, and photographs. Page after page, his hands groped their impatient way through the textures of a teenaged mind and the obsessive images that infiltrated it and incessantly shook it to its core.

As he flipped through the impressions, he painted a picture of Gabriela, daughter of Severin and Estefania, inside his head. With every word he read, every adjective, every image and sexual pose, he constructed Gabriela's identity, body, and imagination. There she was, accessible to him, he thought, ignorant of the fact that years had passed, that an evolved persona had now taken over her body and that she had indeed become a woman after all this turmoil. He focused on the sexual stimulations of a troubled adolescent girl that he never got to know and was forever out of reach for him.

Aimé's fascination grew. He saw her as tortured, recognized parallels between him and her, found comfort in that presumption. As he read her private, immature thoughts, his nerves sizzled like sugar in a heated pan. Aimé's fingertips worshipped the paper she had confided in so long ago in the past. It was as if he could sniff her out, her libido, intensity, and hunger when she grabbed the pen, when she turned the pages to look at sweating bodies rubbing against each other in complete anonymity, diving into the sea of human entanglement to unrecognition, where only touch would reign and sensation, culmination wandering from arm to arm, sex to sex, genderless, fluid, an underground jungle of knotted roots. He felt connected to the new facet of this perverted little girl's mind.

Suddenly, he heard a hum in a corner of the room that was still shrouded in darkness. He got up and his gaze turned to a young woman standing in the middle of the mirror-*paravent*. Only her forehead and hair were visible to him. Her eyes were closed and her smile was crooked. She was forebodingly silent as he slowly approached her. Her hair was braided with silk scarves into a beehive. She was pale, her eyeballs unruly beneath the skin of her eyelids, moving around like maggots in a corpse. Her facial skin, despite its pastiness, had a luminescent blue glow that shimmered across the mirrors that embalmed her body in the silhouette of the *paravent*.

"Who are you?" Aimé was whispering, gasping for breath, his hands turning into fists.

"What are you doing here?" It was the surreal voice of a twenty-something woman with a childlike nostalgia in its tone. The eyes were still tightly shut yet moving around.

"I came to see her." He couldn't say her name. His tongue felt knotted as if his body was releasing its self-control to the entity talking to him.

"What are you looking for in here? You cannot sink. Not after all these efforts. You are way past this room. Why come here and expose yourself? People get stuck in here. That's not what you are meant to accomplish. Her stories are alive in here. You stand there and fumble. I see what both of you envisioned."

"I know who you are. Where else could this be possible? Open your eyes. You are here because of her, aren't you? I am not here to hurt you. I am trying to understand everything and put all the pieces together."

"I grew old. I do not need my sight, Aimé. You have prepared the terrain. What will the completion of the task make of you? She made you listen too much, and now you are stuck in a web, paralyzed, gravitating between forces that may very well quarter you. Are you here out of love? There can only be one outcome. Can you stick to it?"

"I will not speak of the matter. You are invisible and mute to the common ear and eye; even more so to those whose fears rendered them ignorant, so I'm not threatened by you. I'm sorry for your plight, but my pity ends there. You better wash those hands clean before you point your finger at me. Get out of that lair of yours, open your eyes and face me at least. I need your blessing. I know you have a heart."

Without a sound, she stepped out of the *paravent*, her arms taking up a great space around her and her steps anticipating her fragility. Each body part was uncoordinated and somewhat detached from one another as if there was no sensory, muscular, or nervous connection in her flesh. Like a clattering wooden puppet she walked toward Aimé with great purpose and halted a few steps in front of him. As his hand reached out to her face, she grabbed it and held it tightly shut in her fist.

"What on earth makes you think that you can touch me? What makes you think you are entitled to just go ahead and put your unwanted hand on my face? This is my face, and you have no claim to it. There was no invitation, no agreement, no interpretable hint, and no justification allowing your hand to declare my body its tactile territory. She held me tightly. I'm not a traitor. It takes more than this. I cannot let this happen. What will become of me? I was safe. The unravelling started with my death. You cannot deny its impact."

"You are a traitor to what is good. You've meddled before. I'm asking you to step aside, not disappear. She wouldn't want that."

Just after he had uttered the last word, the woman's eyes burst open in fury, revealing lily-egg-white eyeballs and void pupils. When she spoke again, a different voice came out of her ocher mouth, an ancient, abysmal, and rough emasculating voice escaped effortlessly and echoed into Aimé's frightened face.

"You are too secure. People normalize their misery and even get comfortable. You think you have her all figured out. Using me against her, to conquer her? Women play with what you see in them. Your superficiality will break you."

Suddenly the body language of the enigmatic female figure changed, broke almost to the sound of cracking bones. She looked away from Aimé, then back at him with a fury that erupted out of nowhere. She spoke to him as if she had confused the man in front of her for another.

"*You stop yourself at their skin, their appearance, their scent, you have never made it through all that, through the surface. By downplaying every woman you meet, you are the vulnerable one who is ignorant and exposed. Careless you are, the way you trample into their lives. It's almost too late. Murderer. Pretender. Do you really believe they don't decrypt your projections coming their way? You grant them no autonomy. They are the ones who will get under your skin. I will stay there forever. You don't have that deciphering power. You only know your own shallow image of them both, and you have already fallen for it. I've fallen. Lost everything. You took it. Stole it all. How dare you come back to me?*"

Aimé fainted, and his body dropped heavily on the old floor as the woman disappeared. The door opened with a loud creak, lights turned on, and the intimidated silhouettes of Estefania and Gabriela stood in the room, their mouths gaping at the sight of Aimé's body.

"Nothing good can come out of this room."

"Or what you bring into it."

Estefania looked at the man's body, his form, and fell back into a memory she had compartmentalized. Her husband's corpse lay there, without her, speechless, on the floor that had separated them for all eternity. The image shoved its way back into her mind, and she gasped. The air of old memories crippled her rib cage, and the long-lost weight of a bad conscience fell back in place.

The mother sensed her daughter's eagerness to lean forward and help the psychologist, and in her sudden detachment, she gave her a little push to check whether he was all right.

"Let's put him in Gunnar's room. Our home needs a new pulse."

"N-n-no."

As Gabriela uttered the word of resistance, an old terror galloped back into Estefania's stomach. A jealousy she had long considered digested resurfaced, and she was sure that Gabriela intended to use that orphic bond of siblinghood against her again.

"We can carry him downstairs together. There's no need to keep him up here. All his things are in his room anyway," Gabriela said.

The tone of Gabriela's voice did not convince Estefania. It sounded as if Gabriela herself did not believe what she was saying. Out of a reawakened vulnerability stemming from exclusion, Estefania reconnected to the loyalty she had felt for her dead husband and braced herself against her daughter's liaison with her twins that she knew had lived on.

An Anecdote

Is HE STILL SLEEPING?"

"Yes. Your coffee is too strong, Gabriela. I need some sugar in this."

As Gabriela rummaged around the kitchen cupboards, Estefania sensed a weakness in her daughter that she intended to intrude.

"Let me tell you an anecdote about my parents, Gabriela. My father convinced himself that he adored my mother. The man was violent toward her. His own troubles, criticisms, and nags were always hidden in polite subtleties, sweet-voiced verbal punches addressed at her. This man was traumatized by his work and what he had seen, but so was she, because he brought it home and she stood by his side, chasing it all away. He always forgot. He wasn't alone. My mother had to rebuild herself from scratch. It was such hard work that she invested in herself instead of tackling the problem outside of her own body. Maybe she did not want to give him up. Maybe she polished herself up to such a degree so she could deal with him better.

"Their miseries outdid one another. Both were spiraling away from themselves. He always complained that her food wasn't salty enough, that it was tasteless and uneatable. One day she'd had it. She told me, 'Estefania, if he ever lays a finger on me, I will pack my bags and leave,' that's what she said to me. So, one day, he intentionally oversalted his food in a mocking gesture, then complained that now it was uneatable because there was too much salt on it, blaming her, toying with her. She didn't pay attention to his mind game and scoffed in silence, standing in front of the sink, her back to him. That's when he threw the saltshaker at her, and it just missed her ear by a millimeter. He left the kitchen. I looked at her and I was happy. She turned around, panting, holding her ear, stared at me, speechless and frozen. I smiled, anticipating an end, and told her, 'Now you can leave, Mother.' And do you know what she said? She took a deep breath and without blinking replied with a composure that is held together by lies and illusory memories: 'no, he missed.'"

Even though Gabriela knew it was never a good sign when her mother launched into a tirade, she thought what she had just expressed carried some value and sincerity that she could engage with. But before Gabriela could speak, Aimé stumbled into the kitchen and Gabriela, conflicted, ground her teeth; a gesture unmissed by her mother.

"Here's your sugar, Mother. Look who awoke from the d-dead."

While Aimé spoke to Gabriela, Estefania felt like she took part in a show intended for her. Not one word the young man uttered meant anything to her. It all rang so terribly false that she also lost interest her daughter's stance against her biographer. It looked like he was talking to a wall and Gabriela seemed incredibly offended, but not by what he was saying at all. She knew her daughter; she was raging because of something else. Instead of listening, the mother observed, as the words played no role whatsoever in the conversation.

Upon Gabriela's silence, Estefania pressed her face into the mug, waiting for the woman that her daughter had become to burst out, but instead she heard a distinct voice yammering inside of her mind. *What is going on in your head, you don't make sense, all of your stories, gibberish, you lovesick circus clown, you rotating carcass of information, they all hurt us.* Estefania broke out in loud hysterical laughter, splashing the coffee she had just sipped all over the table.

Bored by the artifice of Aimé and Gabriela's dialogue, the mother stared into their faces that looked as if they expected applause. Still subjected to the incessant humming, retrieving, and resurfacing, she looked around the room as if to spot the insect asking to be killed.

Egged on by the humming sound, Estefania tripped around the kitchen furniture, now having the full attention of her daughter and her biographer. She grabbed the saltshaker, opened its lid, and threw salt all over her hair, her ears, over her shoulder blades, until the voice went mute and she whispered in a frenzy, "We'll restore my former glory and splendor. I'm tired of this charade."

A Woman to Fear

GABRIELA SPREAD HER BODY ON THE BED, LETTING THE sun shine on her face, and enjoyed the cloudy breeze rushing through the window. She could hear her mother's steps on the creaking staircase, her gown dragging across the wooden floor, making her way toward Gabriela's doorstep. As Estefania's movement stopped without having reached Gabriela, the daughter turned her head and saw Estefania standing in front of her room holding two cups of tea. The mirror-*paravent* stood between them. Every time she passed it, Estefania felt convicted. Never knowing by whom, exactly. She saw it as a forest of thorns cutting her off from her own daughter, taking her side, and villainizing her motherhood. She felt judged as something evil, as if her daughter needed protection, liberation from her, that she must be kept at bay.

Gabriela acknowledged her mother's reluctance to come closer. She sat up on her bed and invited her in, holding out her hand.

"I'm happy to have a moment alone with you, M-mother. These past few weeks have been stressful. I had no time to think. I really need some p-p-peace."

"Someone died."

"How did you kn-know?"

"Because of your envy."

Estefania put the mugs on the nightstand and sat down beside her daughter in a graceful posture that kept her back straight. Her hair had a slight gray shimmer in the sunlight, and she wore it like a crown. For a moment, Estefania looked as if she had had a good life.

"Why would you th-think that?"

"You've always associated peace with death. You've never had peace." Estefania grabbed her daughter by the chin, her eyes wandering over her daughter's troubled features.

Gabriela remained silent, returning her mother's gaze that slowly drifted off as she caressed her daughter's translucent temples. Without blinking, Estefania continued to speak.

"Always envious of those who could manage to give themselves up to the water effortlessly. To defects. To earth. Fire. Alcoholism. You were never self-destructive even when you were trying to be. You have never ceased to reinvent yourself. That's what sets you apart from your siblings, and you consider it a curse. Survival. If they could only see us, Gabriela, how far we've come. How we've grown. What would they think of us?"

Estefania lowered her head, her hand covering her eyes, ring finger and thumb holding her temples. For the first time, Gabriela felt like her mother had allowed her to come closer, be with her in sincere solitude, to take a look at what had been going on inside of her, her vulnerability, and she almost leaned in, her hand reaching forward, but then something halted her gesture. An automated alert, a setback to reality, a warning in her muscle memory. To be on the same page as her mother was unnatural. She did not trust it. She forced herself not to give in. It was so easy to lose her voice, her determination, in her mother's company, she could not allow herself to be distracted, converted. She made her choice. Peace resonated in her brain as her hands snuck back into her lap. Gabriela did not reply because she knew the answer and her mother did not want to hear it.

Estefania grabbed her mug and looked out of the window, her forehead blemished by a frown. When she started talking again, her voice sounded deeper.

"I, on the other hand, could always feel their envy and rancor. Your sister, how she clung to every fiber of life in me. How she tried to suck it up through me. How she held on to me as if I could keep her alive. Latching herself onto my body, its promise of life. Craving to persist. Jacqueline envied the one with the wound of loss, the one outliving her, you.

"Your brother, how he tried to impress me, copy me, impersonate me, fill me with his own life, and I took it. All of it, away from him. I emptied him to the very bottom until he lost his will to live, his capacity to do so, his joviality and *raison d'être*. I ate it like a cake that he handed to me just so I wouldn't starve of my own hollowness and let him rot in a corner so I wouldn't have to do it myself. I emptied that boy of his love for me until he had none left for himself. I pushed him over the edge. He was so envious that I could ask and take, never give. He tried to be a survivor, but he was made out of a different wood, and I watched him decay in front of my eyes, my son the suicidal comedian."

Estefania blinked without a pause, but there were no tears to withhold. Her mouth was shivering, betraying the dry eyes. Gabriela thought this was the first time that she sounded like a mother, a relatable human being, a person with an actual conscience, with regrets and an awareness of guilt. Gabriela was not the one to grant her absolution. She was her own woman, and her mother needed to understand that. She needed to understand that she was not talking to Gunnar, that she was not looking at him, no matter how long she stared at her daughter, evoking his image, forwarding it into adulthood. He never made it, and thus Gabriela stared back to remind her mother that her eyes were alive.

"I lost him a long time ago. He became so h-heavy. His sadness was o-overwhelming. He d-disappeared into an opacity where I could neither hear nor see anything. His touch became powdery. He never stopped being a b-boy. A transient. He made himself smaller and smaller. His blurry face surfacing out of hesitant waves only appears in my powerless d-dreams."

"Always taking the safe road, my little Gunnar. What about the other one?"

"I wanted to talk about Agnes and her death, m-mother. Not about Jacqueline."

"It's what keeps us alive, isn't it? Talking about what is not there anymore, what others deem decayed."

"I noticed that some of the brightest and most opinionated girls, even the most cultivated ones with good taste, became mutes in the presence of boys. They suddenly became st-statues, a silent artifice of monotonous colors. These girls crouched willingly under the hovering male air that ventured around them. They were trapped into thinking that their s-silence and adornment would impress the boys more than their conversation and intellect. Who had the prettiest girls in their group, that's all everybody could see. Girls with so much to offer competed against each other with a twisted smile and their t-tongues in a knot to decorate the boys and forget their own identity.

"I saw the sparkle in the girls' eyes when they spoke about their literary heroines or historical anecdotes in our common rooms and bedchambers. A s-sanctuary unblemished by their outer p-personae. Outside, in the company of boys, that sparkle eva-nesced and a matt filter neutralized their inner passions, posing in generic lines.

"In case a participating sign of life was required of the girls, they would try to blatantly outdo the boys, adapting themselves, smoothing their edges for the comfort of their male counter-parts. Girls are voodoo dolls; they are p-pierced by their very own n-needles. The boys were merely entertained observers and bystanders, betrayed by a system of images and expectations as much as the girls without being aware of it. Who was this show for anyhow? Who was w-watching?"

"And the connection to Agnes?"

As her daughter spoke, Estefania lost sight again of the girl she used to know and felt confronted by this woman Gabriela had become outside of her grip. This articulate woman felt estranged, aborted from her, as if she could only fully exist without Estefania's presence. Estefania was not sure that she was being talked to in earnest. It seemed as if she were dead already and she could not allow her daughter to drown her in that sphere of non-existence, pretending to converse with her while erasing her.

Estefania felt an impatience, a disentanglement, thankful for her daughter's stutter through which she regained her comfort and connection. The longer she pretended to listen to her daughter, the more she assumed that this story was not even meant for her ears, had in fact nothing to do with her and was dedicated to Gabriela's evocation of her own peace of mind.

"When Agnes was dying, she became an *objet d'art*. Statuesque. A d-dead w-woman at the height of her b-beauty. Beneath her skin hovered a translucent yellow. Agnes' veins were unnaturally highlighted. Her breathing sounded like that of an old woman, and yet she was surrounded by innumerable admirers whom none of us had ever seen before. Led on by her p-parents, who, after lengthy preparation, seemed to gl-glorify her much-acquainted death that would end their sufferings of waiting and sitting around for the eventual loss of their d-d-daughter.

"The crowds of friends and followers assembled around Agnes' deathbed and stared in awe of her much-praised angelic posture. Reading poems to her, lulling her to s-sleep, sketching her features in pastel colors, taking coordinated and posed photographs with her without ever laying a finger on her sick body, which was ambivalently beatified from a d-distance.

"Too weak to engage in a conversation, Agnes relied on the communication her eyes could provide, and she directed her gaze toward me. I was standing in the middle of the sensationalist crowd, really looking at her. I had to follow strict instructions given not only by the family itself, but also by the board of the school, to not engage in overt overemotional behavior that might upset Agnes. To be with her and be granted access, I had to keep my mouth shut and give the f-f-family's beliefs their space. And I thought, what rights does a family truly have? Was it really her family in the end considering the way she felt?

"I bit my lip so hard it almost turned blue. I had to control my s-sobbing as our eyes interlocked. Tears rolled down her powdered cheek. Nothing about this procedure was right. They disempowered her. Intimacy had nothing to do with this. Agnes was imprisoned by the slowly failing organs inside her body. Her evanescent skin had become a projection surface to an audience of well-wishers and reality-deniers. Agnes' reality. She lay there, expiring like meat in the sunlight of a marketplace. Everybody treated her as already decayed and felt so incredibly flattered to be in her fleeing presence. N-nobody touched her, caressed her hair, spoke words of comfort and love. She wanted to be held. Disgust lay in the overcrowded air, as Agnes had started to smell. N-nobody's love seemed to be grand enough to genuinely be by her side and hold her frail h-hands."

Estefania clasped her mug. Everything that came out of Gabriela's mouth, she associated with herself, as a subtle punch directed at her womanhood, making every piece of this story hers. Estefania wouldn't let this woman attack her motherhood. She had no right. She grew up away from her. As the widow twisted every word in her mind, her mistrust in Gabriela's intentions blew out of proportion.

Gabriela was so immersed in her story that she did not realize that time stood still on her mother's face, and behind its flesh, a chaos that plotted against her was erupting.

"The s-sketches people drew looked distorted and idealized. They deified her body without having known who she truly was. Every drawing I saw had been a m-misrepresentation of Agnes' character. The crayons pirouetted across the paper. Their lines hollowed her out, erased her personality. She did not want to be remembered this way. All the women present were powdered white and yellowish to resemble the dying girl. A purified beauty in their eyes. Prayers were spoken, but none had any significance for Agnes. I kn-knew her well enough. Generic eulogies that had nothing to do with her left her ice-cold. This hypocritical ambiguity filled the stiff air in the room, and I could hardly breathe. She was in agony, and everybody was smiling and congratulating her. Agnes was painted with a surreal smile that I hadn't seen for a long while and certainly not in that very moment. A smile that made her look like a goddess on the verge of eternal life. Agnes felt like prey waiting to be baptized by several heavy heaps of earth.

"And then Agnes broke the rule she never consented to follow. She mustered up all her effort and stretched out her arm to me. All she could do was m-moan, and her eyes were those of a b-beggar. I wouldn't have dared to resist this last reaching out of hers. I couldn't bear it, to not hold her as long as I had her with me. I wrestled my way toward her. I rocked her slowly back and forth, humming, until her rattling stopped. Agnes' fingers became l-lifeless. Drool cascaded out of her open mouth, and then her eyes stood still. She had died in my arms. In p-peace. That's when I left the room that held me in contempt. I didn't care. I had given Agnes the shelter she deserved."

"Why would you tell me such a despicable story, Gabriela?"

Estefania held her empty mug in her hand and swung it about. The tea bag slouched in the corner.

"Doesn't it remind you of your own l-life, M-mother? Who you were in the past? Doesn't it do something to you?"

Gabriela took her spoon and stirred her tea. The scarlet bag hemorrhaged in the depths of the metamorphosing water and the daughter looked up at her mother. Wherever she looked and stirred, she saw death, its stains and remains. Her mother was right about that.

The doorbell rang, and Estefania's old fears of her child arose once more, an eeriness, and on the verge of collapse, she posed her body in contrast to her emotions. She stood up, her mug like a weapon in her hand.

"I'll get the door." Gabriela jumped up, spilling her tea on the sheets. She ignored the stain and walked out of her room to open the door.

In that moment, Estefania sensed an eruption within the *paravent*. With her back to it, staring at the red stain on the sheets, she forgot to breathe. A stampede ripped through her body, and she felt dragged toward the bed, face forward, but then she shut her eyes and revolted against the imposed energy. Estefania turned around and with a resolute swing, she threw her mug against the wall, its pieces dispersing in the *paravent's* midst. The widow ran out of the room, covering her ears.

When Gabriela arrived in the entrance hall, she could already see her friend that Rhubarba had let in.

"Hey Gabby, haven't heard from you since graduation. Is everything going all right?"

A tall woman stood in front of them both, her energy taking up the entire room. You could feel her in the furniture, in the mugs, in the cold coffee sitting on the stove, in the banana peels in the compost bucket. You could smell her presence, warm and engaging, spicy even, persisting through every piece of clothing. Her black hair hung heavy and loose, partially braided and otherwise unbrushed, around her entire upper body as if she had rummaged through the roughest of winds, her ash-leafed woody scent spiraling around the glowing darkness of her skin. She was the most breathtaking woman Estefania had ever encountered.

Estefania stood on one of the last steps of the staircase, holding onto the balustrade as if not to be dragged toward her demise. Estefania's intuition never failed her and yet she always ended up ignoring it. Something inside of herself attracted her to self-destruction. Women had always been her undecipherable nemesis. She had been most wounded by her own sex, distrusting them all to the very bone, especially the ones that had managed to bond with her daughter before she did. Estefania felt betrayed by motherhood, convinced that she, as a mother, had always been rejected, leaving her in an in-between state where her identity did not make sense to anyone.

Estefania forced herself to remain aboveground for as long as she could, observing the young unknown woman that her daughter was talking to so intimately. As she felt antagonized by this new unannounced presence in her home without an exchange of words, her body directed her into a state of defense that was filled with adrenaline. Estefania heightened her senses to find the leak of imperfection, the wound, the blood that would tell her the whole truth about this woman, the one that people tend to hide deep within themselves. The mother's heart raced because it took longer than expected, and introductions would soon be made. She knew she couldn't handle the woman without being aware of her weak spot, and she needed to have the upper hand from the moment she was introduced.

"Mother, this is Jada Fleur Blanche. I invited her. She will sleep in my room with m-me. I thought she would be a valuable asset to our *tableaux vivants* sh-shows."

The mother froze on the staircase, trying to escape in her mind. Jada's energy reached her before the woman herself did. As she was approaching the mother, stepping onto the staircase, without fear and bursting with resolution, Estefania felt violated in her private space. Jada's upbringing was similar to Estefania's, and yet the young woman did not seem to apprehend her childhood as a weakness or something to remain quiet about. When Jada reached the mother, halting just below her, she reached out her hand. Estefania knew she would not retreat. The widow interpreted the gesture as meaningless in its blinding formality and it felt more like a goodbye, a conclusion, than a well-intended introduction. A woman of opposition, Estefania, sharpening her edges, brought forth her own hand to make physical contact on her own terms, but then she sensed that she had entered Jada's territory, and that terrorized her like fog.

Both hands found each other, and every time Estefania's palm tried to initiate a retreat, Jada prolonged the gesture, challenging her hand to endure. Estefania was unable to control the irritated twitching of her hand. Jada felt at ease within Estefania's discomfort. When the widow least expected it, the young woman's hand pulled Estefania's entire body down a step. After they had looked at each other at eye level, Jada released her hand, smiling, and a thick energy ran through both women's arms.

Estefania knew better than to start a scene to scapegoat her daughter overtly, especially in front of this woman, and she composed herself, turning toward Gabriela and abandoning Jada on the step.

"Well, in that case, I have to see her naked. You know that. The models need to have the adequate body type to represent the masterpieces we have chosen."

As the widow was convinced that women, in contrast to herself, felt uncomfortable in their own skin, especially when showcased and nude, she heard Jada's contralto voice addressing her for the first time, disrupting her power-drunk reverie.

"Why not touch me and find out?" Jada suggested it with a voice that could belong to a man as much as to a woman. Estefania's horror increased, her gaze begging silently across Gabriela's face.

"It's nothing haptic. It's purely visual," the widow uttered without turning around, her neck in a shudder.

"Oh, you know better than that, Lady Z. It is all about the touch. You have felt it yourself. Come here and find out."

The widow was terrified that if she turned around, she would see Severin on the step. She felt disoriented and cornered, as if a lifeline toward the dead had been re-established, the white noise finally erased, her old self coming back to life in a way that she had not known. Something inside the house had shifted back into gear. The presence speaking to her behind her cold back grew bigger and felt like a mirror piercing through her stomach. This was a woman who had been subjected to the unbearable in her girlhood, catapulting Estefania back into her own infantile skin.

This young woman actually felt openly comfortable in her traumatized skin, asking to be touched by a stranger. Estefania could not understand how Jada could be so reckless with her own life. The young woman came across as a blank page to the mother who did not know from which angle to approach her. Estefania had wrestled all her life with vulnerability, desperately craving to teach Jada a lesson that nudity had nothing to do with sexuality, but she knew she had the wrong woman.

In that moment, the widow got an idea how to subvert Jada's expectations and imbalance her, wanting to throw her off her high horse.

Estefania approached the young woman with her nose first, landing on her face, her nostrils over Jada's eyebrows, coal, over the eyeballs, the familiar salt, the air she exhaled, the skin above her lip, walnut honey, and her full lips, a cushion, a stream of roasted almonds coated with cinnamon rose water and hot caramel. Estefania's tongue hung loose inside her mouth as she daydreamed over the facial features of this unknown woman. Then her fingers, as if to pluck an apple, grasped the depths of her hair, her skull, her skin with all the ant-colony-like roots, massaged, scratched a bit, and she put her fingers under her nose, skin and wax filling her nails.

A profound nostalgia was unhinged in Estefania's bones as she let go of Jada's face, feeling as if she had touched her own from decades ago. It had nothing to do with youth, but with life; Jada's skin was so full of it and had innumerable stories to tell, whereas Estefania felt like a scratched pan that had been left in the cupboard and forgotten about. She contemplated that this young woman could have been her if her choices had been different. She could have been this fearless and imposing, but more than anything she envied Jada's energy of freedom. Estefania could not detect when exactly this emptiness had taken over her life.

As Estefania resumed her haptic inspection, Jada followed her gaze with unfatigued and shameless curiosity, anticipating every movement of these unknown fingers. Estefania's hands glided down her neck, gently, exploring what this woman was made of, the female backbone, and, as she could sense the oddest of heartbeats calling out to her, stopped her excursion to the breasts, the navel, or genitals, her left hand halting right over her heart. That's when she saw how Jada's pupils hung deep down in the lower corners of her eyes, challenging, disarming. Estefania saw what had happened to her for such a long time. Jada's skin warmed, and the room itself felt inflamed.

"Your father." Estefania's hands shivered, and she curled them up.

"Yes?" Jada stared back at her with unyielding eyes. The young woman's voice sounded wooden, as if she had walked through fire and survived.

"It's too common a thing. It's almost banal. A woman's heartache."

"Our wounds are very different, Lady Z. And most certainly, we treated them in our own ways and found our proper cures, or maybe made them worse."

This young woman had a face that did not move. There was no fluidity in it, no revelation. Jada's features had been fossilized, her pain engraved in her invisible pores, her life locked in a miniature inside her pupils.

Estefania felt like a beggar in front of the young woman, in dire need of acknowledgment that they were alike. Jada denied Estefania her unspoken request, lacking respect for her for rejecting her responsibility and remaining silent when her voice was most needed, for disappearing into a world where nobody could follow her. Jada saw that Estefania had bathed in her misery and dragged everybody down with her.

"I haven't made my wounds worse," Estefania yelled uncontrollably.

"You had a family."

In a guilt-crazed motion, Estefania pointed at Gabriela and could not cry, vividly gasping at her daughter.

"I have my daughter." Never did the distance between mother and daughter feel greater. It drove Estefania mad that her offspring fell back into her childlike silence that she never failed to misinterpret and always thought was used against her. "I have my Gabriela." Estefania's voice rang false in her own ears.

As Estefania's last sentences dissolved in the dark air, she tried not to collapse. She put her hands on her hips, breathing heavily through her nose and trying to demean Jada to make her less of a threat.

Jada held Gabriela in her arms and they prowled away. Jada turned her head, met Estefania's deranged eyes, then shut hers tightly for a long moment in compassion for the woman, or rather for the younger version of herself. Jada clasped her jaw and looked ahead, tightening her grip on Gabriela's hips. Estefania realized Jada had been invited to fill a void, and as she observed her daughter's relaxed body, she understood that Jada's intentions were set against her.

The widow fell onto an armchair, put her circulating hand on her throbbing temples, and whispered to herself, "What have you brought into this house again, child? Have you seen what I've seen? I bet you have and now she is here. Here with me, with us, with him."

Deceit

IN THE EVENING, AIMÉ, ESTEFANIA, AND GABRIELA SAT IN the reorganized and cleaned salon, going over the plan for the first opening *tableaux vivants* ceremony and selecting a variety of artists who had applied to participate. Estefania drifted off into a trance that put her on a stage with an all-expectant audience and she had never seen a script, nor did she know her character, and upon the sheer panic in the limelight, her teeth started to fall out and it didn't even hurt, though they left her mouth with a pebble stone texture. The audience frowned at the sight of her as blood ran over her lips and chin, and people started to flock to the exit doors.

"I don't want her in my house," Estefania screamed, her palms weighing down the armchair and disrupted her biographer's and daughter's conversation.

"*Your* house?"

"Yes. I won't get any sleep with her under my roof. I want her out."

"This house is where I come from. Where you brought me as an infant. Where life and death never cease to cycle. Where you lock away parts of m-me. I have earned the right to invite my best friend. I will not live in isolation anymore. That has always been *your* choice for all of us."

Estefania looked at Gabriela, her daughter, the silent orchestrator, and became unsure who the real source of hostility was. She had lost her sense of orientation in her own home, not knowing where to turn for safety. This mansion had been a magnet for decades and had become too crowded, too many stories hung loose across the walls, too much undying matter, echoing voices that would never be heard, banished into the pipes, curtains moving like body bags in her head.

"A home is an intimate space, Gabriela. I had to protect my family. I couldn't just let anybody come into your lives. People see things and think what they want. Everybody has an opinion and they all babble. We couldn't afford the wrong kind of talk. We had relationships to maintain to assure our future in this town. *We* needed to be the normal ones, your father and me."

"Stop talking about the past, Mother. It's o-over. You project all this b-baggage onto Jada. She has nothing to do with your fears. You conjure up all of these insane and paranoid thoughts. Give it a rest. Nobody is after you."

The wooden floor creaked, a shadow evanesced across the hall, and Jada appeared in a long Roaring Twenties robe, in between rooms, her figure standing out of the frame, transcending the door, her mossy eyes glistening in the shady corners of the light. She reached out her hand to Aimé without stepping forward.

"You must be the infamous Jada. My name is Dr. St. Irresis. It's a pleasure to make your acquaintance."

"I'm very familiar with your work, Dr. Irresis. Very controversial indeed, and that's why I am in awe of it. You seem to be hovering above mankind, seeing things very clearly, with a common sense that is lacking in most minds nowadays. You are often misunderstood because people antagonize you and refuse to listen to you, even though your insights would come to their rescue. It's a shame people try to categorize you, and they're always wrong. You base your work on facts and experience. Women have spoken to you for years now. There is a reason. As you can see, I'm more interested in your psychological work."

Estefania studied Jada's behavior. The mechanics beneath her face did not seem to fit her apparent age, which disturbed

Estefania terribly. The way Jada articulated herself felt from a different time and space altogether.

There was an indecipherable tension in the air, and Estefania felt invisible for the first time in her life; she felt like a conclusion, something that had been dealt with, case closed.

"It's refreshing not to be attacked for my work, for once. I'm pursuing my journalistic endeavors at the moment. Of course, I cannot quite separate the fields," he replied, clenching his teeth under the flesh of his smile.

Estefania felt intimidated by the biographer's words, as she had forbidden him to do a psychological profile from the very beginning. Jada raised her right eyebrow slightly so as to avoid a microcosmic smile and took a seat. Aimé refilled his glass with wine and slithered past the bookshelves, studying all the titles that caught his eye, his ears never retrieving from the conversation.

"Isn't it interesting that people always have the highest expectations of mothers? How people pressure mothers to not fail, to not fall apart and become this perfection of a life-giving woman, even though history is full of women taking lives as much as giving them? Why do people always think of mothers as saviors? Protectors? Nobody asking questions about fathers lurking in the background machinery. All eyes are on motherhood. Screaming alpha males and yielding women looking the other way. I despise fear, submission, intimidation; terror has no gender."

After Jada uttered those words, she leaned into Estefania's lap, looking at her face from below, closed her eyes, and then whispered, "Are you ready to talk to yourself, Lady Z?"

"Jada, not now," Gabriela interfered with a penetrant hiss.

Estefania chuckled maliciously at Jada's comments, her discomfort trying to convert what she had just heard into comedy to deny the young woman's control over the situation. The mother grabbed Jada's chin, an energized violence in her hand, and examined the young woman's black eyes in the chandelier's light. "So young and already so bitter. You invade my home and dare antagonize me? I know your kind. Don't you dare think you're special. Are you getting bored already with all this misery left behind you? Do you know who you are without it or do you think you need it to be able to characterize yourself and poison my daughter's brain with your vengeful philosophies? We share the same roots, perhaps, but the comparison ends there, believe me. This house is not a joke. You better watch yourself. It's no place to play games, dolly."

"You killed her because he loved her more, because he wanted to save her." Jada stared into Estefania's fiery eyes, which upheld her gaze rigorously.

Estefania pressed her forehead against her new houseguest, who sank into the cushions on the floor. Estefania pointed at her own head, tapped it, and yelled, "What happens in here is my business. Mine. I won't let you in, do you hear me?" The widow's eyes were wide with sadness. "I had no choice. She was weak. I was too young."

"Oh no, Lady Z. She was your strength. She held you together. She is the big missing piece. And you feel it. You've eroded yourself. How overwhelming your self-loathing must have been to commit such a barbaric thing."

"I didn't know better. I just wanted to hide her. She never came back. I couldn't stand the darkness anymore. I refused to look at it. The darkness never stopped."

"Your mother let you down, didn't she? And you tried to overcome everything at the cost of your own skin, Lady Z."

"Everything has an origin. Every emotion. Every action. It worsens in a hereditary, vicious circle. They all keep going, oblivious, lazy, finding themselves in their shadows, aggrandizing them and getting comfortable with their worst selves. Families. Ancestors."

Jada wiped tears off her face and her tongue slid over her lips for a second to allow a breath to evaporate. Gabriela's back was turned away from her mother, her arms crossed in front of her chest, her shaking head facing Aimé. The mother sensed Gabriela's rage but eviscerated it in her mind.

The daughter would not allow herself to succumb to empathy and pity. She had to remain strong for her own good. Her head needed to stay clear. To have the ability to see through her mother was the hardest task. She had no interest anymore to find out what was real about her mother or not.

Estefania stood up, wiping the sweat from her upper lip, and said: "Whatever a father's activity or passivity, he must never be neglected in a narrative. They chose each other for a reason, melting together in the worst ways. And she watched, didn't she? Letting it happen. She even became jealous of you. Of her little girl. You had no idea, or did you? All her complexes were reawakened. Her inferiority complex. Competitiveness. Mother and daughter needed to deal with daddy and his desires. The centerpiece of a household. She hurt you, didn't she?"

Estefania realized that her suspicions were true; Jada had sharpened senses, a higher awareness, was doomed and blessed with a sensitivity and receptivity for energies from all the layers of the world and consciousness. The young woman's belief system had been so established and strong that she must have had regular exposure to what common people deemed dead. Jada's arms reached back centuries. The young woman's confidence was so rooted that communication and contact entered verbal stages. *She must have seen everything*, Estefania thought in her paranoia. She felt the weight again, a woman like that in this house could only wreak more havoc. She knew that Jada had found her way into the dreaded *paravent*.

"You foolish, excessive woman, you. Who were you hoping to talk to in that dreaded hole? Are you even sure you found the right person in there? You can never know. Their identities are always veiled. They enjoy their anonymity, while you are never anonymous. Can't you understand that? They are the empresses of deceit down there. They are the ones in charge. They let you believe you're conversing with your own self. It's in your body. This *paravent* has a cruel history. You silly little girl. What you must have unleashed. I overestimated you. You will stay here and deal with the consequences. Do you understand me?"

"I never intended to leave in the first place, Lady Z. You know what my father and I did. What Gabriela and I have done. If my body feels it, is it a lie?"

"Always question the source. You don't know its intentions and the power it can hold over you. You should know better. You will not force me to look into my own abyss. I see. He hasn't touched you. Not a single time. It was hard, wasn't it, not to be touched by your father? In the weirdest way. He had no affection for you. Didn't see you as his own daughter. Treating you like his plaything. Keeping his distance. Protecting himself. Teaching you all that is wrong with the world and calling it love. And you wanted more. Of course you did. How could you not? You have been so deceived, little Jada."

"I have cried my tears," Jada said. "I have helped myself. I made myself whole and sane. I looked him straight in the eye. Innumerable times, I faced him until he started to shrink. Until my fears vanished and I derived strength from our separation, independence, happiness even. I developed a sexuality without him, my greatest triumph, forgetting him when I desired. Touching my own skin without feeling him there, his platonic, non-existent touch, its derailing meaning and intent. My life and lust without feeling ashamed, without competing with other women. I erased them both, my mother and him."

"And yet you curse her more. Why is that?"

Jada's hand pounded against her chest, and she raised her voice. "I blame her more because she let him rob her autonomy, because she made herself small for him, because she gave me up and made me her enemy for something she let happen to please him, to be the good wife. She gave birth to me so he could have his fun. She knew exactly what it was like and repeated all the same patterns. She never faced her own devils and wounds. She wouldn't help me because she wouldn't help herself. There was no love in that household. She knew what it felt like, what he felt like, all of them, and yet she handed me over like a piece of meat. She made me to protect herself."

"Betrayed by your own sex. And your mother tried to destroy you because he never grew tired of you. Jealousy is a powerful thing. She became a woman unseen with nothing left to do. Her life revolved around your father. The wrath you must have absorbed. She was convinced that what she created, she had the right to undo with her own hands. Did you know it was wrong, what they did to you all those years?"

"I existed in my father's parameters of what was right and wrong. I felt the damage once it was over. I always thought of myself as their good little daughter."

"Mother, Jada has revealed quite enough, and you should stop d-digging now. You've established your kn-knowledgeability and your insight. And before you dissect Jada's relationship with her p-parents, you should wash your hands cl-clean yourself. We should get back to the applicants. Jada is very v-v-versatile; it is possible to fit her into a few p-paintings."

"I know, Gabriela. Versatile indeed. I'm sure of it. The little darling had to play many roles for daddy. One more thing, is she still alive, your mother?"

"Deceased."

"I think it's her. You made her find you."

"If only you knew the truthfulness of the words you speak."

Togetherness

ONE NIGHT, WHILE THE FEROCIOUS WIND WHIPPED UP the heads of the trees outside the house, Jada and Gabriela headed to their shared room after dinner. The two women sat opposite each other, their legs spread, forming two bonding pyramids. Gabriela's notebook and the old photo albums lay in the middle. They both put their hands on them, bowing their heads, breathing, slowly and extensively, with their eyes closed, waiting for Jada to initiate the conversation once their bodies loosened up.

A crawling could be heard in the room, a crawling on eggshells, an inconspicuous body breaking things to move onward, extracted by the young women's bidding from a faraway room. Its knees splattered and bruised, crackling along. A scratching against the mirrors of the *paravent*, the nails aching from beyond. A being as young as it was old emerging out of netherworld clouds.

When the foreign movement halted, the energy in the room paused like a fragile animal for a reaction to its presence. Jada's body became translucent, its surface a fluid mechanism to inhabit, the skin opening its shores, the mouth gaping to let the cold get in. The climbing onto Jada's body went unseen, mimicking the facial expressions of a grown woman, a lost and separated face that would never come to exist. The energy's mute howling scraped across Jada's eyelashes, soaking up the exhalations from her nose. With a swirl across the inner cheeks, the force found itself a host and a voice.

"Gabriela? How old are you? Is it you? What are you doing in my room?"

Out of Jada's mouth came the voice of a girl, a voice of repression and heartache that made it sound older. Gabriela shuddered at the sound of it. She recognized the tone of abandonment. Beneath Jada's eyelids something whirled, and the energy succeeded in opening the eyes, but they weren't Jada's. The gaze appeared like the ones on ancient busts, no pupils, affront, no soul perhaps, a lost world, half-dead. Then the eyes looked at Gabriela's hands, and with a crackling of bones, Jada's fingers were guided toward them.

"These are my hands. My beautiful hands. They were taken. What they had to do. They didn't know better. They were the hands of a child. A trusting child. A girl that believed in love. We all fall on our faces. They misdirected my hands. My young small hands. They were initiated into a world that would forever reject me. What they did to them. And now I look at them, and they belong to a woman. I lost my hands. My own matter. There they are. Without me. How could they survive? How are you able to sit there without me being a part of you?"

A hot storm gathered around Gabriela's stomach. Her heart cramped, and she could barely breathe. She craved to hold herself close and feel complete. She wanted to apologize and justify her actions, explain to her younger self how sorry she felt and that she wouldn't live without her. She thought of herself as her own harshest judge, and that led to the biggest mistake in her life. She had the revelation that she needed to continuously learn how to love herself and live with herself. She needed all parts of herself to truly accomplish that. She would never again chase away the stations of her life, her identities, and let others make her feel ashamed of them.

Gabriela knew that peace and unity were far from this energy's mind. It was deeply hurt, envious, and suspicious. She needed to maintain a peaceful situation, subtly mimicking every gesture that Jada's body produced.

"You left me here to die," the voice in Jada's mouth said. "You left me here joyless. Incarcerated. Condemned with the saddest of faces and hearts. This room is no friend of mine. And yet you didn't look back to see me. The room of a dead child anticipates every train of thought of its nostalgically lingering guests. The never-ending mourners and their desires. The room derives its energy from it. The more desire leaves the guest's heart, the more it grows and twists that dying aspiration around until the guest is no more and the room conquers all. This gangrenous room where you left me infected. Abandoning me in an open churchyard. And she locked the door. She wants to be in charge of time, letting it stand still. Our mother. Always at her mercy without corporeal autonomy. How could you suppress me like that?"

"These are not the words of a child. You haven't given up hope entirely. There is a chance for re-reconciliation. You have survived without me, and yet our connection has not splintered entirely."

"You made a degenerate out of me. Who could love me like this? You? You left me when I was radiant. You don't know what it feels like."

"To be me?"

"It's been years. Nothing worse could happen to me."

"I came back for you. I have heard you. All those years. You know it. And now you are going to face me. We can finally l-live. Grow old together. Walk hand in hand. I will hold you forever."

"I am so sore. I can smell myself. My finger is all wet. I don't know if this is right because my heart beats so fast."

"Don't go back there. It's over. We've survived it. Don't relive it. We're in a good place now. Try to f-feel it. Can you feel our strength? You are not alone, are you?"

"*It happens all too often that we confuse the flutterings of moths in our stomach with those of butterflies.*"

"This is not you talking. Who else is there? Who's with you?"

"You didn't want me to see you. *See you getting fucked. They threw you away like trash. Once more. They always do. Girl trash. Who makes us mentally ill?*"

Jada's body trembled, her hands pounding her chest, grabbing her throat, clawing through her hair, screaming without a sound, holding her knees and rocking back and forth. And when complete stillness calmed Jada's body, her face hanging loose on her chest as if she were sleeping, she whispered in a distorted voice, "I don't like the way I smell down there. I need to wash it all the time until it all goes off. *And boy, do they go off.*"

"Don't let her infiltrate you. Don't let her c-control you. She is hurt too, but this is what remains of you, and it is already too fragile. Please, don't let her push you over."

"They leave it on me every time. You don't listen. You don't want to see me, and I'm left alone with her. She thinks I'm hers. We've been wronged. Her girl had not seen the world yet. *I am a good little girl. I am a clean little girl. This is fun. This feels good and this is what we women do. This is what makes us little darlings happy. They put me in a coffin. And she doesn't listen.*"

"Clémentine."

"Clémentine, Lavandine. The *paravent* makes toxic concoctions of us all. The mirrors make everything worse. Close the *paravent,* and our hands are tied!"

"I know of their misfortunes, but I can only help you."

Gabriela sensed an increased twitching coming from Jada's feet, her legs unsteady, vibrant, and then she felt the punch of an impatient fist against her own foot.

Jada lifted her head abruptly, wide-eyed, frantic, her teeth exposed and her hand wrestling with Gabriela's hair. Gabriela grabbed her notebook and albums and threw them out of their intimate circle, and Jada came to her own senses.

"Your mother was right, wasn't she, Gabby? It wasn't just one. I'm sweating all over. What did she say to you? Did you reach her?" Jada opened the window, stared at the clouded moon, drank a lot of water, wiped her mouth and stuck her arm into the humid air; a thunderstorm was close, tons of rain.

"We found her. We f-found them all. The pain of centuries, the wrongdoing, but we have the present in our hands. That must count for something, Jada."

"It's a very challenging task for them, and once you get them to open up, there is no guarantee of what could happen. The most atrocious things have happened. It's not easy for both sides, and things can get very messy. It's very rare to get both parties on the same page, though. You're dealing with your own selves, which you think you know so well. It's unsettling. You need to be in charge at all times. Don't let them get to you. You can never really estimate how much hostility toward yourself you actually have, how many detrimental emotions like resentment, aggressions, remorse, guilt, and self-sabotage are brooding around in there. It's even scarier to see that this version of you, the one sitting in front of me, is, in my opinion, the version that turned out best, so you're waking up the worst in there. They weren't so lucky and were drowned in misfortunes and never reached a helping hand to connect them all. That's why you feel so hollow, why your happiness seems so shallow, but at least you are alive and healthy."

"I will never be the best version of myself without her," Gabriela said. "Without the lot of them. But it's not just me in there. Everything's tainted, their stories interwoven. I will not go over my dead body to live in peace."

"As I said, it is very deep inside of you. Hard to dig there. The bottom alters with time. Stories and their reconfigured retellings are burgeoning on top of each other, slowly breaking the neck of the original. You see her as weak, perhaps, as shameful and repulsive. You know how hard it is to rebuild those emotions that she had to identify with and make her believe in love and care for her now, making her feel secure with you, the disjointing butcher. Her misery is her comfort zone. You harmed her and put her there in the first place, but who can blame you, really? Who put you there in the first place? It's always the victim who ends up in this shithole."

"I'm concerned about the other women. They have suffered too m-much too quickly. Suffering changes people, especially if they die wrongfully."

"The fact that she is so young does not work in her favor," Jada said. "Or maybe it does, it's still unclear to me. Mirrors make everything worse. You told me that it was your doing?"

"Yes, I liked the endlessly duplicating effect they created when you closed the *paravent*."

"Mirrors work in many ways. They can block and unleash, enhance and overshadow. If you hand the dead a mirror, they will never let it go. It's a platform that allows them to merge, a second chance to live, projecting themselves onto you and you will see them, gradually, in your own face. They will infiltrate your features until you fail to recognize yourself. To think that you have eight mirrors at their disposition in a haunted *paravent*. Who knows who kept you company all these years you lived here? This thing is a magnet. I'm not sure whether its long state of isolation in your locked room weakened or reinforced it. There is a reason your mother stayed out of your room, that's for sure.

"A mirror facing another one keeps the soul prisoner, ever-reflecting, ever-duplicating, ever identity-depriving," Jada continued. "The *paravent* allows both states: closed-off concentration and freed elaboration. Think of it as a functional heart, the systole and the diastole. There is a catch though. The longer you keep the *paravent* closed, the stronger the unity within it becomes, and who knows what could be unleashed when you spread the octagonal mirror-walls apart."

The Weapons of a Mother

THE FOUR OF THEM WORKED FOR WEEKS ON THE *tableaux vivants* show. The cast left after an extensive rehearsal day in the mansion that had become a stage flooded by a never-ending draft, as all the windows and doors in the house were kept open. The overpowering scent of Estefania's garden roamed through all the rooms, its spiciness burning in the nose on hot days.

Among the grandeur of the poisonous flowers and plants, there was a clearing where Estefania was comfortably surrounded by the dangerous plants she had nurtured. Nobody followed her there.

Rhubarba and Jada were cooking together in the kitchen; they complemented each other's culinary talents and specialty cuisines, and for Jada, cooking was an activity to let it all go, a meditation of creation that nourished her, which she had learned to do at an early age.

Gabriela wandered through the house, reliving the memories that had formed her, letting them sink in once more, putting things in perspective, trying to find her own voice in the echoes of the past. She moved from the basement where her father had succumbed to his self-directed demise to Jacqueline's shrine where everything began, the madness of her mother, and ended up sitting in front of the open door leading to Gunnar's unchanged room.

She looked at his old-fashioned toys, his limitless imagination spread out in his childish room, how easy it had been for him to fill it with the images in his head; he had been so innocent. How everything in this room came to a halt embittered her skin, and she cried for her brother, for her long-lost twin. She ignored the stagnant signs of her mother, that she had wanted to destabilize the twins' union and had felt cheated by them. Instead, Gabriela focused on the hopes of growth and identity in Gunnar's room. As his sister, she should have known, she thought. *Gunnar was the sensitive one. He had so much to give, and he always did.*

Her mind knew better, but her heart went there anyhow. *I could have kept him alive. Sometimes it only takes a few words. A possibility. An inspiration. A perspective of a different life. It was in his hands. It started so early. The disturbance of our hands. The perverted rejection. The emotion of being unwanted. Gunnar was not meant to die; he had so much life in him.* Gabriela's mind could not demonize only her mother, it was the entire family tree, how nothing was ever done, how everything just repeated itself, how misery was accepted and they all tried to outdo each other. What Gunnar desired more than anything was a family. He wanted to be loved. And that was too much to ask.

Gabriela crouched in the doorway of his room, her legs shut together, her hands folded in front of her face and touching her knees. As she heard her mother sing through the windows, the sound of her voice hollering from her garden, Gabriela apologized to her brother. She never stopped asking for his forgiveness, and she whimpered. Her head landed on the floor, her hands grasping for his absent feet, his life to come back, drag him back, back to her and to the hope that she had lit up in herself. To become one again as adults, who had overcome all the pre-teen tragedies and who knew the worth of life and dreams. The heaviness of her brother's name as she whispered it was lifted with every utterance, and she let her love for him grow inside her and his suicide disintegrate.

In that moment, the strongest rainstorm Gabriela had ever encountered poured across the sky, chasing her mother out of the garden. Rain dripped inside Gunnar's room, bursting through the window. Gabriela approached it with unmeasurable glee. Her face wet, she danced in Gunnar's thunderstorm, in his tears of final contentment, the element he surrendered to, and she felt whole again, forgiven, loved by her beautiful twin. Gabriela spread her arms to be embalmed by every drop the wind brought in and let herself be soaked to hold her brother again.

Aimé, who had quickly closed all the windows in the house, appeared in Gunnar's room. He stood still, unacknowledged, in awe, gazing at her with admiration and enchantment.

Gabriela realized Aimé's presence, spread out her arm to him, and smiled. Infatuated, he stepped forward, his eyes wandering over her wet body, the tight clothes, her feminine figure, the soft curves, and as he held her face in his hands, his lips cherished every bit of her neck, kissing her lips, absorbing them, sucking on her tongue, his cheeks gliding over her ears and her hair. Aimé shoved her toward the window. Gabriela moaned, ecstatic, sticking her upper body out of the window, her head in the heavy rain, her long hair floating and dripping. Never had she felt so exhilarated and free, thoughtless and empowered.

Aimé undressed her, threw her clothes out the window, and grabbed her breasts, convinced he was touching the skin of a goddess. He squeezed them together and propelled his face into their flesh, her nipples hardening across his temples, her arms holding his shoulder blades. The rain ran across her features, in and out of her mouth, her eyebrows. She wanted this man then and there. Nothing else mattered.

Quivering with lust and moisture, she slithered back into the room, his strong arms holding her from beneath. She looked him straight in the eyes, and he had never felt so alive. He let her lie down in front of him, all of her body exposed, the ivory legs, her burning sex, her young feet. Never had she felt more sincerely desired. The windy rain kept showering her body through the window, and Aimé plunged his face into her, his tongue sliding across her lips, inside her flesh, her humidity. He discovered every part of her, cherishing the taste of her, this intimacy, and he felt that she had completely let go, every corner of her hidden flesh caressed by his tongue, his fingers, softly, rhythmically, amorously, opening her up with his suction. Gabriela transcended, holding on to the long curtains, her legs cramping. She pushed her entire lower body onto his face and shoulders. They fit perfectly, her body vibrated, thunderstruck, salivating out of every pore.

The moment Gabriela's pleasure reached her subconscious, images penetrated her mind. Gunnar's poor blue lips, in flames, eliminated, her mother's eyes, her father's hands, fingers, dirt in the long nails, and Jacqueline's heart which was hers. Her heart raced. There it was, a thunderstorm of heatwaves. Her shuddering was out of control, her hips almost in seizure, her tongue hanging straight out of her mouth like a stone, her legs entangled around Aimé's neck and face. His muffled sounds were incomprehensible, his hands grasping hers, and he could feel the intense and unworldly energy that electrified her body and went through his. He clutched her wrists to hold her still and tried to liberate his head from its position. He knew something was wrong, but he needed to breathe. She had become so strong she was close to breaking his neck. He tried to resuscitate her, call her back from the depths she had vanished into. He wriggled inside her like a fish on a hook, and he put his entire body to work to disentangle himself.

It wasn't Aimé's strength or Gabriela's awareness that liberated them. It was Estefania's voice, talking as she watched them, leaning against the door with her arms crossed.

She trampled with a pretentious delicacy over their bodies to close the window and shook her head at the puddle they had created with their carelessness on the fine floor.

"Children, children, I really wondered when this would happen. My little Gabriela always had that certain taste that led her into trouble's claws. Is this your grand overdue revolution, daughter of mine? Is it sex? With my biographer? There are some things you need to understand about my daughter here, Dr. Irresis. We were apart for years, but I haven't lost touch. I feel the cutthroat pain in her bones, the unanswered desire and those desperately longing dreams that evaporate in her reality. I feel them sieve across my skull like a dense pestilent cloud, a boat cracking continuously against the rocks on a shore only to wake up anew to the same torment every single day. I stare from a distance and listen to her suppressed sorrows, which fail to drown in the waves she evokes. I remain silent, vigilant, and harbor the tomb that will engulf us both."

Gabriela lifted herself up, her knees wobbly, her head faint, and leaned her arms on her legs as she barely managed to stand. Her hair shielded her face as she recovered from the convulsions her body had put her through. She forced her heart to slow down. Aimé was still coughing and holding his throat, his head resting on Gunnar's dusty bed, his legs spread on the wet floor.

"Why don't you come to me, sw-sw-swim to me, if you see me d-d-drowning, Mother? You just stand there, as always, waving your hand, examining me, asking yourself how could this creature stem from me, *my magnificent body*. Is she worth saving? No, you just wishfully stand there and let disasters afflict me, waiting with your arms open, that way you seem motherly from afar. You want me to come back to you because compared to the h-horrors of the world, you don't seem so vile in the end. You, standing there on your d-dry shore, that brutality in your face, your righteousness, your p-pretense. You dug my g-grave on the day of my b-birth and will only succumb to cradling me within it when we both make it there. You can only go when I go. I shall live no longer than you. Not without you; I have no right.

"You make the ocean dance savagely until my b-body washes up against your feet and my wet hair binds you to me once more, a deadened c-cord between us, choking me post-mortem, and only then, M-m-mother, do you pick me up, hold me in your c-cold arms. You sit down, my head in your suffocating l-lap, that's when your sick love awakens, your sense of m-motherhood and own-ership after destruction. There are so many doors surrounding you, doors to your disastrous p-past, and you resist them all and only open a few among the many, the ones shedding a good light on you."

"There she is! I thought I could never tickle her out of you. So I see, not a lot has changed. How dare you dishonor your brother's room like this? And I thought you had become chaste. What an idiot am I? You know how much this room means to me, and you brought back the water. How could you be this ignorant? All this water. In his room. It always finds its way. I should never have named him. You don't name the dead. Now his room is destroyed too. You! You always manage to make everything fall apart, and then you leave. Why did you do this to me? This room was holy."

Aimé regained his normal breathing. Listening to them both, he observed the pandemonium he had created with his feet in Gunnar's train village while he pleasured Gabriela. And then he thought, it had finally reached a state of honesty. The houses bro-ken, the people fallen over, spread apart, the rails derailed, the trains crashed against each other.

"The poor boy is gone," he said. "He is not here anymore. This room is chasing ghosts. It is unhealthy. It is not him and it will never do him justice. It cradles despair and will drive you both mad. Let him rest in peace. How can he, with this havoc you both wreak around him? How can you two live like this?"

"Dr. Irresis, my son does in no way concern you at the moment. I see my daughter here has finally gotten to you. How marvelous. Was this different for you, Gabriela? How did you feel? Validated? Intimate? Floating on chemistry and energy? What's the word, loved? Did you take what you wanted like a good girl? Did you erase the man from the act? Did you make his body yours? Sex by disassociation? Are you indeed a woman now? How does it feel?

"The girl whose girlfriends, if she had any, were always preferred, the girl who always stood in the shadows of other girls, unnoticed, uncherished, no matter how much time she invested in her socially invalidated appearance, her fitting-in makeup, her copied hair, her artificial scent, all those hours spent surrounded by hopeless mirrors lying to her about other versions, alternatives, exits, only to end up in the same dead end called invisibility and extinction because, see, nobody else could detect how beautiful and breathtaking she really was. She herself didn't believe it after a while.

"That girl was only worth using in a degrading way, she came to think. Boys reacted to her sexuality, and that would become her sad illusional weapon, her luring-in mechanisms, her only way in. She reduced herself to an object and a vessel of pleasure that could never be paraded like a trophy in the revelatory sunlight, must always remain hidden and get fucked in silence, in secrecy, undeserving of further engagement, of emotion, of love, of sexual gratification even. They still didn't care, those silly little boys in men's bodies with their pumping dicks.

"But she believed she was appreciated when they came on her face and went back to their girlfriends. The Seductress. The Lover. The Concubine. The Courtesan. All these roles she perfected, for herself or for them? She forgot all about her self-worth, personality, intellect, and love, and all they cared about was her willingness to provide them with splayed legs and pretended exhibitions. A dream come true for a few moments of egocentric ecstasy. The indoctrinated girl who kept quiet, in blasphemous solidarity with the cheaters, the abusers, the alpha boys, the big shots, condemning their girlfriends, finding pride in the backchamber that harbored her and their genitals, her heart locked away, beating too loudly, disturbing the treacherous peace, the conscience, her body.

"They were ashamed of her, of fucking a girl like her, the creature that must remain extinguished from the limelight that would rotate their decorous oblivious girlfriends. The whore must remain cankered in the cellar in the basement, used only when necessary. Alone she stood, this little girl who was looking for love for so many years and found a cheaper way, the only apparent option. Everybody wants to be seen and appreciated. So what if this made it possible for her, attracting the deadbeats?

"This sexuality is not hers. She lied to herself, moaning like she knew she was expected to while she felt nothing during the penetration to make them feel like conquerors and heroes, just how they knocked her soul out of her, her integrity. She didn't know how high the stakes were; nothing came back her way.

"They're backstabbing boys, and yet girls always blame themselves and each other instead of grabbing the cock by its head and disengaging.

"She started to buy into the idea that after having been so special, she was worthless, random, exchangeable, pretending to be tolerant when not sufficient anymore. The martyr-mistress going to extremes to please was a hurting child who tricked herself into thinking this was what she had indeed deserved and this was giving her pleasure, that this fucking and desecrating of her parts was adoration and affection, even though she ended up like garbage in utter darkness, still elevating those perpetrators and toxic narcissists, lying to herself, idealizing, projecting an idyll in a raging war zone that left scars that would only emerge later, much later.

"All these men that had the simple audacity and the misguided entitlement to touch her body because it screamed compliant victim, an uninvited smile, a kiss on the cheek unasked for, the prolonged holding of her hand, a nasty hissing directed at her from a sinister corner, the eyes devouring her. All these devastating men who think they hold an unstated ownership over her body just because she appears to be so polite, such a *Liebmädchen* that needs to please and be kind to everyone but herself. Let herself be torn apart to not offend, walk home with the bruises that nobody sees, burying herself deep underground, throwing herself away into the hungry manholes. What a scarring texture sex can call forth. Where is she, Gabriela?"

Estefania's monologue made her daughter bury her face in the puddle, nude, exposed, shattered into too many tiny pieces that would splatter across the room and she didn't have enough hands to catch them all. She remained crushed before her mother, the moisture inside of her burning an acid hole in her womb, burning her up from the inside, revolting against the treacherous medicine, the sickening stigmatizing fluid that had poisoned her against men and herself, the fluid that could do so much damage and took such a long time to appreciate and grow comfortable with.

"Stay like this. Dr. Irresis, call Rhubarba to get my painting bag. I will name it *Philophobia*."

Aimé was baffled. Everything made perfect sense. Every conversation, every tear and heartache. All the reasons she listed. Something in him stirred and broke, making him determined once and for all. He had witnessed it with his own eyes and understood what Gabriela had to run away and recover from. He wanted to cry, looking at this young woman lying there with all these terrifying words still flying around in the thick air of the room, the torture chamber. The way her body became silent, one with the floor, contrasted to the enraptured woman from before. Her past would never let her go. It would always find a way to attack her and make her feel guilty and unworthy of validation.

Yet Aimé was immoveable. Gabriela's body would dissolve under a touch other than her own. He saw her in her entirety, from beginning to end, the fetal woman, and he wanted to shove the mother's head into the oven or throw her out of the window, but nothing would help. Nothing could help her, and he felt so guilty watching her shiver, like a spider that had been threatened with fire.

"You're a murderess, Estefania."

"And yet here she is, my beautiful daughter. Still alive. One doesn't die that easily. She's proven that."

The Image of a Child

OVER THE NEXT FEW DAYS, AIMÉ ARRANGED ALL THE technicalities and refreshed the promotion of their event around Arracheusebourg and ended up taking a long walk across the black lake's silhouette, contemplating the context of the Zweighaupt house.

Estefania had never felt more energized and inspired, drawing and painting her frustrations away in Jacqueline's memorial room. The coolest and brightest room in the house. Gunnar's room has been blemished, so why not bring Jacqueline's palace back to life? she thought, her brush caterwauling across the canvases, splashing her colors over the walls and the marble floor. *Let's be sincere in this house.* We are all impure, life tainted us all, she told herself while her hand foxtrotted in despair and savagery. *They all paint over the past, nothing ever happened, so let's paint, let's paint and create, they preach.* Her thoughts deranged themselves and her body went on. *Everything has lost its worth in here, nothing matters, start anew, kill the old, the mantra of new generations. And where does that leave me, you stupid little children? This is where he picked me off the floor when I brought the color in. Severin with his pastel colors. You were never a pastel color, Jacqueline. You were bright yellow. Massacring this family, you little baby. Don't look at me like that, little lady, you know what you did.*

Jada and Gabriela went into the basement to clear Severin's atelier and rid the room of its history by throwing out the life-size doll that imitated her father's body for the grotesque museum guests years ago. They put the erect doll with its back against the wall right outside of the atelier, which gave them a lot more space. The event that they planned would accommodate more viewers than ever before, and an additional coats room was required. Severin's unused atelier proved to be the perfect choice.

"Do you ever wonder what your parents were like before you were born? Whether they were happy?" Jada asked.

Gabriela took care of the trash, slamming it into her garbage bag; to her, this room felt like a hoarder of death, holding on to human wastelands. It had nothing in common with her father, and yet she didn't know how to reply to Jada until the truth shot out of her mouth without a second of filtering.

"They never meant to be."

"And their happiness was not your responsibility either."

"They entered this union as two broken people who never took care of themselves."

Jada removed a chest of drawers and something fell on the floor where blue paint had dried. Its white surface caught Gabriela's attention, and she read her father's fragile handwriting: *My Gabriela.*

Her heart stood still as she picked it up; she knew it was the one missing picture, the one she had never seen, and now she knew why: because he took it, her father, who had secretly loved her and known she would survive and stand here one day, discovering his forget-me-not. As she turned it around, she saw herself, her younger self, standing proudly on the patio of her home, holding the column, a solitary heroine who had it in her to fight for her life. The sight of her smiling face, her strength of character and the posture of this courageous girl, moved her deeply, and Gabriela felt overwhelmed with admiration, respect, and awe. This was her, the missing piece, and there had never been a reason to expel it, and she felt now to the very bone that she loved this young warrior with every fiber of her being and wanted her to come home to her.

Never again would she be judged. She held the photograph and pressed it against her chest, thanking her father for keeping it safe.

"This is me," Gabriela said, and she cried.

"You're majestic," Jada told her friend, putting her chin on her shoulder. "See, there is no reason why this little queen should let herself be attacked. Look how ready she is."

Gabriela acknowledged that Jada spoke the truth, and yet the image of her mother as a young girl came into her mind. Before she started to feel sorry for her, she retreated back to her own self; she could not carry them both; Estefania's girlhood was not for her to reclaim.

"I always felt like I couldn't leave Estefania because of her r-rage. What she would do to me. What she would take away from me. Everything that I could be blamed for. I petrified and imprisoned myself with all these fears. I sustain her still. We became part of the same statue, and no one and nothing would ever chisel us apart. I'm unlearning everything she t-taught me. She hasn't changed, neither has she apologized for anything, nor has she understood how badly she affected all of our lives. Instead she throws away every sense of responsibility and truth. It's her endless lament, her *via dolorosa*, the s-story of her failed life and unreturned s-sacrifices."

"You stopped the vicious circle of this family that has been going on for too long. You will interrupt the pattern and start anew. You have never shied away from the darkness, and yet you focus on what matters in your own life and all the good things that keep you going, even if you are still hurting. You can't go back to your old ways and the schemes of this house and what it represents. Don't let the toxic air of the past get to your lungs. You are already changing things around here. You see through your mother. You are not your mother's little girl anymore, but she still is that haunting mother figure from your childhood. She will never change. Don't crawl back into that hole now. You belong to yourself. And don't let her shame you for your sexuality. There are things that sneak up in us and take over. Sometimes we manage to control them, and sometimes we can't and surrender and give in to our primitive callings even if people get hurt, but everybody gets hurt once in a while, you know that all too well."

"Death is not an option for me. I've been living on the edge of it my whole life. I feel it in my body. There is Gunnar and Jacqueline. They are d-death. Sometimes I look at my legs and I can't relate to them. I look at my breasts and sense they don't belong to me, they can't. I don't recognize my features, my reflection. I feel haunted and terrified by myself, but I'm whole, an entire body in d-disarray and discoordination."

"You are not a monster, and those who condemned you in the past have the biggest piles of dirt stocked up on their doorstep, believe me. They see parts of themselves in you that they hate and reject, and therefore they make you the scapegoat for their cowardice and frustration. You cannot change what is dead. Don't conjure it up anymore. If you resurrect the past, it can still affect you as you meddle with the echoes of your feelings. Your education carved out your strengths and talents. Stop justifying yourself and your actions and don't be so apologetic as if you owed everybody your best self at all times. Trust your own instincts."

"I've had this recurrent dream at school," Gabriela said. "My mother would be kne-kneeling in front of a tall mirror, ornamental, heavy, framed with different shades of gold fading away. Her lilac nightgown would hang loose around her chest. I was invisible behind the mirror, looking right back at her. She would be so vulnerable, and I would gaze right into her soul without her consent.

"We would never share this moment together. I envied the intimacy that she shared with a mute medium. I never became visible to her. Her love would always be tw-twisted. This vision of herself that was landing on my face felt inauthentic on my skin, dishonest. This warmth and tortured self-love coming from my mother was not meant for me, not directed at me, and yet I soaked it up gluttonously, without skepticism. I envied the mirror itself, the affection and dedication it received. I could access a picture I would never be in but so desperately longed to. I had been ejected into a d-darkness that no one wanted to acknowledge, no light should go there.

"My own awareness suddenly d-draws me in. There I am in the corners of her mouth that hang low in sadness and regret. There I am, in the hard edges of my mother's grieving face, the minimalistic truth, pulling her down, a facial intruder holding on to her mouth, her hands gliding over me and what I try to leave behind, smoothing the edges, eliminating my language, her maternity mutilating it to beauty and p-perfection. The terrifying idyll where nothing seems to twitch. To gain access to my mother means never to be born, never to die."

The Widow's *Chef-d'œuvre*

E STEFANIA THREW HER COLOR-DRIPPING BODY ONTO THE last canvas in an artistic hurry, brushing and stroking aggressively across the blankness. Jacqueline's memorial room looked like a sanctimonious circus. The booked models and actors peaked into the room from the doorframe. All of Estefania's body was tainted with color. It seemed as if she had tried to recuperate parts of her old self, reattaching the pieces that had escaped her a long time ago. She tried everything to reinsert herself into the house, the rooms, the sense of belonging somewhere and not drift into nothingness.

The widow remembered her daughter's crouched posture well. She painted her daughter's distress with her entire body, crawling, hitting the air around her, rolling on canvas, revolting, hammering her fists and splashing the color everywhere, protesting against her very own mother.

The widow wanted the artists to be a part of the process. They had to acknowledge how much energy and truth went into it, how much torment and heartache. Estefania wanted witnesses that would have access to the sentimental weight and essence of it all, and they were moved. Knowing nothing. Feeling everything. Estefania was an artist in her own right, and she insisted the actors see it too. Day in and day out she tormented them, forcing them to experience her intuitive knowledge of their deficiencies. If they were afraid of the darkness in themselves, they could understand the substance and backbone of each of her paintings.

At one point, Estefania collapsed while she used several brushes at once, her hair unwashed and full of different hardened colors, her body dripping and sullied in sweat, blood, and bruises yet sparkly with glitter, her heart pumping through her chest like a rat scavenging for food and scratching its way through the surface to find it. She lay barefoot in the soup of her creation, and the observers stood in shock. But a moment later Estefania blinked away the hallucination of her mother and rose as if resurrected from death.

"It is indeed hideous, this shallow space, this quenching closeness between love and hate, dependency and obsession. This is where I lie with her, the milk as sour as always, the plants growing around us, poisonous, the roots tearing us apart in unison. We feed off one another, unable to leave. Your pain is mine. I, too, was hopeful once, but I have lost it all. Lost it all too early, too soon. I believed in life once. On my own. How it slithered away from me. Did I let others take it away from me? Does it matter? I held you in my very core, strangling you from the inside, making you bitter and denying you the warmth that was killing me.

"There is no difference between your scent and mine. We smell the same, and it frightens me to death. You expose me every time you lay your eyes on me. I am shattered too; they are my losses too. You don't get to engulf all that heartache for yourself. Everything came to life through me. I was the sole gateway. I'm defined. I am fire, Gabriela. Water has been so cruel to me, to you, water moves things away, flushes them down, wandering from systems to sewers, to rivers and puddles, coming back, haunting us, tormenting us, forcing us to never forget these movements of our past, our shadows and ghosts, circulating underneath us, washing us impure; they are everywhere.

"I am fire, my daughter. I want no rests, no aftermaths and leftovers. Reduce to ashes everything that wants to hurt me, remind me, judge my worst self and eliminate the best of me. We lie here together in this puddle that is our tomb. Too proud to die, too scared, maybe. I don't know what your beliefs are. I know our wombs are enclosed as we watch each other decay. It has always been that way, because that is how we know we are still alive. Will you run away from our fluid, child? How old are you? I think the water plays with your age. You vary, you elude me, daughter of mine, why have you never caught fire at my bosom?"

Rhubarba entered the room. Gabriela was not present, and thus she sent the artists to their chambers, some of them horrified, some inspired, and some strangely exhilarated. As Rhubarba chased them away, Aimé and Jada wrestled their way into the room through the crowd of actors. Aimé kneeled down beside Estefania, who was still beside herself, breathing erratically. Jada perused the paintings she had created and was baffled beyond belief.

"Sometimes the most violent beast has the deepest insight and gift, but they always need to hunt first. Just look at these, Dr. Irresis. I have never seen anything like this. This is Gabriela as she lives and breathes. How much more lifelike can a painting become? This is unbelievable. She might be the only one to know her daughter after all."

"I don't think you know what is really happening here, and that's the seductive beauty of it. She is a hostage of her mother's mind, that's what I see. It is what her mother makes out of her, the identity that everybody perceives, the collage over her actual persona, which ends in the fact that nobody believes who she really is."

"Rhubarba, please bring me to bed," mumbled the delirious widow.

As she carried the disoriented Estefania out of the room, Aimé exited too. He turned around and glanced back at Jada who stood there, bashfully tearing up.

"Think about it and look at them again."

Jada bowed down in front of the paintings on the dirty floor, the sullied surroundings, the platonic crime scene, and cried as if she found herself amidst the mutilated corpses of a massacre that always remained speechless in between the fine lines of the mother's scripture and testament. She felt Jacqueline's infant eyes on her, nailed to the wall, her dying eyes, everywhere in the cold room. Suddenly, she heard the sound of a young girl's voice, a girl she had never met as such but knew. Jada sensed the fragility of her presence and kept her eyes closed and listened.

"Estefania sees everything that is dead as alive and hears everything that is alive as dead."

"They are still alive?"

"Find them before it's too late. I don't belong in the dust."

Revelations from a Fallen Muse

T HE WIDOW'S BODY WEAKENED. BEDRIDDEN FOR DAYS, SHE did not move a finger, and yet her mind's machinery never traveled far. Estefania's mind felt like an undiscovered trench in the ocean's midst, captivating, arresting, fear-inciting. In the mirror of her brain, death pure and simple, how could it ever be her own? She was the one accelerating waves, dominating the masterdarkness, swallowing what was hers. The only thing that moved were the tears that never found their way out of her eyes, set to stone in her own mechanism, the widow's head humid with heat. She had engulfed herself in her own unlived life.

"Women sense when their time is up. Not me. I'm blind to my own demise. I feel it creeping up but no more. Beds have always been the centerpiece of my life, the execution place, the gradual rot of matter, the accumulation and loss of love, the end of perfection and projection, the terrifying brain behind the human face, the shielded depths of insanity, our dreamlands, no-woman's-land, the chasm between sickness and health, the silence of life."

Rhubarba dunked the blue sponge inside the iced rose water and dabbed it on Estefania's forehead, cheeks, and neck.

"Calm down. You've outdone yourself this time. You're not well at all."

"I might be tied to this bed, but I still know what's going on around me. I've never been untied in my life. Beds absorb the most frightening versions of ourselves and harbor our darkest secrets, desires, and alter egos. I tell you, the bed remains while I perish in it. I appreciate the absence of lies in this very piece of furniture. My oldest ally, you might say. I don't mind at all, Rhubarba. I have always been observant. I've always existed in my head."

"You shouldn't talk this much. You always exhaust yourself and go places that make you throw fits and smash you straight back into unconsciousness."

"I saw him in a dream. He came back to me. Standing in my garden, waving, reaching out to me. He felt comfortable for the first time in his life, sheltered. I wasn't sure about his intentions. I hesitated, staring at his hands, and they were unsteady. He tried to smile at me, but did he mean it? I thought, if this is heaven luring me in, it must be damn treacherous, because this is not how I pictured it.

"Do I dare step toward him? Was he crouching in the wings awaiting my soul to bring me straight back to hell, just to make sure I got there safely?"

"Our dreams are better left behind," Rhubarba said. "They are ephemeral. There is reason why they can be barely remembered. The line between dreams and nightmares is thin. They all should remain in their proper realm. They have no business in the world of the living. Stay awake, Estefania. You know how they can overwhelm you. Don't give in to their visualizations. Keep them where they belong."

"Rhubarba, I haven't left these drenched sheets for days. My pulse is thrusting against my temples like a jackhammer, and I look like a dried prune. My disease killed off every piece of beauty I ever possessed. My face is gaunt. I am not this old. He painted me this way; that's how he saw me, and I looked away. They want to eradicate me. Severin's hazardous widow."

"Who wants to eradicate you, Estefania?"

"She never healed, you know. I was born with the cord around my neck. She did that on purpose, the tossing and turning. The very, very unhappy woman. What a fraud. It was all fake, I saw it.

It was her language that betrayed her, exposed her insane malignancy. Everybody was fooled. It was all a show. Very resourceful. The mischievous nature. It was all intact. It was never a secret between us both. Sanctimonious. All these years. I know death well. The absence of a conscience. I started to play her demented game and forgot all about the darkness. Can you imagine how resolute and headstrong I must have been to persuade myself that everything was bliss? And then Severin came into my life. He retrieved it all. Scraping and scouring my beatifying murals that covered the mold."

"Nobody goes to their graves with a clean vest."

"I'd prefer a good dry-cleaner."

"You are a cultural legend, a universal myth, the Widow von Zweighaupt."

"I stopped being a mother a long time ago and turned into something else that I can't face in the mirror. There is a reason I don't go near Gabriela's mirrors. I'm childless. I'm selfless in the worst way. Owned by death itself, like a copper shackle. A legend is best kept behind thick curtains for no one to see, or they would spot the fraud, the dishonesty of half-goddesses. We decay just like the rest of them. There is no spectacle. How did I end up here? Dissolved into old photographs decorating the void in this room with their pretentious beauty ideal?"

"You need your peace after all these endless years of struggle, and I'm here for you. This has been my home since I can remember. I don't dare look any further for companionship. These halls have always been with me. I will be by your side as time has come for you to rest. Life has been too intense for too long."

"Sometimes I forget how we might be the same clockwork, you and I. I've overstayed the welcome of my own body. I will attend the opening night show, however, in person. I mean, it's my last *chef-d'oeuvre*, after all."

"You never shied away from the extra mile, Estefania."

Estefania erupted into a laughing fit, then collapsed into a horrid grimace.

"And look where that got me: here in this bed, in my forties, what a distasteful joke. I cried as a young woman. I stuck my head into the sink and let my face drip away into that dark hole. I cried my eyes out. And he never found out. Never asked. I came out, splendid and polished, and he never questioned a thing. Severin, the almighty observer of women. How many hours my head was stuck in there. My sink. It was my sanctuary. Went back to it years later, but nothing came out. A mute woman screaming into a dirty sink. And you know what, Rhubarba? I never knew why I cried, what it was that dragged me to the sink so irrefutably. I had no idea what was wrong with me. I had no words. Feelings were all I had, and what did I do with them? I let them perish down the drain, never asking myself why."

"Those times are over now, Estefania. You had an unlucky marriage. These sentimentalities are all too common, I'm afraid."

"It's this house that is accursed. Everything I thought I helped build dissipated in my grasp. On purpose. I was but a cross on the map. Who does that? This face everlasting and reoccurring all the time. This one face, everywhere. In his paintings. In various forms and backgrounds. At different ages and sexes, and yet, it's always that same face, and it pretends to wander and hide, but it laughs at me, pointing its finger at me. What a torment it must be for the brain. Lacking the imagination to come up with new faces, the ones that go unseen, that need to be evoked from scratch. The prophesying faces and bodies in our dreams are anchored in ourselves forever, never to be forgotten, always shifting, it's a nightmare, this recycling of our memories and heartache, a rotated carcass that we need to learn everything from. They might be dead and gone, but never will they leave the premises of our brains at night. The endless cavalcade of ghosts. You know how I found out that something was wrong with me? That something actually was the matter with me? My tongue exposed my sickness to me, Rhubarba. The rest of my body still doesn't know of its sealed death. My tongue's sudden defiance and revolt against the words I saw formed in my inner eye. Good riddance, it said to me, and it turned floppy, gradually unable to hit the roof of my mouth, my upper teeth, the sound of certain letters and syllables. I know you can hear it, my deteriorated manner of speaking, my degenerate mouth. I feel your impatience as I speak, and with every breath and effort, I lose my expression. I am ill. The movement will cease entirely, and it won't take long to take me down and defile my speech completely."

"Please, smile again for me, Estefania. Your tongue hasn't deserted you yet. Hold on to the words you need spoken."

"A woman smiles when she pleases. What good does a fake grimace do anyway? What am I, a clown? Can't bear to see me like this, I reckon, presumably defeated? This is not how I feel inside. I might be sick, but my heart is still pumping. I may not yet look like it. When did appearances tell the truth anyhow? I don't feel sick. I'm still very clear in my mind. I decide when it will take over and invade me wholly. I own my soul. I'm taking it with me wherever I go, it is mine, not to trade, not for sale. Will she do right by me, my Gabriela, or will she look back in horror and condemnation?"

Rhubarba patted Estefania's hands in a patronizing gesture that felt more like betrayal than genuine empathy or consolation.

"You should rest for your appearance on the opening night. We're sold out. You've always belonged onstage, my dearest Estefania."

Irrevocable Women

T HE ROOM-DIVIDING DOORS WERE ELIMINATED, AND THE room with Rosemarie's dolls and the room with Amond's collages became aligned for the show. The *grande salle* was full, and people had high expectations. The art journalists and critics had the best seats, temperamental discussions already mingling with cloudy cigar smoke. Everyone was curious, some nervous with anticipation, sweaty hands scribbling notes on a paper pad, the decorated room feeding corner rumors. A special *tableaux vivants* exhibition, the lifework of the Widow von Zweighaupt that cost the awakened artist her health and made her stand out independently from her long-deceased husband.

The red curtains caressed the wooden stage, anticipating Estefania's entrance. The dead dolls glared at the crowd from their captivity behind glass, ecstatic in anticipation of the child who had finally become an artist. Everybody expected to see Estefania in all her radiant and devil-may-care beauty, the upright widow and stubborn artist, the charismatic muse of the past, all made up and shiny in extravagant *haute couture*, a woman of big statements, the drama queen of the town ready to be bathed in the limelight. When she actually entered the room, nobody noticed until she reached the higher level of the stage and looked down on everyone else, her secretly capitulating body embalmed and slightly torn apart by the clicking of the cameras.

Barefaced and shameless, her hand-holding body positioned itself in the middle of the stage, so honest in its exposure that no untruths could be projected upon it. Nobody knew if this modest moment or display of naturalism was worth capturing on camera. Everyone was baffled, holding their breaths, beholding her in fascination, bewilderment, shock, maybe feeling bashful for her, which was not her problem at all, maybe thinking of her as brave to appear in this manner, or was it crestfallenness, acquiescence, even?

There she stood, the audience's gaze slowly wandering toward the uncontrollably shivering hand of a woman who looked older than she was. The hand she held was much smaller than hers and was invisible to the puzzled audience. Her tremoring lips were pressed together to constrict the convulsions storming through her body. A silence-breaking voice from the gaping crowd shouted out, "Bravo, Madame Courage!"

Madame Courage had lost her voice; her tongue had failed her mouth and identity, a cushion of flesh that lost all mobility and willpower bowing to an unconquerable illness that had sunken into the dissolving functions of the widow's body. Estefania's face was a grimace of truth, a distortion, desperate to make a sound, to make sense and have a meaning. Her mouth was gaping, her saliva holding on to both lips, her tongue immobile, her breath collapsing within her gut, and she felt like she had been sent into a prenatal state. The crowd realized the ordeal and, moved by her fate, they were confronted with her physical downfall for the first time. One hand was wildly gesticulating around her throat, shivering, and the other was clasping something invisible to the audience, an audience that gradually became scared of her and secretly begged for a takeover.

Estefania's muscles constructed a crying face, and yet no tear would fall. Defeated, she pressed her lips together as hard as she could and looked up. She tightened her grasp, put one hand on her mouth, closed her eyes, and sobbed to herself. Nobody would listen to her ever again. Nobody would hear the sound of her voice ever again, and it would never age further. It had been put to rest.

As she walked away, almost choking on her breath, a paragraph was projected onto the red curtain.

I tried to make Gabriela my third failure so that nothing would remain to drag me through the mud and that nothing of me would survive without me. I didn't want to be betrayed. I put all my children in one basket. They all ran away. Maybe because I chased them. Maybe because I never let them go. The garden is poisonous, ladies and gentlemen. I found my little daughter in the darkness. I finally heard her scream, and it's not too late. I will show her who I really am. My unspoiled little Gabriela gave me a second chance. We finally found each other, and I'll never let go of her again. It is incredible, really, what women are capable of enduring through their vulnerability.

As Estefania stepped out of the room, still holding the hand of a girl nobody could see, two people in the crowd stood up and followed her.

As the widow made it back into her boudoir, she sat down on her bed, panting, holding the little hand that was not hers with one hand and her own chest with the other. Her mouth was foaming, and her chest felt as if it were imploding, as if everything inside of her were too loud to be contained, too unbearable to be kept under control. She hurt so much that her silence throttled her rib cage, rattled across it, set her innards on fire. She kept pressing the inaccuracy down, the rage pillaging her blood vessels, suppressing the war in her regretful bones, pushing and hammering the wrongdoing and paranormal kidnapping away. She was sitting there in agony with the little girl next to her when a voice interrupted her forceful intimacy.

"So this is the room that you've chosen to start your marriage and independence in? The room where those nutters demolished themselves? You really begged for misery, Estefania. Of course it came to this. Isn't this the window the first bullet went through? I can't believe you. You should have known better. How naïve of you. Sleeping in here. No wonder your love rotted. You look so small, I can't even pity you. You hoped for a better life away from the knowledge we had and taught you. Attaching yourself to those ignorant Zweighaupts with their industrialized sense of art, a light-headed world where money and normalized overwork rule, suppressing everything that withstood centuries, the core of every being and the one before, how we correlate, call it primitive; I call it in tune with the goings-on, eyes wide open. You ran away seeking shelter from the truths that surround and overwhelm us. Now look how everything found its way back to you. When you pushed us away, you also exiled the protection and salvation we could have offered. There are no demons without angels. Let go. She is not for you to hold."

A voice with the impact of hellfire for Estefania, a voice that she hadn't heard for decades, that she tried to abort from her memory, arrowed its way back into her life. Gabriela had sent for it, and Estefania knew this voice would not confront her without actually being physically present. When Estefania turned her head, her nightmare had found its most accomplished form, and out of fear she almost crushed the hand of the little girl she held.

Rosemarie and Amond stood there, her forlorn parents, well-traveled wanderers, piercing their intimidating eyes through their sick daughter, an all-too-familiar sight, trying to bring her back to reality. They looked at her as if she was the one ghost that they had allowed to roam freely, an unruly presence in the lives of those closest to her, someone so damaging and obsessive, someone so alive that she killed others around her, someone who simply didn't know how to live on her own, exhausting the lives of others, crawling under their skin and staying there like a tumultuous hermit.

The worst case they ever had was their own living daughter, the undead, the monument that never left the premises of her confinement, never changed or went anywhere, a daughter lost in time and space, vanishing all the time, reverting to herself like a casualty that could never bear standing on her own two feet except to slowly extinguish herself, an emotional state she had become familiar with. Estefania's parents realized for the first time that they had irrevocably failed their own daughter. They got a bitter taste on their tongues as they watched her hold on to the little hand.

"It's not too late, Amond. The little one is strong, and she can do it."

Estefania searched for love in her mother's old face, below her wrinkles, in her blind eye and in the healthy one, in the entire texture of the face that she had tried to forget, that she had tried to differentiate from her own face. These were the features that had made her wet her bed for years, chew her nails. Nothing good could ever stem from this woman, and no matter how hard Estefania thought she had tried to deviate from her mother's image, she had never been more right in her assumptions. Then there it was, the smirk on Rosemarie's face, the malicious provocative smirk that she merely exposed to her daughter and had misled others to believe in her sheer innocence and well-intentioned heart, the smirk of betrayal, of truth, the indicator of her mother's true, unaltered state of mind.

"This is not you, Estefania. She is not yours."

Estefania's mother's voice rang like a curse in her ears. She knew exactly how to accentuate certain words. Her diction had a terror in it only her daughter could perceive.

Estefania grabbed her portable blackboard and started scribbling viciously onto its surface.

I made her, she came to me!

Estefania's handwriting roared while she avoided eye contact with her parents whom she had shunned from her life. She couldn't look them in the eye, as she needed to keep a clear head, and it was too easy for her parents to get under her skin.

"You don't own her. Stop this vile nonsense. You misguided and fooled her with your open arms and tormented longing for motherhood. You are harassing her and depriving her of everything she needs to find her way back! Everybody needs to admit when they failed, ladybird. There are no perfect mothers and fathers. Let go."

Rosemarie smiled again, mocking the widow, while the focus of the room was fixated on Estefania's misdemeanor. Rosemarie's body was a mighty one, a conjuring one, and as she started waving her hands slowly up and down, her daughter clenched her teeth. Estefania knew exactly how her mother used her body to manipulate people. Shaking her head, she scribbled sentence after sentence on her blackboard.

They never showed any interest in me.

There is always the possibility of reciprocal love.

Estefania's hands were shaking, her chalk stomping on the surface, screeching, and as soon as she wrote a sentence and it was read, it was erased again, wiped off with her sleeve. It was heartbreaking to watch her.

"She belongs to Gabriela. It *is* Gabriela. She has no idea how to deal with you. Can't you see it? You confuse and overwhelm her. It's not too late for them; let her go. Don't destroy more lives than your own. Look at you."

It was unthinkable to Estefania to give in to her mother, the one who wounded her so deeply in the first place. She couldn't let her take over, not her.

You always left me guessing, Mother.

It would always be you.

It was just a matter of time.

You let her back in, Father.

She brought out the worst in you.

You should have protected me.

I will never rest in peace.

Look at me indeed.

Estefania pointed at her face, up and down her features with her free hand that also held the shrinking chalk. She revolted against her mother surviving her. She was undeserving. There was no reason for this woman who had hurt her so much to be triumphant. Estefania felt humiliated to the core, that after all this time they entered her life once more to accomplish her mother's dream and that the room seemed to agree with the act, the crime, as legitimate and necessary. The betrayal of the father was never far away from the mother's decisions. His voice sealed Estefania's defeat along with the charlatan mother's annihilating intentions.

"Your mother is right. You cannot thrust Gabriela onto the same path you chose for yourself. You cannot make your life better that way. You have to face every single choice you made, even if it hurts and you're ashamed and you might end up alone. Gabriela has lived in your shoes for too long. Too long has she endured your pain, your madness, too long has she listened to you. Surviving you instead of living. It is time for her to love herself completely. That is the hardest task. She has never seen it in her life. She needs to make peace with herself, and you cannot take that away from her. You owe her that much, my love, let her find it, let her find herself. Can't you see that she has lived for you all these years, stuck with you through all this torment and heartache? What did you give her in return? You're projecting. Let the child go, Estefania."

Estefania pounded on her chest, frowning her eyebrows and looking at them both in agitated disbelief.

Where did mine go, then?

Why did Gabriela come to me, then?

"Because you abused your motherhood. None of them are left. Of course she would trust you and come to you, you lured her in. She saw your hope, but not through it. She believed in the good in you. You can't deceive her, not at this stage. You cannot be opportunistic and take her for your sake, you know what happens then. She is not for you, not anymore, not like this. Everything is fully formed. Just look her in the eyes. Do you see yourself or what you did to her?"

The nerve you both have.

Invading my house.

You have been summoned.

Gabriela's unfinished business.

Estefania's hand had reached exhaustion, the chalk breaking away from her wrath. She thought of everything that she needed to say to her mother, thought of it with every fiber of her being, the thoughts filling her entire weakened body, her head bursting with pumping, agitated blood. Her mother could read her all too well. No words were needed indeed.

What a victory that must be for you, Mother. My daughter begging you to finish the deed that you had intended since I grew in your womb. To have the blessing of everybody in this room.

If I cannot trust the woman that created me and the woman that I have created, then what will become of me?

Women always know best where the blow hurts most.

You have made a fool out of me.

No, no, no, the garden is blossoming, I don't understand, even if poisonous, it lives, it flourishes.

This is my family.

"You've sacrificed them all, Estefania. Your life is an endless blood trail. Your fate is your own. Your family is eroded."

No!

"They were standing in your way."

No!

Estefania underlined the word three times in her mind, hammering the chalk on the board, her skull.

"You outgrew them all. You took their whole life force for yourself and pushed them into the shadows. You extinguished them, rendered them useless, orphaned and mute."

I put my head under water to hear Gunnar's dying heartbeat.

To find him.

The sound within my womb.

Bring him back.

Estefania started to ram her fists into her stomach, still holding the invisible child's hand, bashing it against herself, tearlessly crying and wailing, sounding shallow and blunt, protesting the truths that her shunned parents now divulged to her.

"Leave her out of this. Can't you tell how frightened she is? She doesn't understand what is going on. Let go of her hand, Estefania!"

She left me.

She left me.

They all did.

"You tell yourself that to make yourself feel better. You've always felt comfortable in misery. Why should anything good ever happen to you? You never allowed yourself to grow. You destroy it with your own hands immediately because you can't deal with it, happiness, isn't that so? It tastes too foreign in your mouth, too surreal for your palate. You need to reverse it back to what you know, what you think you deserve. They didn't leave you. You just couldn't stomach their presence. You've made yourself blind and ignorant. If only you knew how long they really stayed by your goddamn side, child. They fought for you, for themselves. One and the same. Ask yourself why you need to lie to yourself that they all left you. Why are you still the victim here?"

Estefania evoked all her forces to stand up, throwing the chalk across her mother's ear, approaching her motionless body and forcing her forehead against hers. She transmitted her thoughts and feelings as fast as her body could keep up with her determination.

Mother, you barbaric bitch.

You always come back to me as if nothing ever happened.

As if I had no reason to wish you were dead.

You were a constant threat to my life, and I needed to protect myself from you my entire life.

I've put myself in storage to get away from you, and no distance has ever been far enough to recover from the wounds you inflicted in the first place.

You never tried to regain my trust, you just glossed over your crimes and pretended they never happened, you erased my wounds while I was still bleeding and hurting.

I tried to keep you close to make you less frightening, showcasing all your dolls, to keep you in check, but still after all these years of separation, you get under my skin and I need an armor to stand my ground in front of you and your earthquakes.

Did I ever have a true chance to not become like you?

Did I fight too much against it?

Did I fail without even noticing it?

With one brisk and strong-armed gesture, Amond snatched the girl away from the aging mother, his defiant daughter, and listened to the little one running away, knowing that she was headed toward her rightful host, Gabriela. The father's eyes wandered over to the grimacing, disfigured facial features of the grief-stricken widow who had just realized from head to toe that she had lost everything life had given her and was confronted with her mortality, ruin, and early invalidism.

Visualizing her defeat, Estefania looked up to her father. She had been trapped in this aging body all her life, his traumatized young girl, edging against her organic confinement, her leathery prison, unable to grow and evolve, too afraid to move and expand, sick and discouraged, always escaping into the dark, the materialistic, the world of brushed and stroked colors and shades that died down as they dried, but not for her. She would put her life to it, the eternal canvas of her identity.

The father stared at his daughter with the most heart-shattering woe and soul-crushing disapproval, mostly of himself. No words needed to be spoken, as he saw before him the saddest ghost he had ever laid eyes upon, a blood-related spirit suffering the most devastating bane, unconquered and unleashed. A ghost that eluded him for a lifetime where he let it wander about without a cure, a diagnosis even, a ghost he let suffer in self-chosen isolation.

He ultimately succumbed to make-believe when she met the love of her life and concurred she was his responsibility no more, and he felt relief.

As Estefania gave in to her devastation and disillusionment, she regained her knowledge of her parents' profession; that they were on a mission. They had been summoned by someone close to her, someone who couldn't bear her presence, who felt haunted and terrorized. The Vienneses weren't in the business of killing people, no, and they had no intention of healing their daughter, because they saw her as a demon. They were here to provide the other extreme, to confirm Estefania's damnation.

In that moment, Estefania felt her mother turning her on her belly, holding her arms behind her back, putting her weight and tenebrous strength against her daughter's deteriorating body to keep her still. Amond came into the room with one of the mirrors from Gabriela's *paravent* and laid it right underneath Estefania's chest, as her heart was the source of her torment. She lay there, staring forcedly into this panic-inducing mirror that in its octagonal configuration had frightened her beyond relief for all these years.

As Estefania was rapidly breathing onto the moistening surface of the mirror, she saw her thoughts appear on her cloudy reflection. Every word. Every sentence. It was a mockery, a hellhole.

I knew this mirror would be the end of me.

I knew it.

I must have done it. She let you get away with everything, that sensitive little thing.

I wanted to live. I needed to survive.

Estefania shrieked and howled. Nobody could hear her. It had always been that way.

Rosemarie leaned in to address her distraught daughter once more.

"And who do you think you were as my daughter? Never saying a single word. Too much time and imagination to retreat and digress. Always thinking, seeking solitude. Always so pale and silent. Looking like a ghost.

"All of these painters put some color over you, made you believe in a product. Then Severin came, and you thought you could fly and be shrill and stand tall and flamboyant. And you accuse me of faking everything?

"You were born anyway; you didn't care. You wanted out, and then you have the nerve to complain? I didn't give birth to a buoyant woman; no, you're as despondent as they come. I had to live with you, but there was no devotion. On either side. There was nothing I could've done.

"Tell me, where is your beloved Jacqueline? Do you have any idea what you have done? What she has done? You messed it all up. Have you not learned anything from being our daughter? Nothing would have been more logical than to keep us by your side, you self-destructive coward and collector of the dead.

"You underestimated both of your daughters. They are the reason certain people entered your life, invaded your home, and the reason behind the objects that never left the premises. You nightshade. If you could see what I see, you would be incapable of sleep. I will listen to the living in this house, but I won't meddle with what has already been too much in the making. You fed them all, Estefania. You are not alone, daughter of mine, not at all. And you've been betrayed."

Rhubarba approached Amond, handing him his toolbox, then turned around and grabbed something else. As Estefania raised her head toward Rhubarba, she saw that she was holding Jacqueline's glass jar. Only now it was filled with ashes, her heart gone. She also held Gunnar's urn that contained the teeth he lost premortem and that his mother showcased for herself.

Fire doesn't leave traces, annihilation asks for fire, but water, water always finds you, that rotten water.

As Estefania's tampered thoughts were still blemishing the surface in a haste, Gabriela entered her mother's room with a sealed flask in her hand. Amond prepared the scarlet powder and unleashed it on the surface of the mirror as his daughter trembled and yowled, her thoughts looking like thick white scars on the red background and reminding her of burned skin. Rhubarba set Jacqueline's and Gunnar's ashes free amongst the red color, alike in substance on the cold surface of the mirror. The widow felt it on her skin, her children's substances, their fire, their deaths. Estefania's rapid breathing disseminated their molecular remains across the glass. They became one, they moved in unison, filling out the entirety within the frame, closing down Estefania's world. Estefania looked at the little teeth, and she felt him again rising in the pit of her guilt-suppressing stomach.

Please don't separate me from my children. Please!

The exposure of her thoughts felt diabolical to her, like a slap in the face, a confessional box without the absolution, a room without doors. Her thoughts spread out across her children's remains. Gabriela kneeled in front of her at the other side of the bed, piercing her mother's eyes with an accusatory gaze. She slowly tipped the flask.

"Do you know what this is, M-mother?"

Gabriela, I'm just trying to survive. Please, let me survive.

"This is the blood from my greatest wound. My miscarriage that you flushed down the toilet. It kept coming, the blood, the pain, the loss. Rhubarba told me to conserve it. She told me I might need it one day. Faith is a powerful thing. Everything is attached to it.

"I pictured you as a daughter and felt sorry for you. I had an understanding of you, but, Mother, you quench everything so well.

"You rendered our home barren. You send my brother to his grave; a mother can't be this blind.

"You sabotaged us all. We failed you from the very beginning and maybe I plotted against you, but only because you never stood on my side.

"I invited everything in that challenged your character, and you withered. You summoned the inescapable.

"I tested you. I tried to push you. Outside of your walls. Outside of your own *paravent* walls, but you kept knocking your head against them, imprisoning yourself and accusing everybody else of robbing you of your freedom. You are a corseted spectacle for yourself in there. It started as a game, as entertainment for me, but you always took me so seriously. You never stopped seeing me as your nemesis. How could I have been born with love with your constant desire to eject me and abort me from your life?

"You confuse me, Mother. You've always wanted me in the pit with you, but then, when I actually kept you company, you smashed my head against the cold stones. How can you not see it?

"You are still in that room with your mother. You are still hiding under your blanket. You never left that house. You have buried yourself. What you did has not protected you. You took us all with you to live in that horrendous room. And yet your eyes are closed. There is no clarity in your thoughts.

"You are still that child, that little tormented girl who knows the truth, but you are the great smotherer, Mother. You are like the twin cities at the edge of the Dead Sea.

"I can't accept you as a child anymore. I have to see you for who you are, what you did, for years, all these terrible consequences of your existence and your choices.

"We need to part ways. I want to live. You need to go back to the source, to a time when I have not yet existed, none of us. Whoever you will face in there will have a greater knowledge of yourself than you. And you need to let go."

Gabriela poured enough of her blood onto the mirror to create a thick paste to overshadow her mother's reflection entirely.

Gabriela's life force. She left the room without looking back. Rosemarie tore the wedding ring off her daughter's finger, and as Amond stirred glue into the mix, she tossed it into the paste as it became firmer.

One last row of sentences appeared on the surface.

Are you enjoying your gluttonous synesthesia, Mother? How does my misery taste? Blood of my blood. My ashes? Don't think I can't see it. Daughter's delight. Don't swallow the shards. They will get to you. I should have jumped like Jeanne when I had the chance. My life has lost all its meaning.

Rosemarie chuckled. Amond took a brush and smoothed over the surface, wiping his daughter's face away, the reproach, the bond between them, erasing the life he had created in the manner of chasing ghosts away. The living were the ones being exorcized, cleansed from themselves if necessary, posing threats to others, standing in their own way.

Amond could see the wounds she had left on Gabriela. He could see that Estefania, if she would have had the courage and willingness, could have healed her own wounds over time, maybe kept Gunnar alive, maybe Severin would still be here, maybe she wouldn't be dying. But she refused and got sucked into her mind's misfortunes and disabilities, holding on to grudges, agony, and self-loathing instead of loving herself in the first place and not pretending or giving in to more appealing projections of an alternative self that others believed in and held dear but never corresponded to the truth.

Amond only needed one tear out of his daughter's eyes. She hadn't cried since Jacqueline's death, but now, faced with the dissolution of her family, the reality of her life hitting her in the ruined face, the remnants she had designed, the ashes that remained dead and silent, tears fell right into the pond that would drown her insanity once and for all.

Amond smashed his daughter's head against the surface, the glass beneath the brew breaking, wounding the *paravent*, opening up a new outlet, new potential. The glue and liquids filled in the valleys amongst the immoveable shards, and they married their daughter off to her own devils. As Rosemarie cut off Estefania's jumper and glued it to the bottom of the mirror, she let go of her despondent daughter and let her collapse onto the floor as a part of her brain shut down.

A roaring round of applause hollered through every particle of the house as Gabriela, Jada, and Aimé embraced each other onstage.

Rhubarba stayed with Estefania that night as her parents disappeared again to help people across the globe; because sometimes it's better for ties to be cut in due time and family to be apart. As soon as the mirror dried, it was hung on the ceiling over the widow's bed. She had lost all sense of ownership, control, and identity.

A Garden's Embrace

THERE SHE LAY, ESTEFANIA VON ZWEIGHAUPT, FIFTY-FIVE years old, around a decade after the night she was condemned to a lifelong degeneration to her desolate and despotic deathbed.

Sometimes the death-obsessed take the longest to die.

Underneath her chambers, the gallivanting of the renewed tours went on from room to room in the mansion, the hushing and shushing, the narrating and philosophizing, and yet she was not able to hear a thing. Of everything that was alive, she could only hear the dead muteness, the stagnancy, the conclusion of every being that drove her mad during her last years. Her home had become lecture halls for men and women of all ages, a mecca for creativity while hers was at its most deteriorated state.

Estefania's body existed in a savannah of make-believe. What had been dead and decayed for years regained its form in her eyes, regained life. She dove her face into their fresh corpses, embracing them, kissing them, cradling their cold bodies to celebrate their re-acquaintance. They were all unknown to her, family and strangers alike, she could not tell anymore, a body was a body to her: company. They all visited her, parading around her bed, lying next to her, and their eyes looked so alive that she thought she was happy among the pit of death.

Gabriela, now a renowned lecturer at the local university, explained to her listeners that looking back into the past is like driving a car forward while continuously staring into the rearview mirror: at some point you will crash. Gabriela never discredited her own past and that of her ancestors, as it taught her valuable lessons, made her understand things, why she was how she was, where everything came from, and in leaving the examined past behind, she realized a better life for herself.

Estefania pondered death every time the nurse cleaned her throat, changed her tubes, or the physicist washed her forsaken and lackadaisical body in the oversized bathtub where she would try to hug Gunnar's body with her flaccid limbs. In moments of lucidity she came to the same conclusion: she would give death its way. What she wanted most of all in moments of clarity was a ceremonious suicide by stuffing her face with toxic plants, bathing naked in the hazardous colorful field of blossoming death that she herself had created, and perishing away in a matter of minutes in the midst of her own nature. But death wouldn't be so kind, she believed.

Death treated her slowly, dishonestly, as it disabled her as much as the garden would have, just in a slower manner, more brutally, recklessly, with an agenda maybe. She fantasized about what each different plant and flower would do to her body, how they would evoke and highlight each of her sick features and death-infected weaknesses, how she would thrall in color and become one with the flora and fauna she had bestowed upon herself, how she would die unrecognizable among them. Then she would deviate to the thought that she would die a cliché, which her ego wouldn't endure, yet another heroine poisoning herself, no, it was out of the question, she needed her own great death. Would death itself grant her this favor?

Her mind plundered through the variety of suicides; none sat right with her. They all found their own way, these literary and historical heroines. To find hers would be so much more difficult. It had always been that way anyhow, but she insisted on her grand exit.

She acclimated to the idea that a character like hers was a match made in heaven for death, that she was made out of the right kind of wood to face death in all its glory and conquering nature, to meet it head-on without perspiration, doubt, regret, or fear. She grew as comfortable as she could get and let herself sink into her silken sheets, awaiting it with the flirtatious nature of a corruptible schoolgirl.

The room filled itself with the scent of *Le panier aux fruits embrassés par la lavande*, tiptoeing around her bed. With shuddering knees, the widow stood in front of her colorful window that reflected its patterns on her skin and light nightgown. Suddenly, Estefania heard the wildly trotting steps behind her. With all her might, she turned slowly around to know what was happening. Just as she saw the face of her attacker, her body was thrown through the window.

The fall was not noticed for quite a while. The widow's body landed in her lethal garden, her skin exposed to the plants' hazardous particles. They ate at her while she was dying and rattling away. The stuffy air around her was engulfed in the perfume of foul eggs and burned flesh once again with a hint of spilled gray milk.

In the widow's bed, beneath the white silk of the neighboring pillow, a gasp of exhaled air rustled, and the features of Severin's death mask appeared outlined, slightly grinning in peace, softened by the death of his wife.

Four people were present at Estefania's garden funeral. After the priest had blessed what had been a lost cause, he moved through the newly created pathways of the garden. Gabriela, Aimé, and Jada held hands in front of the grave, remembering when they had all met for the first time at school as they envisioned a life without the war drums of their human demons. Estefania's death was finite, and the vicious circle had come to an end. The graveside of Gabriela's mother, a source of happiness that Gabriela had orchestrated for both their sakes, granted her life. The love she had encountered along the way had given her the will to live, to restore herself, to indeed outlive her mother, whose death unshackled her. Gabriela reclaimed a childhood that she was robbed of, a state of free-floating hope and forward-facing dreams and most importantly, fearless courage, outbound from the home whose blessings finally opened its doors to her as the Zweighaupt mansion went up for sale.

The Soul of Gabriela's *Paravent*
Post-Mortem

N INE DAYS AFTER ESTEFANIA'S BURIAL IN HER POISONOUS garden in front of the *Casa Padronale Dell'Arte*, a corpus of six books by Maldorosa Compassat was sent to Gabriela. Attached was a note and a list with the titles of each work:

1. The 1st Marchioness of Blutkutsch: Her Secret Pregnancy and Unexpected Death

2. An Unideal Husband: The Marquis' Despisement of Children and Seclusion from Society

3. Death of the First Wife: Splitting the Belongings: the Comb, the Corset, the Powder Box, and the Paravent

4. The 2nd Marchioness of Blutkutsch: Inheriting from the Accursed

5. The Immoveable Butcher: Horrors of the Paravent

6. Life-Bearers and Unwanted Mothers: Deaths of Pregnant Women and What They Leave Behind

"May they finally complete your own private collection, Gabriela, and help you to contribute your part. Love, S. M."

Acknowledgment

I WOULD LIKE TO EXPRESS MY GRATITUDE TO WIDO PUBLISH-ing and E. L. Marker, especially Joseph Jones who believed in my story from the very beginning, MaryAnne Hafen who taught me a lot about editing and asked all the right questions and finally Karen Jones Gowen who guided me through every single element of the publishing process.

About the Author

A LOVER OF LANGUAGES, LAURA FOUND AN EARLY INSPIRA-tion in German, French, English and Italian culture. She wrote her M.A. on "The Decadent in Love with his Psychopomp: Thomas Mann's *Death in Venice* and Adrian Lyne's *Lolita*." Deeply interested in Dionysian and Apollonian imbalances, Laura seeks out Decadents in literature and film. She studies the women she writes about, their constellation, identities, language, violence, sexuality, behavior and physicality.

Laura's MLitt by Research focused on "Romanticising Deca-dence and Aestheticising Death: Women as Projection Bodies and Mimetic Identities in Zola's *Thérèse Raquin*, Schnitzler's *Dream*

Story, Süskind's *Perfume: The Story of a Murderer* and Eugenides' *The Virgin Suicides*." Decadent symbolism is naturally incorporated in Laura's fiction. Her predomi-nantly female-centric poetry concentrates on the psycho-sexual com-plexities of girlhood and womanhood.

Laura firmly believes that acting on one's

creativity and fulfilling one's purpose resiliently contribute to a wholesome state of mental health, joy and meaningfulness.

Learn more about Laura Gentile at her website and blog: www.croquemelpomene.com.